Praise for *The Mary Shelley Club*

"A smart, serpentine, propulsive thriller with an ending
that will make you gasp. Don't try to read this
one right before bed if you want to sleep."
—Jeff Zentner, award-winning author of
Rayne and Delilah's Midnight Matinee

"This club is SERIOUSLY. MESSED. UP.
I loved everything about it."
—Lygia Day Peñafor, author of *All of This Is True*

"A bright, smooth candy apple with a razor blade inside.
Goldy Moldavsky continues her white-hot streak of
unmatched brilliance in the world of contemporary YA."
—Derek Milman, author of
Scream All Night and *Swipe Right for Murder*

★ "This twisty tour de force . . . is at once a gripping
teen melodrama, an incisive meditation on fear, and
a love letter to horror and the genre's tropes."
—*Publishers Weekly*, starred review

"An atmospheric page-turner about loving scary movies,
longing to belong, and uncovering the many masks
people wear." —*Kirkus Reviews*

"Moldavsky manages to both pay homage to and poke fun
at traditional horror tropes . . . and the final fear test is
keenly chilling." —*BCCB*

LORD OF THE FLY FEST

Goldy Moldavsky

Henry Holt and Company
New York

Henry Holt and Company, *Publishers since 1866*
Henry Holt® is a registered trademark of Macmillan Publishing Group, LLC
120 Broadway, New York, NY 10271 • fiercereads.com

Our books may be purchased in bulk for promotional, educational, or
business use. Please contact your local bookseller or the Macmillan Corporate
and Premium Sales Department at (800) 221-7945 ext. 5442 or by email at
MacmillanSpecialMarkets@macmillan.com.

Library of Congress Control Number: 2022908067

First edition, 2022
Book design by Michelle Gengaro-Kokmen
Printed in the United States of America

ISBN 978-1-250-23012-6 (hardcover)
1 3 5 7 9 10 8 6 4 2

LORD
OF THE
FLY FEST

1

RAFI FRANCISCO REALLY STEPPED IN IT THIS TIME.

She was lost and alone in the middle of a Caribbean jungle, wearing an ill-fitting shirt that clung to all her sweat-filled crevices.

There was an incessant bug, big as a bullet, buzzing into her neck, lured there by her ridiculously poor choice of candy-scented body spray.

Her backpack seemed to be getting heavier, and banged into her lower back with every step she took.

She was thirsty and tired and scared, and this colossal mistake of a trip had cost her two thousand dollars—aka her life's savings.

Yes, Rafi Francisco had definitely stepped in it. But like, literally.

She knew the moment she did it, feeling her shoe slide forward on the sticky stuff. Rafi winced as she lifted up her foot to examine the damage. She didn't want to think of the kind of animal that could make such a massive mess. With her luck it was still close by and watching her through the trees, ready to charge. Thirty minutes on this island had already proven soul—and *sole*—crushing. She scraped the bottom of her shoe across the base of the nearest tree trunk until most of the gunk was off.

A few hours ago Rafi had been on an air-conditioned plane, eating her third bag of free chips. Now she was here, regretting her life choices. Instinctively, she took her phone out of her pocket, but then remembered there was no service here. There was something so silly about a phone in a jungle, like holding a bouquet of flowers in a blizzard. Like things that belonged to two different worlds trying to coexist.

And while Rafi had been here only a short while, a lot of things about this place felt *off*. Rafi had flown to the island of Exuma with a plane full of concertgoers, and then they'd all subsequently boarded a ship that had taken them on a half-hour-long journey here. The island was big enough to take days to explore fully, but still small enough that Rafi couldn't find it on a map. She thought she had once, and studied it long and hard before realizing it was a blueberry muffin crumb. But what was really strange was that when they all got off the ship, there was no one to greet them. Not an organizer or owner or even a volunteer. Which was how Rafi had ended up in the jungle, looking for anyone who could tell her where to find her luggage.

Thirty-five minutes in and Rafi had the sinking feeling that she and everyone else here had been duped. But the biggest tell was the island itself. It looked nothing like it had in the promo video.

Fly Fest had gone from rumor, to viral fact, to the hottest ticket in town in a matter of days. But it really came alive in people's minds when the promo video dropped. Sandy beaches, Jet Skis, and supermodels. And, of course, there was the now legendary voice-over that played over the stunning imagery.

> Fly Fest is a question. An answer. An enigma. A messiah. A sandal. It is all and it is nothing. It will push the limits of boundlessness into an endless quest to enlightened fulfillment you didn't even know you desired but also never really longed for. It is air. It is foundation. It is sand, it is SUPERMODELS. It is the way the sun feels slipping through your fingers, and the way water feels blowing out your nostrils. It is standing at the top of Mount Everest and discovering the lost city of El Dorado. It is the Loch Ness Monster. It is the moment right after Mount Vesuvius exploded but right before the people of Pompeii turned to ash. It is the delicious mix of mental ecstasy and physical ecstasy and synthetic ecstasy. It is yachts. And it. Is. Fly.

So yeah, things were definitely not as advertised. Silver linings, though: At least no one had seen Rafi step in poop.

"Hello!" a voice called.

Rafi turned to find someone rushing toward her. Someone about her age, with a pageboy haircut and phone in hand. "Finally! What is the Wi-Fi password here?"

"Excuse me?" Rafi said.

"You work here, right?"

"In . . . the jungle?"

"No . . . the festival."

"Oh," Rafi said. "I don't work for the festival."

"But, your shirt . . ."

Rafi looked down. Her shirt was neon pink with the hashtag #LiveLaughFLY written across the chest in white cursive lettering. When Rafi bought her ticket to Fly Fest, she realized she had no idea what the appropriate attire was for a weeklong music festival in the Bahamas. Her wardrobe consisted mostly of comfortable sweatshirts in varying shades of gray and taupe. But she wanted to blend in on this trip. She wasn't sure her choice of shirt had worked, though. The moment Rafi set foot on the island and saw what all the other concertgoers looked like, she felt instantly different from them.

Her black bob with bangs stood out in a sea of flowing blondes and shimmering browns. Even though they were in the tropics, everyone looked so manicured, not a wisp of hair blowing in the island breeze, while Rafi, in a rush to make it to the airport on time, hadn't put any product in her hair. She hadn't even packed any. Everyone also already looked like they'd made a point to get tanned before showing up, which just made Rafi, who spent probably too much time indoors, feel suddenly Casperish. The pink shirt was the brightest, most carefree, and most expensive T-shirt Rafi owned. When she saw it on the Fly Fest website, she figured it'd be perfect. Though, now that she looked at it, she saw it for the generic thing it was, and couldn't be one hundred percent certain that the word STAFF wasn't written across the back.

Looking at her new companion's shirt, she noticed a button pinned on the collar with the words THEY/THEM on it.

"I'm Rafi, by the way. She/her."

Her introduction was met by a skeptical look that started at the top of Rafi's head and swept slowly down to her offending shoe. "Peggy Yim."

"Hi, Peggy. I don't work here, by the way. I've actually been looking for someone who does. It's weird, right? That there isn't anyone in charge?" She waited for a response, but Peggy was preoccupied with their phone, holding it up to the sky in search of reception.

"I tried that already," Rafi said. "It won't work."

"I have a satellite phone. I'll get online," Peggy said. "It's just a matter of time."

"You a tech whiz or something?"

"Yes." They offered nothing else, but Rafi liked the short answer, how assured Peggy was when they said it. They were probably one of those STEM coder people who were going to rule the world and knew it. Rafi needed more of that in her life, the boldness, the confidence. She'd come to Fly Fest to be bold, do important things. She suddenly felt bold enough to share something about herself, unprompted.

"I'm kind of a tech person, too. I have a podcast."

Rafi paused, in case Peggy wanted to ask a follow-up question or maybe murmur their approval. But the only sound that came was the squawk from a toucan flying overhead. Maybe Peggy's silence was their way of telling Rafi to go on.

"It's called Musical Mysteries. It's about mysteries in—"

"Let me guess," Peggy said. "Music."

"Right. I already have one season in the can. Eight episodes. It was pretty successful."

"Never heard of it."

"Well, successful in the independent podcasting world. It got written up on a few blogs. And Michael Panz called it 'promising,' and he's a contributing sound producer for NPR, so. Yeah. I'm proud of it."

Peggy kept checking their phone, and although they were walking away wordlessly, they also weren't changing the subject, which was new for Rafi, since at this point in the conversation about her podcast, most people usually did. "I'm focusing season two on River Stone."

"Isn't he supposed to be here?"

"Yes!" The word came out way too loud, but Rafi was just glad for the engagement. This was officially a two-way dialogue now. Her podcast was a topic of interest not only to her, but to Peggy, who was clearly a smart and interesting person. "Yes, he's supposed to be one of the musical acts. Which is why I'm here."

"Stalker."

"No, no, no," Rafi said, quickening her step to keep up. "No, I'm like a journalist. I'm chasing a story. And if I'm right, it could break a lot of things wide open."

"The girlfriend disappearance thing?"

"Yes," Rafi said. She was pleased that even Peggy seemed to acknowledge how that story seemed implausible and strange. Which made it perfect for the podcast.

"I heard River canceled his trip here."

Rafi stopped walking. "What?"

"All the musicians canceled. The models, too."

Rafi quickened her step to catch up with Peggy, who hadn't stopped walking and pointing their phone to the sky as though beckoning a higher power. "But I'm only here to meet River."

"Bummer." Peggy's tone did not in any way convey that this was, in fact, a bummer. Maybe their arm was finally too tired, but Peggy put down their phone, letting it bounce against their hip as they leveled Rafi with a serious stare. "There is no one affiliated with Fly Fest anywhere on this island. You know what that means, right?"

Rafi shook her head.

"We're stuck here," Peggy said.

It sounded too heavy, too bleak, and to counter that, Rafi's instinct was to chuckle. "We're not stuck here." If the festival really was canceled, then someone would be around to come get them. A boat. Surely. "Help is coming," Rafi said. A second ago she wasn't aware they needed help, but now nothing in the world seemed more true.

And yet, Peggy did not look convinced. "I just hope help gets here before all hell breaks loose."

Another thing that made Rafi laugh, though the sound that came out of her throat was more like a toad choking on a fly. "Come on. *Hell breaking loose*? Everyone here seems pretty cool."

"I take it you haven't been to the seaport yet."

2

WHEN THEY ALL DISEMBARKED FROM THE SHIP EARLIER, it was the seaport that greeted them. It appeared to be the lone human-made structure on the island, the only real sign so far that, before today, other human beings had set foot here. But it was also a sign that someone had abandoned this place, because it didn't look quite finished.

The building, if you could call it that, was only partially enclosed, with three walls and a few columns in front holding up a thatched roof. Its wooden beams were splintered, plaster-swollen, and chipped; the welcome signs warped with age and moisture. It looked like someone had plans to make this island a place for visitors, and they started with the seaport but then ran out of money. Like the building across the street from Rafi's house back home. It'd been under construction since she was eleven years old, and now, seven years later, it was still only partially done, with half the walls covered in insulation and the other half a skeleton of steel. The seaport was a promise that someone had taken back. But right now it could've been a town hall for how crammed it was with angry people.

When Rafi walked in, the first person she encountered was a girl who looked slightly younger than her, sobbing.

"Are you okay?" Rafi asked her.

The girl looked at Rafi, her eyes twin geysers. The sight of her instantly put Rafi in panic mode, and she did a quick surface check to see if there was something physically wrong. "Are you hurt?"

The girl held up her hands, which Rafi examined for blood or scratches. But they were as pristine as a nail-polish model's hands. "Where," the girl began, pausing to take a shaky breath, "is"—*sob*—"my"—*gulp*—"villa?"

Right. Some people had paid thousands to spend the week in luxury villas on the beach. Rafi had opted for the cheapest accommodation, which the Fly Fest website had described simply as "room." But there weren't any rooms that Rafi could see, let alone villas.

She didn't know what to say.

The girl, exasperated, let out another wail and skulked off to someone else who might be able to help her. But it didn't look like anyone in here could. All around the seaport people were crying, yelling, getting into each other's faces, asking their own desperate questions. It was discombobulating, and Rafi felt adrift in a sea of confusion. She sidled back up to Peggy like they were a life raft.

"Someone has to calm everybody down," Rafi said. "Maybe you should say something."

"Me?" Peggy said. "Why?"

"You're the only one in here not freaking out."

Peggy was extraordinarily calm, still looking down at their phone, trying to make it a little less useless. "It's a condition I have where I don't care about things."

Rafi nodded, though she couldn't tell if Peggy was being serious or not. Their monotonous voice made everything sound sarcastic.

"But you should definitely say something," Peggy continued.

"No, I couldn't." On her podcast, Rafi spoke to her listeners with no issue, but that didn't mean she was comfortable speaking in front of a real-life crowd. Especially not one as angry as this one. Without headphones on and a mic in front of her, Rafi couldn't even be sure she had a voice at all.

"THIS GIRL HAS SOMETHING TO SAY!" Peggy shouted. Turned out their voice could stay expressionless at a much higher octave, which surprised Rafi. But what truly horrified her was that Peggy was pointing directly at her.

"No," Rafi said. But it was too late, Peggy had already gotten the entire room's attention, and they leeched on to Rafi, the force of their questions strong enough to make her back away. Unfortunately, she backed right into the check-in desk at the far end of the room, and it seemed that the only way to get some distance from the increasingly angry horde was to climb onto said desk. So that was what she did.

"Where is everything?" someone from the crowd yelled.

"Where is our luggage?" another person asked.

"The website said there'd be on-site massages!"

"I want a piña colada!"

Rafi tried to keep everyone calm, but she couldn't even hear her own voice over the din. And then she thought maybe she *was* the perfect person to talk in front of this crowd because she had just the tool for exactly this situation. She swung her backpack forward and unzipped it, fishing inside for her portable microphone. It wasn't as high-tech as the one in her studio, aka her closet, but it would do. And the great thing about it wasn't just that it could record audio, but it could amplify her voice. She found her portable speaker in her bag too and set it down by her feet, plugging the mic into it with a thick cord.

"Okay, everyone, calm down!" Her voice boomed over the crowd like a heavy blanket over a bonfire, instantly putting out the questions and concerns.

She glanced quickly at Peggy, who kept their eyes down on their phone but still managed to raise a thumbs-up Rafi's way.

"I'd love to answer all of your questions, but I don't work for Fly Fest," Rafi said.

The crowd, still silent, looked collectively confused. "Are you sure?" a voice asked.

"Why does everyone think I work here?"

"You look like someone who has to work for a living," a boy said.

"You're like, what, thirty-two?" a girl said.

"I'm eighteen," Rafi said, appalled. And then she figured it out. *It must be the microphone.* It was authoritative and adult and impressive. *Yes, it was the microphone*, she thought.

"It's your shirt," someone else said.

Rafi looked down at her shirt and wondered for the second time that day what it was about the brightly colored, generically hashtagged, shapeless tee that screamed STAFF. "This shirt is cute and stylish," she tried to explain.

Their confused silence seemed to be gathering strength. Some of them shook their heads to disagree. Rafi pretended not to see those particular people. "Look, I might not work here, but I do know one thing: It doesn't look like anybody on this island works here either."

Heads began turning, looking at each other, as though checking to confirm that no one from Fly Fest was secretly among them. But there were no more bright pink shirts with generic, festival-approved slogans on them.

"Maybe they're coming on a different boat," Rafi continued. "Or maybe they're on another part of the island, and we just haven't seen them yet."

"Does this other part of the island have the villas?" It was the girl who'd been crying to Rafi, tears now drying on her cheeks.

"The other part of the island has all the yachts!" some guy shouted way too confidently.

"The supermodels are there?" someone else asked.

"Can I get my piña colada on the yachts with the supermodels?" another person said.

Rafi recognized the start of a new angry uprising. She spoke into her mic. "I know we were promised yachts with supermodels." Even as she said this she could see how ridiculous it sounded, how unlikely it was for supermodels to want to party on expensive boats with regular people. "But I think we have to prepare ourselves for—"

"My name is Paul!" a guy said out of nowhere. He was as tall as a goal post and looked like the type of guy who played football at Rafi's school. "And I only have one question: Is O-Town still coming?"

"My name is Ryan and I have the same question!" another guy said. "Is O-Town still doing their reunion concert here?" This Ryan person looked almost identical to Paul. Both of them had short, dark hair, square chins, deodorant commercial auras. Rafi felt like she was seeing double, which was disorienting, but not as disorienting as their weird question.

"I don't know what a Hotown is," she said, "but honestly, it sounds kind of sexist?"

"Are you kidding me?" Paul said. "Do you have any idea who my father is?"

"I don't see how that's relev—"

"If O-Town canceled, I want to get off this island," Ryan said. "Get the boat back. I want a refund, and I'm suing your ass."

"Like I said, I don't work here."

"I don't care!" Paul said.

Rafi glanced at Peggy, hoping for some reassurance, but Peggy only held up their hand again, this time in a thumbs-down.

So now not only was she out two thousand bucks and stranded on an island; Rafi also had a lawsuit on her hands. It would've worried her more if she wasn't distracted by something else.

A new group of people was marching toward the seaport from down the beach, a swarm of money and beauty. There was something about them that was different from everyone else. Maybe it was because none of them was currently suing Rafi, but they looked more dignified. Shinier. They were beautiful, and their clothes looked expensive, even if the attire was all wrong for the beach.

The girls plowed the sand with their heels. They wore crocheted halter tops that were both too much for this climate and not enough to provide cover from the unrelenting sun. Some had ropey bikini tops that looked like overly complex bondage situations and a nightmare for tan lines. And there were way too many of the most maddening clothing of all: rompers.

The boys' clothes were simpler, but no less head-scratching in this atmosphere. Designer sneakers and designer oversize sweatshirts and designer pants that got tighter farther down their legs. All of it looked cozy and kind of quilted, and Rafi could only imagine the deluge of sweat streaming underneath all those layers.

There was something special about them, and Rafi watched them like she knew them. It took her a minute, but she finally realized that they looked familiar because they *were* familiar. Rafi recognized them from little stories she'd seen bouncing around the internet, information that she'd come upon largely against her will.

Influencers. It was so clear now, as though she could see

the blue checkmarks or large figures that ended in *K* and *M* floating above their heads.

Rafi recognized the couple who insulted turkey (the cold cut, the animal, and the country).

The boy who adopted seventeen puppies and re-homed sixteen of them.

The girl who came out with a skin-care line that got recalled because it mimicked the effects of snake venom.

The vegan food guru who accidentally poisoned people with his raw mac-and-cheese recipe.

The crystals guy who started a cult.

The fashion designer who started a cult.

The fitness girl who started a cult.

The candle girl who burned down the West Coast.

The guy whose entire life was an elaborate prank.

The girl who broke travel bans to fly to 120 countries in the pandemic.

The person who went to Uzbekistan to do charity work with earthworms.

The guy who started that war using mindfulness techniques.

And sprinkled among the influencers was an even more rarefied group of elites. Rafi recognized them because they occasionally popped up in photos with real celebrities. They were practically celebs themselves. Well, celeb-adjacent. As in, they had the same hairdressers as certain celebs, belonged to the same invitation-only dating apps. They didn't shill anything on their social media platforms because they were already independently wealthy, thanks to their parents. They had no scandals to their names or anything even in the neighborhood of discernable talent, but they always seemed to be smack in the middle of the most glittering lifestyles. Which, Rafi guessed, was what drew them to Fly Fest. They didn't look so sparkling now, though. They kind of sparkled from all the sweat, but that wasn't the same thing.

At the front of the group, leading them, was the biggest influencer of all.

Rafi knew Jack Dewey from his makeup tutorials on YouTube. He was pretty. Not pretty in the typical teen heartthrob kind of way. Pretty in the *Toddlers & Tiaras* way. Like he could've entered a pageant and definitely stolen the crown from a dolled-up three-year-old. He had red hair that swooped over his forehead, and a body as smooth and stick-straight as an eyebrow pencil. He dressed mildly compared to everyone around him (simple tank top and short-shorts), but he didn't need to wear something ostentatious. His face was the real attention-grabber.

Jack was fully made up, with eyebrows painted in high arches, deep cheekbones cut with contouring, and overdrawn lips. It was a talent, what he managed to do with makeup. Rafi had tried following along to his infamous smoky-eye tutorial once, but it only made her look like she worked as a professional chimney sweep.

When he reached the seaport, Jack stopped, and his gang of influencers stopped behind him. He noticed Rafi right away. "Finally," he said. "Someone who works here."

"This shirt was for sale on the Fly Fest website," Rafi

announced into her microphone in her clearest voice. "Right next to the wristbands and the mouse pads." And as she said "mouse pads," it began to dawn on her that—yep—this festival was a scam.

"So who even are you?" Jack asked.

"My name is Rafi Francisco."

"I mean on social. What's your handle?"

"Oh," Rafi said. "Well, you can find me on Twitter under @MusicalMysteries. It's the name of my podcast. I have a podcast."

The silence that fell over the crowd was devastating. You could hear a dragonfly buzz straight from the room out of sheer mortification. The quiet stretched uncomfortably long, punctuated by one of the newly arrived influencers swaying and then finally falling face-first onto the floor.

"Is he okay?" Rafi asked. "He could have heatstroke."

"Pretty sure it's just secondhand embarrassment," Jack said. He stepped over the collapsed boy to get to the check-in desk and join Rafi on top of it. "I'll take it from here," he said, trying to grab Rafi's mic.

But Rafi held on to it tight. "This is actually mine," she said. "I was just telling everyone we should probably check the whole island to see if there's anyone in charge before we jump to conclusions. I've already been in the jungle, so that's covered. Do you want to team up? Head to the other side of the beach?"

Jack's chuckle hit her like a slap across the face. "And go back out in the sun? Absolutely no—"

"I'll do it."

Rafi searched the crowd for the person who had just volunteered. There was an awed parting as people backed away to let none other than musical sensation River Stone through.

The sight of him, so unexpected, made Rafi lose her voice.

Jack was quick to speak for the both of them, though. "The three of us will go, yes!"

3

RAFI, JACK, AND RIVER WALKED ALONG THE EDGE OF the island, first the mile of white sandy beach, which eventually turned into rocky terrain and cliffs on the east side. They stayed away from the center of the island because it was a mountain they weren't too keen to climb: The land was like a bedsheet that someone had pinched in the middle and pulled toward the sky. Rounding that area, they found themselves in a thick forest of jungle. And the whole time, Rafi held back, observing. She did a lot of talking on her podcast, but her most important job as an investigator (and she did consider herself an investigator) was to know when to stay quiet and keep her eyes peeled. And that was what she did now that she had eyes on *the* River Stone.

The one person she was here for.

Rafi zeroed in on every step he took. Even though River wasn't singing, it still felt like a concert experience. The oppressive humidity of the jungle mimicked the stuffiness of a performance hall, with every leaf and creeping vine like elbows and shoulders invading Rafi's personal space. When it came to River, though, the plants grazed and glided over his skin, wicking the sweat off him like adoring fans delicately dabbing his brow after a set. Typical.

Rafi's silence, she had to admit, was a little bit of the stunned variety. She'd spent all her money to come here and meet River, but now that he was only a few paces ahead of her, she was so shocked to be this close to him that she had no idea what to do or say.

Jack knew all too well, though. He walked in stride with River, gushing and asking endless questions.

"There must be a way for you to contact someone," Jack said. "Arrange a pickup? They wouldn't just leave a superstar to die in the wilderness. Does Uber have boats?"

"You know, I actually don't have a phone," River said. "I have people who handle all my social media and emails and all that. I like to be 'off the grid' whenever I can."

"Wow. Incredible," Jack said.

Rafi could not roll back her eyes enough. At River for having "people" to do his bidding, and at the idea of Jack believing that a phone-free life was "incredible."

"Is Hella here with you?" Jack asked.

Hella Badid was River's girlfriend. Dating for two months. She was a supermodel. In fact, she was one of the supermodels who had been prominently featured in all the promo videos for Fly Fest. When people said they wanted to party with supermodels on yachts, they meant they wanted to party with Hella.

"Uh, nah, she missed her flight. Probably for the best, right?"

20

The words poured out of River's mouth smarmy as an oil spill, but that may have just been because he was Australian. Like his answer to Jack's question, River may have seemed simple and innocuous, but Rafi could see right through him. And she saw his smile go crooked. It was something she'd observed about him in her research. River had a tell when he was lying, and that crooked smile was it.

"I only heard that all the other musical acts canceled when I was already on the ship," River said. "I knew something was wrong when I got off the boat and there was no one here to tell me where to go. In my industry, you rely on a team. I may have had the number-one album three weeks in a row, but I wouldn't know how to get dressed in the morning if I didn't have someone to tell me what to wear."

That explained his lack of a shirt.

Jack laughed and agreed about the "industry" as though he belonged to the same one. But Rafi couldn't giggle along with him. She saw right through River's humble-bragging. He slathered on the charm like it was a bottle of cheap cologne, and he stank of it. Did people really fall for his shtick? His arresting smile? His muscley physique? The way his shiny hair kept spilling over his eyes, and every time he brushed it back with his fingers it seemed to volumize with so much body that if little tiny people existed, they would take their teeny surfboards and ride those waves into the sunset?

The answer, of course, was yes. People ate it up. River had exploded onto the music scene two years ago, and he remained one of the most popular pop boys around. And Jack seemed to be falling for him in real time. Rafi noticed he would find any opportunity to casually rest his fingertips on River's forearm. River didn't seem to mind. His forearm had probably felt the touch of a lot of hands. His forearm was a swell covered in sparse, golden-haired foliage, coming to a point at his wrist, which was slender but strong. From it branched his hand, wide with long fingers. Looking at that hand, swinging idly by his hip, Rafi could so easily picture it wrapped around a knife.

Or a crowbar.

Or maybe pulling a thin rope taut until there was nothing but stillness on the other end of it.

"What smells like poop?"

Jack's question shook Rafi out of her reverie, and she noticed that both boys had stopped walking and were looking at her. Jack's nose was tipped up, lip curling as he sniffed.

"It's not me," Rafi said quickly. She dipped her right shoe behind her left, hoping the awkward motion was enough to hide the smell that was apparently emanating from her. "I don't . . . smell like poop."

"I don't smell anything," River said.

"Me neither," Rafi said.

"I have a scary-good sense of smell," Jack said. "I once smelled the glaucoma all over my great-grandfather. He died two days later."

He kept sniffing, and no matter how many steps Rafi took away from him, Jack's nose led him to her. Rafi backed away until she backed right into a tree and there was nowhere else for her to go. Jack bent low and when he straightened, his green eyes narrowed with certainty. "It's your shoe."

Rafi fixed her features until she felt they looked appropriately shocked, then lifted up her shoe so she could pretend to inspect the bottom of it for the first time. "Oh nooo," she whispered, elongating the small word so it sounded, ironically, Australian. "I must've stepped in poop."

Jack shuddered with disgust. "You just stepped in it? Where did it come from? Did someone just *go* out in the open? We haven't even been here three hours and people are already going in the wild? This is madness!"

"It's natural," River said. "Everybody goes. Even me."

The conversation was steering in a weird direction, and though Rafi was glad it was in a direction away from her offending shoe, she felt the need to get it back on track. "Um, I'm pretty sure it was not human poop."

Jack snapped his face in her direction. "What do you mean '*not human poop*'? Then what kind is it?"

River watched Rafi too, both of them waiting for an answer that she thought was pretty obvious.

"Animal?" she said. "Probably a boar." After bingeing the show *Lost* a few years ago, Rafi knew that the only things that lived on deserted islands were boars, polar bears, and smoke monsters. And out of the three, boar was the most likely culprit.

"Are you saying there are wild hogs on this island?" Jack asked. "If I wanted to party with wild hogs, I would've gone to my cousin Lionel's seventh birthday."

There were three tiers of passes to Fly Fest. Rafi had paid

for the kind that got you "room" and "limitless water." Jack must've paid for the kind that came with private villas, infinity pools, and no poop of any kind, human or otherwise.

"I think we need a change of subject," River said. "I mean, look at this place." He gestured toward the crystal water view shimmering through the trees to their right, the lush jungle to their left, the tropical birds cawing at them from above. It was hot, but there was a strong aroma coming from all around, from flowers or fruit, or both. There was nothing but the blue sky, the fresh air, and nature all around them. "There aren't any power lines. No people. No cars. Not a single cell tower," River said.

"It's a shit hole," Jack said.

"It's beautiful," River said at the same time.

"*So* beautiful," Jack agreed.

River seemed suddenly more interested in exploring the newfound beauty of the island than he was in continuing in a straight line down this expedition. He veered deeper into the jungle, following the sounds of birds in the leaves. Rafi kept her eyes on him, intent on following his every move. She couldn't stand to look at him for too long, but she also didn't want to lose sight of him.

But when she made a move toward River, Jack blocked her way.

"I hope I'm not overstepping here," Jack said, "but I thought I might give you a beauty tip, since it's kind of what I'm known for." He unzipped the black leather fanny pack that he wore around his waist and retrieved a tube of shiny lip gloss.

"It breaks my heart when I see a girl who's never heard of makeup before."

"I've heard of—"

"This goes on your mouth," Jack explained slowly, extending the tube to Rafi. "Your lips are so pale I can't be certain you even have a mouth. This gloss is clear so it won't totally fix the problem, but it's something. And you really need"—he looked her over, the expression on his face darkening—"something."

"Thanks," Rafi said, though she wasn't sure that was the right word to use. "My lips probably look like this because there's a ninety-five percent chance I'm dehydrated."

"Oh, I can tell you're thirsty," Jack said. "How many followers do you have?"

Instinctively, Rafi turned around to see if anyone was trailing her, but then realized what Jack meant. "Around five hundred on Twitter."

Jack's eyes narrowed, confused. "Are you, like, a nano-influencer?"

Rafi didn't know what a nano-influencer was, but she was pretty sure she wasn't it. She shook her head.

Her answer seemed only to confuse Jack further. "Nobody our age listens to podcasts, unless they're losers or incels. When do you have time for TikTok?"

"I don't."

"YouTube beauty tutorials?"

"Also not."

"Of course, of course. Your whole look is starting to make

a lot of sense." As he said this, Jack wiped the sweat off his forehead, unwittingly smearing the penciled-in color of his brows over the side of his face.

"You've got a little something," Rafi said, gesturing to her own face as a map for him. But though she'd pointed to her forehead, Jack proceeded to wipe the sweat from his upper lip instead, painting a swath of his chin pink.

Rafi looked, slack-jawed, at his multicolored face. But instead of saying anything, she found herself giving Jack a thumbs-up.

"Hey, guys? I think I found something," River called.

They couldn't see River through the trees but followed his voice until they were standing right beside him. And in front of an enormous shipping container.

"Oh, thank goodness," Jack said. "Our luggage is here."

They'd been informed that their luggage couldn't all fit on the boat that brought them to the island and so would be arriving separately. But Rafi never imagined it would be like this. At least they found it. She could finally change out of her Fly Fest staff shirt.

River took hold of one door and Jack the other. Together, they opened the container.

It was not their luggage.

4

AT FIRST IT LOOKED LIKE A WALL OF WHITE BRICKS, BUT when they got closer to the shipping container, they saw that the bricks were actually Styrofoam boxes. Rafi dug her fingertips into the skinny crevices between each box until she was able to retrieve one right out of the center. She reflexively winced, expecting some of the surrounding boxes to tumble out too, but they stayed packed in place, cemented like a brick wall after all.

Rafi opened the box. Inside was the last thing she expected.

"A sandwich." Something she'd seen a million times before, but this sandwich was different. She couldn't exactly ascribe a personality to the food, but there was no denying the thing looked defeated, sad, and kind of sweaty. Rafi could relate. She peeled the top layer of sliced white bread back and found a single square of American cheese. No butter, no sauces. A pale lettuce leaf lay miserably wilting on the side of the box like a boxer against the ropes in the third round of a fight.

Jack peeked over Rafi's shoulder. "What is that supposed to be?"

"I think it's our food."

Jack shook his head. "I paid for the VIP gourmet-chef-prepared organic vegan meal plan."

Rafi checked the side of the box to see if it said anything about this being the VIP gourmet-chef-prepared organic vegan meal plan, but the small print she did find said only: DO NOT REFRIGERATE. CONTENTS MAY DISINTEGRATE.

Rafi glanced at the wall of boxes again, all of them identical, all with the same small print across the bottoms of the boxes like the surgeon general's warning. "Well, it's definitely not real cheese, so I'm pretty sure it's vegan."

"This wasn't on the menu I saw online," Jack said. "Where are the twenty-four-karat-gold-flecked, Incomprehensible Chicken Wings?"

Rafi lifted the sandwich out of the box, searching for anything else underneath it, but there wasn't a speck of gold anywhere.

"What about the diamond-infused water?" Jack asked.

"There's . . . lettuce."

"What about the Tahitian ice cream made with Madagascar vanilla bean, Maui mango compote, and Cook Island caviar?"

"You're looking at the same box I am, right?" Rafi asked.

Jack whimpered but River seemed to take the news in stride. "Hey, it's something. And I don't know about you but I'm pretty hungry." He plucked his own box out of the shipping container, grabbed the cheese sandwich, and took a big bite out of it before violently spitting it back out. He coughed, grimaced, wiped his mouth. "No."

"Can we go?" Jack said, stomping his foot and smearing

more makeup with the back of his wrist. "I feel like I'm melting."

He also *looked* like he was melting. Every ounce of his makeup had started to resemble what Rafi imagined that Tahitian ice cream looked like.

"Okay, we need a plan," Rafi said.

"Turn around and never look back?" Jack offered.

River began to nod, but one look at the expression on Rafi's face, and he started to shake his head instead.

Rafi took this new sandwich development as a progression of what she'd started in the seaport. She'd been bold enough to speak publicly, and she'd taken the initiative to come on this exploratory search. Now she had this. Although the food didn't look good, finding it was. It was a new piece to this weird, music-festival puzzle. It was something. And something was better than nothing. "We should take as much of these boxes back to the seaport as we can. We may not have found anyone affiliated with the festival, or our luggage, but at least we have this."

"People will starve before they touch that," Jack said.

"It's food," Rafi said. "They'll be happy."

Jack shrugged. "Lettuce pray."

The sandwich went whizzing past Rafi's head. "I can't. Eat. *Gluten!*" said the girl who'd thrown it. It was the same girl who'd sobbed to Rafi about not having a villa, sobbing now about the gluten. "Or dairy!" she continued. "Or any food that comes in boxes!"

Rafi wasn't sure what to say to her, or to anyone else, because literally everyone was complaining about the sandwiches. Some people set the open boxes down and took pictures of the sandwiches as though they were art exhibits. Others threw the sandwiches against the walls, the bread and lettuce falling limply like confetti (the cheese, however, sticking to every surface like putty).

One of the jocks who Rafi couldn't tell apart—Ryan or Paul; it was anybody's guess who—held up his sandwich to Rafi's face. "Do you want another lawsuit on your hands?"

She looked around for Jack or River, since they helped bring the sandwiches too, but they were suddenly MIA. The other jock showed up with his own sandwich, a look of incredulity clouding his chiseled features. There was no way he was eating this thing, and his reasoning was simple: "Do you have any idea who my father is?"

More sandwiches flew, like a scene from a college frat movie, or maybe a war. Rafi ducked through the crowd to avoid them, but everywhere she turned there were more people with complaints.

"Guys, this is the only food we have!" But her voice was drowned out. "Guys!" she tried again through the flurry of sandwich missiles.

Hardly anyone could hear Rafi, but even the ones who could didn't seem to want to listen. She found Peggy near the back, a mountain of cheese boxes at their feet. They opened a new box, discarding the bread and lettuce, and flung the square of cheese to the thatched ceiling. It did not return. "You're never gonna get through to them," Peggy said.

"We need to preserve the food," Rafi said. "And it's going to be night soon, we need to make shelter." A rising panic was taking shape in her gut, the reality that there was no good food and no one here to help. "We need to do *something*."

"Most of these people already have shelter," Peggy said, tossing another piece of cheese.

"What do you mean?" Rafi asked.

"You know," Peggy said. "Tent City."

"Tent *what*?"

Five minutes later Rafi and Peggy stood before an encampment not far from the seaport. It was made up of rows of domed structures built with plastic frames and waterproof canvas. The kinds of tents you see on the news to help displaced people going through natural disasters. Which, Rafi figured, Fly Fest was.

They weren't the villas people had paid for, but at least they protected from the elements. They were perfectly suitable for one night, and Rafi felt a surge of relief when she saw them. There was even a set of three porta potties off to the side— more signs that someone had at least been working on trying to make this festival actually happen.

Tents and bathrooms. Rafi couldn't believe her luck. She

gripped the straps of her backpack, ready to set it down for the first time that day and take a breather. "Which tents are empty?"

"None," Peggy said.

Rafi turned to Peggy slowly, bemused, not sure she heard them right. "There's a nun?"

Peggy shook their head, took care to enunciate. "*None.* The influencers got them all first thing. That's why they showed up late to the seaport, when you were giving your speech."

It didn't make any sense. There had to be at least fifty tents out there. If people bunked together, there could be room for everyone. But Peggy seemed to read her mind and shook their head.

"These people don't do roommates, unless it's a TikTok incubator in Calabasas."

"You keep using words that don't make any sense," Rafi said.

Peggy put a hand on Rafi's shoulder and tried to make it as clear as possible. "You're sleeping on the beach."

By the time Rafi got to the beach, the sun had set and a smattering of people had already claimed their spots for the night. Some of them were trying unsuccessfully to build fires, others were using driftwood and the spare sweatshirts and coveralls that they'd packed in their carry-ons to build shelter. Most of them were midway between the tree line and the ocean, but that was too close to the water for Rafi. She found a spot by the palms, away from everyone else. She'd done a lot today, spoken to enough people. At this point all she wanted to do was decompress and be alone.

In theory, it should've sounded romantic: sleeping on the beach, a blanket of stars overhead, the low tide acting as a calming, natural noise machine. Instead, she sat cradling her sneaker, using a twig to try and scrape off every last bit of wild boar fecal matter that might have remained. And even though the bottom of her shoe now looked good as new, Rafi couldn't hold back the sense of dread that was building in her chest.

There really was no food. (As not a single person had actually eaten the cheese sandwiches, the jury was still out on whether they qualified as edible.) And that was only the start of it. The realization of just how screwed up this situation was came crashing down on her like a series of waves trying to pull her underwater.

There was no shelter for half the people here.

All of their checked luggage had been lost.

There was no one in charge.

They had no way of reaching anyone in the outside world.

For the first time, Rafi was facing the fact that she was stranded on an island with people whom she was beginning to suspect were total morons.

Worst of all, she'd spent every last penny she had for the privilege of being here.

Coming to Fly Fest had been a splurge, but she'd convinced

herself that it would be worth it. That she'd get her story for her podcast and maybe she'd even get to enjoy herself along the way. She'd let herself daydream of a world that was so foreign to her, one in which she could rub shoulders with rock stars and party like she was a celebrity herself. She had to admit she bought into the luxury and exclusivity that the Fly Fest social media accounts had been touting for months.

But she wasn't glamorous like the other people here. She'd paid for a ticket, and yet she still found a way to stay just outside that tight, exclusive circle of elitism. She couldn't even get a disaster relief tent to sleep in.

Rafi tossed her sneaker aside, giving up on the delusion that it would ever be as good as new. It was just one more ruined thing. She looked around at the denizens of the beach, settling in for the night: the people who weren't lucky enough to score a tent in Tent City. Their mood seemed to match her own. They'd all paid so much for the promise of paradise, but they'd been shipwrecked.

"Excuse me, you threw this at my head?"

Rafi startled at the voice, which was too soft and preternaturally calm for what it'd just said. The girl it belonged to cradled a sneaker in her hand like it was a baby dove with a broken wing.

Rafi scrambled to her feet, spraying sand in every direction like an ostrich taking a dust bath. "That was—I didn't mean to—" She took back the sneaker.

"People always try to get me to wear their products—"

"Oh, I wasn't trying t—"

"As a rule, I don't do that, and I'm sorry but I won't start now."

Rafi only nodded. Explaining why she'd thrown her shoe didn't seem worth it, and anyway, this girl didn't seem all that bothered. She wore a crown of flowers on her delicate head, which was framed by the most beautiful soft, curly hair. It was beachy and carefree, yet not a strand was out of place. And somehow, though the sun had set long ago, her hair pulled every bit of light from the sky, making it look naturally highlighted. The ethereal beauty bore no signs of the outrage that Rafi herself would have displayed had a projectile shoe come at her out of nowhere. She looked expensive and contented, like her life was a fragrance commercial. A gauzy shawl that looked like it was made from golden thread spun by Rumpelstiltskin himself struggled to keep from slipping off shoulders as smooth as chocolate ganache. The only sign that this angel on earth was a real, human person was a single blemish on the nape of her neck, positioned where a hickey might be. A wine-colored birthmark, roughly the shape of a heart and the size of a strawberry. A gold necklace bisected it, coming to a point with a charm that nestled in the dip between her collarbones. It spelled out a single, perfect word in loopy script: *Sierra*.

Rafi felt like a clump of shower drain hair just looking at her. She could tell from the way Sierra held herself (and from the fact that she did not shill products) that she was a cut above the rest of the influencers on this island. At the very least she definitely did not belong on this beach, mere steps from people crying into their sandwich boxes. But strangely, she remained, looking out to sea, fragrance-commercial life in full swing.

"My name is Sierra Madre," Sierra said to the sea, and maybe also to Rafi.

"Wow, like the mountain range?"

"I'm not familiar."

"You've never googled your name before?"

"The first thing that comes up when I google my name is me. Is there another Sierra Madre? Is she pretty?" When Rafi didn't say anything, Sierra turned to her, her eyes imploring. "*Prettier*?"

Rafi was beginning to realize she didn't know how to communicate with these people. They seemed to speak in a language she'd never been taught and didn't have time to learn. But Sierra wasn't going anywhere, and the awkward silence was a buzzing static in Rafi's ears. "No, you're prettier."

Sierra ironed out the furrow in her brow and turned back to the sea.

"So, it sucks that Fly Fest was a scam, huh?" Rafi said.

"I suppose." Sierra sighed. "But don't despair. Everything will be fine."

"How do you know?"

The girl's glistening shoulders rose and settled again just as quickly. "Because it always is."

Definitely a language Rafi didn't understand. She was out two thousand bucks and had nowhere to sleep. They may have been standing on the same patch of sand, but Rafi very much doubted Sierra knew how devastating that was.

"I know just the thing to turn your frown upside down," Sierra said.

Did it involve a two-thousand-dollar check? Because Rafi could really use a two-thousand-dollar—

Sierra lifted the flower crown off her own head and placed it atop Rafi's. "There," she said, looking at Rafi like she was a cake she'd just finished frosting. "I don't need this anymore."

The tone of her voice tricked Rafi into thinking that was a compliment, though she was slowly realizing it wasn't. "Thanks."

"And hey, you've always got your . . . little recording hobby."

Rafi's heart, which had felt as limp and deflated as a week-old balloon, began to expand again. "My podcast? You were at the seaport when I talked about my podcast?"

Sierra Madre nodded and finally wrested her gaze from the sea to look at Rafi, her eyes glinting as brightly as her gold necklace. She placed a palm as soft as a soap bubble on Rafi's cheek. "I don't know what a podcast is and I've never listened to one but as soon as I get off this island, I will listen to yours, alright? I promise you that. Just don't ask me to plug it on my social platforms."

"I wasn't goin—"

"Because I've never done that, and I won't start now."

Rafi nodded, once more at a loss for what to say.

"If you need anything from me you can always find me in Tent City, where I will be going now. Bye-bye." And just like that, Sierra Madre walked away and down the beach, like a breeze wisping flakes of snow off a mountain range.

Their shared moment had been a strange one, to say the least. But it had somehow made Rafi feel slightly less like crap. And Sierra was right. Rafi had at least one thing going for her.

She grabbed her backpack and unzipped it, deciding to take inventory. She'd packed all of her clothes in her checked bag, but everything in her carry-on, when used together, made up the one thing she valued over everything else she owned.

Her podcasting kit.

She laid it all out in front of her the way some people on this trip arranged the "flat lays" on their Instagrams. There was her BoomN2 Handy Mic. A cable. A portable speaker. Headphones. A wireless receiver. A charger. And her phone. Put them all together and they made up the most useful tool she had in her arsenal to give her life purpose. Looked at another way, it was the most useless thing you could have when stranded on an island.

But with nothing else to do, Rafi figured she might as well record the first episode of season two of "Musical Mysteries."

She picked up her microphone, cleared her throat, and hit record.

MUSICAL MYSTERIES
Season 2: Episode 1
"The Australian Outback"

What do you have to do to get away with the perfect crime?

It's a heavy question, but one we've all probably asked ourselves at some point in our lives.

Do you have to plan meticulously until "premeditated" isn't just a word to you—it's the code you live by?

Do you have to develop the kind of personality that would make you seem nice and charming and super simpatico all in an attempt to trick people into thinking you're the best thing since sliced bread?

Better yet, do you take advantage of all your newfound attention and goodwill to become a hugely popular entertainer? After all, wouldn't catchy songs and a sparkling smile be the best wool you could pull over people's eyes?

I guess what I'm asking is, can you be one of the nation's biggest pop stars *and* the perpetrator of a heinous crime?

If you're River Stone, the answer just might be yes.

I'm Rafi Francisco, and if you're anything like me,

you've been pretty skeptical about River Stone and his meteoric rise to fame ever since he showed up on the scene with an old guitar and a tragic backstory.

A backstory that includes love, heartbreak, Australia, and a big dollop of mystery. Or should I say . . . murder?

I know there was an investigation. I know there was evidence to support the abandonment story. And even as I say these words I can feel some of you hearing them and getting angry. *What happened to River was horrible and what his girlfriend did to him was unforgivable; can't we leave the poor boy alone?*

Well, dear listener, no, we cannot. Because what if I told you that River wasn't abandoned by his girlfriend in the middle of the wilderness as he claims, and was, in fact, the very person who made her disappear? What if I told you I've uncovered clues—undeniable evidence—that directly contradict River's version of events? What if I told you that River Stone isn't as innocent as you might think?

All of this might sound like outlandish accusations, but I promise you: By the end of this series you *will* have conclusive answers about what really happened that summer night in the Australian Outback. And I'm not talking about the restaurant, folks. I'll even promise you an exclusive interview with River Stone himself, where I ask him the questions that other reporters have been too shy to bring up.

What really happened to Tracy?

That, and more, on this season of . . . "Musical Mysteries"!

This episode of "Musical Mysteries" was brought to you by Nobrand. Ever wish you'd packed a snack because the only food around are cheese sandwiches that might poison you? Why not try Nobrand protein bars? Nobrand makes everything from food to cleaning supplies, and their products definitely won't disintegrate if refrigerated. Go to Nobrand.com and enter code RIVERKILLER for two percent off your next purchase!

Nobrand was Rafi's sponsor for season two. A big get, and also the only company that responded to her inquiries about possible partnerships. They sent her a list of products that she could plug every episode, and said she could write her own copy for it. It made her happy just thinking about it, and recording this first episode had also helped to lift her mood. She'd have to add more in post, edit in some sound effects and musical cues, but for now it was a pretty good intro episode, if she did say so herself. The problem was she was almost out of battery on her phone. She thought she spotted some electrical outlets at the seaport. She'd have to go back tomorrow and see if she could charge up.

But night had fallen, and though she wasn't tired, she longed for sleep. The morning had to bring good news. It couldn't get worse than this.

She bunched up her backpack full of bulky electronics and placed it under her head. As far as pillows went, this definitely was not one. But Rafi couldn't entirely blame it for her inability to get comfortable. The sand was powdery but it didn't yield to her body at all. And there was a weird sound coming from the trees just behind her head.

A rhythmic hacking.

It was a small sound that could've been anything and Rafi could've just ignored it, but the investigator in her wouldn't let it go.

Rafi stood up and made her way through the jungle. The moonlight shone just brightly enough to cast silver outlines of the trees. She was getting close, the noise coming clearer now. She knew that sound. Not because it occurred naturally in nature, but because she'd heard it in movies a lot. It was the distinct sound a knife made when it came violently down on something.

The hacking was both scraping against something hard and hitting something that squelched. It was the kind of sound that made the back of your throat tickle. It was the most sickening thing Rafi had ever heard in real life, and she suddenly wished she had her mic with her so she could record it. Something bad was happening. The stench of it filled the jungle air.

And then she saw the outline of a man. He was crouched on the ground, bent over something, his arm coming up and down violently, hacking away. The knife was clear now, wrapped in his fingers and glinting in the moonlight, and every time he held it up, it came back more liquidy than before.

Rafi only stood there, stunned. She tried not to make a noise but she must've not been quiet enough, because the guy turned around. And when he did, Rafi could see River, his bare chest covered in moonlit blood and guts.

5

"RAFI."

Her first thought, ridiculously, was surprise that he'd remembered her name.

But that thought was quickly wiped from her mind as she tried to process what she was looking at. River standing (shirtless), covered in guts, holding a knife, and getting closer.

Rafi took a step backward, and she must've looked as scared as she felt because a questioning crease formed between River's eyebrows. Usually when girls looked at him it was with heart eyes and lust. But to Rafi, his whole deal was super predatory. The moment stretched out longer, with Rafi wide-eyed and backing away and River trying to seem docile and nice while *holding a knife*. Then he seemed to remember his weapon and the splattered bare chest.

"Oh, this?" When he pointed at his chest it was with the tip of his knife, which didn't do much to mitigate the situation. "I'm sorry you had to see me like this."

Rafi looked past him, her eyes darting all over the jungle ground in search of a corpse. But all she saw was a fish, long as her arm and dead on a bed of banana leaf.

"I know, it must be weird, you've probably seen me in magazines in designer clothes and now I'm a total mess." There was a chuckle in his voice. "*Ick*."

A fish. Not a dead body. Rafi breathed deep, but not too deep. Yes, she'd jumped to conclusions, but this could also just be a warm-up for him. He did seem really comfortable holding that knife. Which begged the question.

"Where'd you get a knife?"

River looked at the weapon in his hand like he'd forgotten it was there. "This? Someone must've smuggled it on the plane. Anyway, I asked around if anyone had one and lucky me, somebody did."

"You asked around for a knife?"

"Yeah, I needed something to sharpen my spear with."

"Wait, there's a spear now?" How many weapons did this guy have? They'd only been here a day, and he already had an arsenal.

"To go spearfishing with. Of course, my spear was a little more rudimentary than a speargun, but under the circumstances it was all I had."

There were too many guns, spears, and knives in this conversation, and Rafi really, really wished she had her mic with her so she could record it all.

"So anyway," River continued, "went spearfishing, caught that big guy behind me, and then I used this knife to clean the scales and gut him. Which you found me doing."

"That is . . . not how you gut a fish."

The quirk in River's smile was slow and deliberate, like

he'd been caught in a lie even though, to his credit, there really was a dead fish behind him. "It is in Australia."

Rafi knew very little about Australia and would have to take his word for it. "Okay, but why are you hiding in the jungle?"

For some reason, this part of River's explanation warranted a toss of his hair, a twinkle in his eye, and a slowly spreading grin. "Because it's a messy job. And trust me, nobody wants to see their favorite musician covered in fish guts."

"Presumptuous," Rafi muttered.

"That people wouldn't want to see me covered in fish guts?"

"That you're anybody's favorite musician."

River stared at her, mouth slightly open, and Rafi realized she'd gone too far. The only reason she'd come to Fly Fest was to meet River and get him to confess to his crime, and this was not the way to go about it. She was letting her true feelings for him show, and she needed to keep that under wraps. She needed him to believe she was just another fan.

Rafi was about to put on a smile, drum up a giggle, say she was only joking, when River beat her to the punch. He began to laugh. A deep, carefree thing. *Of course he was somebody's favorite musician!*

"I'm gonna go get cleaned up," River said. "Do you want fish?"

Rafi hated how much she was enjoying this fish. She didn't know what kind it was, but she didn't care; River had served her a plump white filet on a broad leaf dish, and she gobbled most of it up in no time. She also hated that not only was River famous, and a talented musician, and a good spearfisher—turned out he could cook, too. Or maybe she was just hungry.

She hated a lot about him, but she had to pretend not to in order to get her scoop. Tonight, she'd be River Stone's biggest fan.

"This fish is so amazing! You're so good at everything!" Rafi was putting it on too thick, and she coughed, embarrassed. But River took it in stride. He was used to this level of adoration.

"I know there are sandwiches but I heard some gnarly rumors about them. Apparently they're growing."

Rafi swallowed. "What?"

"Someone took a ruler to them. The sandwiches are half an inch bigger in diameter. Allegedly."

"They're sandwiches. . . . They can't grow."

River only shrugged like it was the damnedest thing. He took a bite of fish and gave Rafi a closed-mouth smile, and the strange topic of the growing cheese sandwiches was willfully forgotten.

Since returning to the beach, River had managed to take a quick dip in the ocean to wash up, build a fire, cook the fish, and construct two simple tents side by side out of sticks and random bits of clothing he had in his possession. Rafi didn't even realize the second tent was for her until it was done, and though she didn't yet know how she felt about being River Stone's neighbor (Pro: She'd have eyes on him; Con: He might kill her while she slept), she had to admit it was nice having shelter.

The whole time he worked, River rambled on about the great weather, and how gorgeous the beach was, and how the concertgoers were dope people. Rafi realized it was another talent of his: filling the air with pointless noise—empty and cunningly distracting—without revealing anything of substance about himself. PR-approved interview-speak. Earlier, Rafi had secretly turned on her mic to record him. Now she made a mental note to delete all of his useless chitchat.

The only reason Rafi had come to Fly Fest in the first place was for a chance to talk to River, and now she was getting it. They were alone, together, in private, and she didn't want to talk about the weather. This may have been her only chance to interview a primary source for her story. And suddenly, the fiasco of Fly Fest didn't seem so bad. Because everyone else had come here for a totally lit week of music and yachts and rich people wet dreams, but all she'd ever wanted was a moment alone with River Stone. And now she had it.

Asking about his first girlfriend might come off too weird, out of left field, intrusive. But this might be Rafi's only shot. She had to tread lightly.

River went to crouch next to the small fire he'd made, poking it with a stick until embers crackled and disappeared into the night. He looked over at Rafi and a smile played on his lips. It made him look roguish, charming, laid-back. If she hadn't known the truth about him, Rafi might have considered him attractive. Because River's smile was arguably the most beautiful thing about him. Full lower lip, delicate Cupid's bow. Lips lush and pink like they'd spent the whole day kissing. It was a smile that radiated happiness. Security. Safety. Rafi wondered if it was the last thing his first girlfriend saw before she "disappeared."

"Tracy," Rafi blurted.

The smile skidded off River's face like it'd slipped on ice. "What?"

As far as treading lightly went, this was the opposite. This was a sonic boom.

"I'm so sorry. I don't know why . . . I guess I was just thinking about your album. And that got me thinking about who all the songs were about . . . and then I thought about Tracy and how she . . . disappeared."

As River watched Rafi, she realized her mistake. She couldn't just launch into her investigation of his first love. She was scaring River off. She needed time to wade into those waters. No, water metaphors were bad—she would not be wading into any waters, real or metaphorical. But the fact remained: She needed time to gain River's trust before striking.

"I shouldn't have brought it up," Rafi said. "I'm just nervous . . . about this festival and how it's nonexistent. We're all alone on an island with no cell service and no way to call for help."

Rafi looked in River's eyes to see if she could see a glimmer of glee at that prospect. But River only smacked his hands together, dusting off any remnants of the fish or the fire or his decision to ever sit down to talk to her.

"No worries."

Rafi thought he'd been stoking the fire this whole time, but now she realized he was trying to put it out. Soon there was nothing but ash and sand, and River stood, stamping out any flickers that remained.

"Better get some shut-eye," he said abruptly. And he smiled at her. Crookedly.

It was nothing like his natural smile, the one that made him seem safe and cute. This one was performative. There was no reason for him to even be smiling! But he couldn't help himself. Whether he intended to smile crookedly or not, Rafi knew it was what happened whenever he felt pinned. And he was doing it now.

"And hey, don't worry about being stuck on the island. A boat will probably be here bright and early to take us all home."

He gave her the same short wave he gave to fans whenever he was returning a pen they'd given him to sign a magazine cover with, and then he was off, leaving Rafi alone in front of the ghost of a fire.

If a boat really was going to come tomorrow to rescue them all from this disaster of a music festival, then why was Rafi suddenly filled with worry?

The answer came to her instantly. She'd just had a one-on-one private conversation with her ultimate interview subject, and she'd blown it. She didn't get any good sound bites. In fact, she'd effectively scared him off. What she needed was more time. This island, closed off from the rest of the world, was the perfect incubator for the story she needed to tell. On the island, River had nowhere to go. And no duties to keep him busy now that the festival was a bust. The problem was getting him to stay.

And if Rafi wanted River to stay, she'd need everyone on the island to stay, too.

6

On the beach, concertgoers were waking from their open-aired slumber to bright daylight. Even this early in the morning the sun was already scorching, beating down on all of them. It was a reminder to get up, that as bad as things seemed yesterday, today was a brand-new day. The sun was like that. It made everything seem shiny and new. Things were looking up.

Well, not Rafi, who literally couldn't look up. Turned out sleeping on a bed of sand was supremely uncomfortable, and she winced and sucked in a deep breath the moment she tried facing the sun. Nope, she couldn't bend her neck back, but that was okay. Yesterday had been bad. Possibly the most disappointing day of Rafi's life. But one of the things Rafi liked most about herself was her ability to look on the bright side. To problem-solve. What didn't work out yesterday would definitely work out today. And in the twinkling hours before she'd finally succumbed to sleep, a plan had taken shape in Rafi's mind, one that got her heart pumping from adrenaline and made her forget that her pillow was a bag of bulky recording equipment.

There was a boat scheduled to pick them all up in one week.

That was one week to get an interview with River and turn her podcast into one of the best true crime stories on record. But if word got out that Fly Fest was a fiasco, then a boat might come back any minute to rescue them. Rafi couldn't stop a boat from coming, but she could convince people to not get on it.

Because if people stayed, then there was a good chance River would stay, too. After all, he was the only musical act to have come this far, despite the early rumors of the festival's shortcomings. If Rafi wanted River to stay on this island, then she'd have to keep the idea of Fly Fest alive. Of course, she couldn't put on an entire music festival by herself, but people had come here for more than a concert. They'd come for the promise of paradise. And that was already here. Sure, there was the ramshackle seaport, and the wasteland on which the disaster relief tents were set up, and the dense, sweaty jungle full of buzzing insects and wild boars, and the cliffs that were too rocky and steep to be scaled; and there weren't any yachts or villas or cabanas or mai tais with little colorful umbrellas sticking out of them, but there was a small patch of actual, white-sand beach with turquoise water.

As Rafi pulled back the muslin sarong that made up the doorway of her makeshift tent, she looked out at that sea view and breathed in the delicious saltwater air. The promise of paradise was right in front of her. Now she just had to convince everyone here of that promise, too. It wouldn't be that hard. She spoke to her podcast listeners all the time. Presented the facts and evidence and convinced them of the truth that was right in front of them. Rafi could do the same with the people here.

Yes, today would be a good day. Rafi's plan was simple: charge her phone, and get everyone on the island to believe there was something here worth staying for.

The second part of her mission would not be easy; on her walk to the seaport she'd heard multiple rumblings of disgruntled concertgoers claiming this place was "hella bad" or that they needed to get "the hell out of here" or just plain "We're in hell." People were really set on the whole "hell" aspect of this nightmare. Or maybe they were talking about Hella Badid—Rafi couldn't be sure. Everything she heard came in hissy, scattershot whispers.

She had no idea how she'd convince the people here to stay, but at least she could take care of the first part of her mission and juice her phone. Even though she couldn't use it to reach anyone, she could still record on it, and that was her lifeline right now. Unmoored as they were on this forgotten island, recording was the only thing that could keep Rafi tethered to a sense of normalcy.

At the seaport, Rafi found those square-jawed guys, Paul and Ryan, sitting on the raised platform that led to the main entrance. Her stomach dropped when she saw that they were on their phones.

"You have service?" she asked them, in lieu of a hello.

"No, are you offering?" one of them asked.

"Dude, maid service!" the other one said. "Finally."

"Don't you need a room first?" Rafi asked.

Paul and Ryan stared at her, like yes, they would need a room first, and why was she just standing there and not getting one for them. Wait. "I'm not a maid," Rafi said, coming to her senses.

"You sure?" Ryan (she was pretty sure it was Ryan) asked. "You look exactly like my maid after she woke up from her coma."

Convincing people to stay on this island, Rafi realized, would be impossible. Mostly because she could not stand talking to them.

"I'm gonna go," Rafi said. She tried sidestepping them to get inside but Paul got in her way.

"I'd like to file a formal complaint."

"For the last time, I don't work here."

"This place isn't very money," he said, pretending he didn't hear her. "O-Town isn't here. And when I tell my father what's going on here, there's going to be hell to pay."

Rafi could've just kept walking, but if she was ever going to convince the people on the island to stay, she might as well start with these guys. Also, if she gave them something else to focus on, maybe they'd leave her alone.

"You know, you don't have to be bored," Rafi began. "There's a lot to do here on the island."

"Name one thing," Ryan said.

"Yeah," Paul said. "Name one."

For some reason, Rafi could not, for the life of her, name a single thing. "Just . . . there's opportunity here, you know? People are struggling. What if you could, I don't know, help them out? Imagine going back home in a week and telling everybody how you actually did something useful with your time here. You guys could be featured in an article or something."

Ryan and Paul stared at each other. "Article?" they whispered.

It was impossible to know whether they were imagining themselves in *People* magazine or if they didn't know the meaning of the word, but rather than stick around long enough to find out, Rafi made a beeline for the entrance.

The seaport was about half as full as it was yesterday, with the people who hadn't gotten a tent at Tent City, or didn't want to spend the night at the beach, glued to the rows of vinyl waiting chairs. Rafi searched for an outlet, but most of the outlets were either already charging phones or blocked by someone sleeping in front of them. Rafi did spot an open one, though. She went to plug in her charger, when someone careened into the spot and cut her off.

"Excuse me?" Rafi turned to see the person who was suddenly beside her, stealing her power.

"You're excused," they said.

Rafi couldn't see their face because it was completely obscured underneath a wide brim hat and shrouded in a black lacy cloth like a mourner's veil. But Rafi did recognize the voice. "Jack?"

Jack's shoulders tensed, and he froze, knuckles turning white around the iPhone in his fist. "You can see through the veil?"

"Not really but—"

"Don't look at me," Jack said, splaying his free hand in front of his face, adding an extra shield.

"Why? What's wrong?"

"Something horrible has happened."

Rafi loved hearing horrible things. Not because she was a horrible person but because horrible things made for great stories. She leaned in just a little bit closer. "What is it?"

"I don't have my luggage."

Not so horrible. "None of us have our luggage."

"But I had all my makeup in my luggage!" Jack's voice had risen high enough to wake the dead, but after a quick cursory check, his veil swinging from side to side, he was sure no one else was listening in. "I don't have any makeup on right now. Which would be bad enough, but I don't have any of my daytime or nighttime beauty regimen essentials, which means I couldn't do my morning cleansing and moisturizing and mystifying routine, which means my skin is a *complete* disaster."

Rafi tried to come up with something sympathetic to say, she really did, but her beauty routine this morning had involved splashing her face with ocean water. And if she was being honest, she would replace *splashing* with *dabbing* and *her face* with *her hands*.

"Oh."

"It gets worse," Jack said. "I don't have any sunscreen."

"That's not so bad, right? You'll get a tan."

Jack's veil was too opaque to see through, and yet Rafi could feel a seething shocked rage emanating from within it. The next time Jack spoke, it was slow and deliberate.

"My skin is as delicate as butterfly wings. TeenVogue.com once theorized that I must bathe in organic, unpasteurized goat milk every morning and night. A Japanese beauty company named one of their gel masks after me. It's a bestseller. I have my own line of face serums that's so advanced it's coming out five years from now with formulas that scientists haven't even invented yet. And the day I met my dermatologist, she took one look at me and died. Do you have any idea what that means?"

Rafi shook her head.

"It means I wasn't wearing sunscreen all day yesterday, and now I'm a deformed monster! My nose is chapped, Rafi. *Chapped.* Lips get chapped and that's only if you're gross and poor. Who ever heard of noses getting chapped?" He took a breath to let out a ragged sob. "*Why* do all the bad things in life always happen to *me*?"

"Can I see?"

"No!"

"I promise not to laugh or recoil or say anything," Rafi said.

Jack sighed, and after a moment his veil bounced sluggishly up and down. Carefully, Rafi pinched the edge of it and lifted, bracing for the worst.

Jack Dewey's cheeks were tinged slightly red. and there was a bit of peeling skin on the bridge of his nose.

"It's really not that bad," Rafi said.

Jack pulled back until the veil slipped from Rafi's fingers. "Call me anything you want, but don't patronize me."

"I'm not," Rafi said. "You honestly look fine. You just need to chill out. You know, sun is actually good for you."

"What nonsense are you talking about?"

"Vitamin D, it comes from the sun and makes you healthy and stuff." Rafi knew very little about vitamins and how they worked, but as she spoke, and as Jack listened carefully, she realized this was the moment she was waiting for. Jack was one of the biggest influencers here. If she could convince him that this island wasn't a complete hellhole and a little more time here might be good for him (and his skin), then there was a good chance he could spread the message.

Rafi smiled at him. "I know just what'll make you feel better."

7

"SO I TELL YOU THE SUN HAS A PERSONAL VENDETTA against me and you decide to lead me directly to it," Jack said. "Quite the flex."

Rafi and Jack stood ankle-deep in the Caribbean waters, she looking as out of place as a coatrack in the ocean, and Jack, face still shrouded, looking beekeeper-in-mourning chic. If they'd been on one of the Fly Fest Instagram ads, looking like they did now, absolutely no one would have been tempted to come. But none of that mattered when there was this view.

How could Jack not feel a sense of hope or joy or relief, standing on a beach like this? "I know things look pretty bleak right now," Rafi began.

"You said you wouldn't comment on my skin."

"I meant the fact that we're all out thousands of dollars and we're pretty much stranded on a deserted island and there's no food and no way to make contact with the outside world and we don't have any beds to sleep in—"

"You don't have a bed?" Jack snapped his neck in Rafi's direction so sharply that even his veil seemed to react, creasing in confused droopy frowns.

Rafi was equally as confused. "You have a bed?"

"All the tents have beds."

"What?" The crick in Rafi's neck flared up in pain.

"Don't get me started," Jack said. "They're stiff as boards and covered in plastic. The worst."

"I'm sleeping on sand," Rafi said in a quiet voice. "I woke up with sand under my eyelid."

"You don't have pillows either?"

Rafi tried to say the word "pillow," but it came out like a cloud of hot dust from her dry lips, soundless and evaporating into the air.

"Sleeping on sand is probably good for your skin," Jack said. "Exfoliating."

"Right." Rafi's jaw felt suddenly stiff. "Only slightly less good than sleeping on a silk pillowcase."

"Exactly. Anyway, what were you saying?"

Rafi took a deep breath and squinted out at the sparkling horizon. It would take more than just a view to sell this paradise to Jack. "I was just going to say that I get what it's like to feel insecure sometimes."

"About the fact that you have a podcast?"

Rafi paused. "I'm not insecure about my podcast."

"Why not?"

Rafi would've said something but she wasn't even sure how to respond. Jack started talking again anyway. "You know, I've been on this island for over a day and you still haven't invited me to be a guest."

"It's not that kind of podcast," Rafi said.

"Well, I would've turned you down anyway."

"Okay, I think we're getting away from the point here. I was going to say that I get insecure about my looks, too."

"Oh, I can tell," Jack said. "Bangs *and* dry skin? It's like, girl, pick a struggle."

It was seriously taking everything for Rafi not to tackle Jack to the ground—or ocean, as it were—but she had to remind herself that she was on a mission here. If she could make Jack feel better about being stranded here—well, convince him that they *weren't* stranded but in fact lucky to be on this untouched gem of nature—then she could convince anyone. It would be kind of like what she did on her podcast. When she knew someone was listening to her, when she truly had their ear, was the only time she felt she had any purpose at all.

"I'm sorry," Jack said. "My sass is a legendary force of habit. Keep going. You were talking about being ugly."

"I'm not *ugly*," Rafi said sternly.

"I could give you a makeover," Jack said.

"I don't need a makeover."

"You sure?"

Rafi looked down at herself. The T-shirt had obviously been a poor fashion choice, and bangs were always a bit controversial, but Rafi felt good about her looks. Sure, she was lanky and built like a pile of wire hangers, but she wasn't really aware of her posture and awkward elbows and knees unless she saw herself in pictures. She was tall, which she liked. And while her skin may have been a little dry, it was also clear. Rafi was pretty happy with what she was working with.

Sometimes—especially in a place like this, where everyone

seemed to walk out of their Instagrams with their Facetunes and filters intact—Rafi felt less than. And this conversation wasn't helping any. But she also knew that insecurity was just a state of mind. That she could change how she felt by changing her outlook. And she could help Jack realize that.

"Just because things are especially bad right now doesn't mean we can't look on the bright side," Rafi said. "If you don't like your reality, then . . . make a new reality."

"Make a new reality," Jack repeated.

"Yeah. I truly believe there's beauty in everything. You just have to look for it."

Jack did look. It was through a veil, but he looked all around him at the picturesque postcard he was currently occupying. For Jack, it may have been his first time looking out, rather than in. "Looking, looking, looking for beauty," he said.

"Do I hear you guys talking about me?"

Jack and Rafi turned at the sound of that jaunty Australian accent. River waved to them from the shore.

"Literally no one was talking about you," Rafi muttered under her breath.

Without waiting to be invited, or even asking what they were doing out in the shallow waters, River splashed in to meet them. He still hadn't found a T-shirt apparently, but that suited him fine for swimming. "So, what are we doing?" he asked.

"I was telling Jack that he should try seeing the beauty all around him and stop worrying about what he looks like."

"Oh," River said. "'Cause I was going to say I like the new

look. But it'll be hard to swim in that thing. Why don't you take it off?"

Rafi scoffed. Who did River think he was? Just because he asked someone to take off an article of clothing didn't mean—

Jack pulled back his veil and tossed it to Rafi. "Hold this too." Jack pressed his phone into Rafi's hands.

"You coming?" River asked Rafi.

She looked down at her feet, still crystal clear in the see-through ocean. Water was fine, so long as it didn't go past her ankles. "This is as far as I go."

River shrugged and dipped into the sea, Jack was already out there. River splashed him first, and then Jack splashed back, and pretty soon Jack actually began to laugh. Rafi couldn't believe how easy it was for River to loosen Jack up. But then, it just showed how good he was at manipulating people. Because that was all Rafi saw: a guy who was desperate to please, who would say anything, just to get you to like him. And Jack was definitely liking him at the moment. They splashed around together like little kids in a water park.

It'd only taken River a minute to get Jack to feel good about himself, and Rafi resented him for it. And if she was honest with herself, she resented Jack too, for having the kind of fun in the water that she couldn't. Still, their playfulness was contagious. Rafi clicked Jack's phone on and took a picture of the two of them. She figured Jack might want to remember this moment.

But a picture was a powerful thing, and if Rafi had known how this one pic would affect the course of their time on the island, she never would have taken it at all.

8

WORD OF JACK'S AND RIVER'S BEACHY ADVENTURES
spread like a viral tweet, and soon it was a full-blown party.
With no other means of entertaining themselves, people were
all too happy to jump into the water and relieve the tensions of
the failed festival. There was hooting and hollering and dunk-
ing and people propped up on each other's shoulders, drowning each other in good fun.

Rafi watched it all from shore. The only other person on
the beach who hadn't joined the impromptu water romp was
Peggy. They sat under their tent, which was nothing more
than sticks, shoelaces, and the clothes they'd packed in their
carry-on.

Rafi stood before them. "I can't stand him."

"Who?"

"River." She plopped down next to Peggy. "I was on the
beach with Jack first, you know? And then River swoops in
and lures everyone into the ocean like the pied piper of muscle
beach—and they're all falling for his smarmy, faux humble,
nice guy act, which is so manipulative."

Rafi detested him, even though she had to admit that this
party he'd inadvertently started was a good thing, as far as

her mission went. Everyone was too busy splashing around with a celebrity to remember that they'd been swindled. Rafi watched as River chatted with Sierra Madre, showing her his fishing spear. Every time he lifted it above his head, Rafi involuntarily flinched, expecting a stabbing, but none came. Sierra seemed impressed. She did not see a dangerous man with a weapon, only a pop star and his big stick.

"I mean, is he conventionally good-looking?" Rafi asked Peggy as she watched River readjust the waistband of his shorts. "There's no denying that. Is his face perfectly symmetrical? Without question. Is he the sexiest man alive? *People* magazine seems to think so. Does he smell freshly laundered even though he hardly wears clothes? Of course he does. The point is, River Stone is a liar. He's using his looks and status to deceive everyone, and it's working."

"How do you know he's a liar?" Peggy asked.

"His smile." It sounded like a flimsy theory, but she had the proof to back it up. "It goes crooked when he's lying. I first noticed it when I watched clips of him playing a charity poker game. Any time he bluffed, out came that smile. I've seen those clips a million times. And then I started noticing it in interviews and stuff, as a way to deflect from questions he was uncomfortable answering. I have spent the better part of a year studying that smile."

"So, you like him."

"*Like* him?" Rafi wrenched her eyes from River so she could level Peggy with her most incredulous stare. What she would say next was serious, and definitely controversial, and not something you drop lightly into pleasant conversation. But it needed to be said to disabuse Peggy of the notion that her feelings for River resided even close to the neighborhood of "like." Rafi took a deep breath and assumed her most serious air. "Peggy, I'm here to prove that River Stone is a *murderer*."

She let the words hang in the thick island humidity, allowing for their impact to wash fully over Peggy. And for once, Peggy stopped fiddling with their phone long enough to stare at Rafi.

"You can like someone *and* think they're a murderer," Peggy said. "The two aren't mutually exclusive."

She would have to work on her delivery when she disclosed this fact about River on her podcast, because it clearly didn't meet expectations. "What makes you think I like him?"

"Literally everything you just said."

The idea of Rafi liking River was ridiculous. Beyond ridiculous. Inconceivable! "I don't like him, I'm just . . . really invested in this podcast."

"Why?"

"Why?" Rafi repeated.

"Yeah. Are you doing this out of some sense of vigilantism? Are you just nosy? Obsessive? Or is this just a popularity thing for you? Target the most famous pop boy in the world so you could get a share of that attention?"

"No," Rafi said. Definitely not that. Okay, maybe a little of that.

Rafi's podcast was a stepping-stone to a much bigger dream of having an even *bigger* podcast. "Musical Mysteries" was small-time, independently run by her without any producers or technicians or any of the fancy stuff more popular podcasts had at their disposal. But if it became popular, then it might get picked up by a podcasting network, and if it got picked up by a network, then she could truly say she was a success.

She'd actually reached out to a few different podcasting companies, but none of them had responded except for one. SteerCat said they'd give her a shot if she could turn in a compelling second season of "Musical Mysteries." They wanted to see growth, finesse, and whether Rafi could maintain the musical mysteries theme for multiple seasons.

This was Rafi's shot to prove she had what it took to make a blockbuster podcast. She couldn't fail.

And as far as Rafi was concerned, River Stone was the perfect subject. Beloved by the world but hiding an awful secret. He'd used a girl to get ahead, but society just accepted that as the norm and let him do it. He'd concocted this image of himself as the poor victim of an evil girl who'd broken his heart, and now he was using her life as material for his stupid songs. If it were a female artist doing all of that, she'd never hear the end of it. But since it was a cute boy, it was par for the course. River was the archetype of a successful guy and all the double standards that came with it.

All Rafi knew was that when people saw River, they saw a rainbow. But she was the only one willing to follow the rainbow until she found the pot of gold. In this case, the pot of gold was the truth.

"I believe that something bad happened to Tracy Mooney,"

Rafi said. "I believe that River did something bad to her, or at least knows what really happened to her. And I can't just let the world let him off the hook for it."

"So you're doing this for Tracy?" Peggy asked.

"Yeah. She deserves justice. And if lifting Tracy up brings River down, then so be it." She watched River in the water. "I mean, look at how he's holding that spear. Why is he so good at stabbing fish? Has anybody bothered to ask that? He is too good at stabbing and gutting things. River Stone is obviously a crazy, manipulative killer who's completely unhinged."

Rafi said all this even as she watched River delicately help pick seaweed out of Sierra's hair.

"You sure he's the one who's unhinged?" Peggy asked.

Okay, Rafi had to admit she did sound like she was going off the deep end, and she couldn't fault Peggy for thinking her crazy. Peggy didn't know what River did. All the more reason for her to plow on with her podcast. "Are you any closer to getting your satellite phone to work?"

"No," Peggy said, and Rafi couldn't tell by their inflection whether they were devastated by the lack of progress or not. "But I'll get there."

A sense of unease settled over Rafi, hearing that they might have a lifeline to the mainland soon. But she was full of unease, and it wasn't just that. Rafi felt it as she watched River and Sierra Madre walk down the beach together. She couldn't let the feeling go as she watched them disappear into the thicket of trees at the base of the mountain.

MUSICAL MYSTERIES
Season 2: Episode 2
"The Case"

Before we start this episode there is something
I want to get out of the way. It has come to my
attention that my careful, meticulous research on
River Stone might be misconstrued as obsession.
Some (really misguided) people out there may even
be listening to this series and come away from it
thinking that I *like* him.

Listener, let me be clear. I do not like River
Stone. I have never liked River Stone. And after
everything I've uncovered for this story, I can assure
you I will *never* like him.

The idea is just ridiculous. Personally, it boggles
my mind how anyone can like River after learning
about the case.

I first heard about it before I'd even heard any
of River's music. The story is so out-there that it
was all anyone ever wanted to talk about in those
early days. On the *Today* show, when he performed
in-studio for the first time, they followed the
segment with a sit-down interview. That interview
was so heart-wrenching it got River the cover of
People magazine the next week, and that *People*
magazine got him *Rolling Stone*. River's rise to
music stardom is intricately intertwined with

a quote-unquote "tragic" backstory: what his girlfriend did to him.

Tracy Mooney was a seventeen-year-old blond spitfire with dazzling blue eyes and an unconventional sense of style. If you look up old pictures of her, you'll see her wearing jeans that she used to draw on all the time. Little doodles in Sharpie and pen of her favorite flowers and cartoon characters.

Enter River Stone. Seventeen at the time. A mediocre-looking boy with an even more mediocre talent for songwriting. At parties he would be the one to put a damper on the mood by bringing out his guitar and asking for song requests. We know that Tracy must have had a generous spirit, because she took pity on River by deciding to date him.

According to lore, the two teens fell in love quickly, in the pure way that people compare to puppies and sunny days and stuff. River doesn't like to talk about this time in his life. Says it's too hard to revisit those memories, but the few times he has reminisced about his time with Tracy, it sounded like a dream. Trips to their favorite ice-cream shop, chaste kisses on front porches, love notes between classes.

Are you rolling your eyes yet? You should be, because this is just another boring young love story. And it would've ended that way too, as boringly as it began, with Tracy going off to university somewhere while River moved to the big city to go sing in coffee houses or something, if it wasn't for the fateful night the couple decided to go camping in, as the Aussies say, the bush. That night would be the last time River ever saw his girlfriend, and it would go on to change River's life forever.

It was meant to be a romantic trip. In fact, River told the world that he was going to propose to Tracy that night. Anyway, you probably know the rest. While River was taking a quote-unquote "short nap" at around nine P.M.—one hour before he planned to propose, by the way—Tracy vanished. He says that when he woke up, he found his car gone and a note next to his sleeping bag. It went like this:

River, you are the most wondrous guy I know. Unfortunately, I secretly hate you and we can no longer be together. I am leaving you immediately. AND don't try to find me because I am running away and changing my name and you will never hear from me again. Good evening. Best of luck with the music. I really love your songs—especially the ones you wrote about me—and I know you will do great moving forward in your career. You are a very talented fellow with a lot of promise and any record labels will be lucky to have you.
Bye.

And that's where Tracy Mooney's story ends. A vibrant girl who loved her boyfriend, had a kitty named Tiger, and liked to draw on clothes, was never seen again. The girl she purportedly ran away to become? No one knows her name. Or where she lives. Or what's become of her life.

River, by the way, hiked to the nearest town, where he found his car—much like him—abandoned.

I'm sure you will agree that Tracy's note to River will go down in history as one of the strangest goodbye notes known to man. No? You're not thinking that? Well, you're in good company because the cops never seemed to wonder about that either. But hey, maybe that's just how people in Australia say goodbye when leaving the loves of their lives in the middle of nowhere.

Maybe your first thought upon hearing a story like this is how heartbreaking it is. A boy abandoned in the middle of the wilderness on a night that was supposed to be one of the most special of his life. But all I see when I hear this story is how many holes it has. And I can't help but wonder how River allegedly wrote the entirety of *Songs for Tracy* in one single week after she left. How the album was ready to go out into the world so quickly. And how it was the perfect story to get just the kind of attention he'd been craving for so long.

That's next time, on "Musical Mysteries."

And before it's all over, I give you my word, dear listeners—I will ask River Stone the one question that no reporter has dared ask him.

Did he kill his girlfriend, Tracy Mooney, and make it look like she left him?

This episode of "Musical Mysteries" was brought to you by Nobrand. Ever been stuck in the sun for hours on end like an ant under a magnifying glass? Well, Nobrand has just the thing for that. Try their sunscreen! It's probably chemical-free. Go to Nobrand.com and enter code RIVERKILLER for ten percent off your next purchase.

Until next time, Mysterinos!

9

THE PARTY IN THE WATER EVENTUALLY DIED DOWN. BY
the time she emerged from her tent, Rafi could see only a few
people still in the ocean: stragglers who would rather go pruney
and pink before letting the festivities end. But someone dark-
ened her doorstep, blocking her sea view.

"You took a picture on my phone," Jack said.

Was he upset she'd used his phone without his permission?
"Just thought you'd want to have a memory of something
nice."

Jack made a snorty, spitty sound. "As if anyone remembers
memories."

Though he didn't sound too pleased, she definitely detected
a smile in his voice. He held out his phone for Rafi to see. On
the screen was the picture she'd taken of him and River in the
surf. She had to admit it was a beautiful shot.

The two of them were waist-deep in the water. River was
frozen in the middle of splashing Jack, the water a perfect
crystal arch sprouting from his fingers. And Jack stood with
his back toward the camera but still glancing over his shoulder, eyes closed but mouth open in the biggest expression of
glee. It was as though the two were old friends who'd known

each other all their lives and just happened to be caught in a candid moment on one of the most beautiful places on earth.

But there was something a little too beautiful about the photo that made it look almost unnatural. The edges were too sharp while the faces were too soft. The colors too bright. The composition too square.

Rafi's spine cracked, she straightened so quickly. She saw the geo tag. Jack's handle. The caption, little emojis (sandy beach, star, eggplant). Rafi gasped out loud, a jolt as fierce as an electrical shock running through her. "This is Instagram!"

Jack grinned, so many of his teeth on display it was like he was smuggling a blister pack of gum in his mouth. He nodded.

"You got on the internet!" Panic rose in Rafi like bile. "Did you call for help?"

"I only had a connection for a few minutes," Jack said. "I had to use my time wisely."

Rafi stared at him, not entirely sure Jack answered her question. "So you didn—"

"No, duh, I only had time to post this pic," Jack explained. "Do you see how many likes it got? Worth it."

The page was frozen, and no matter how many times Jack thumbed the screen, nothing moved or blinked on or off.

"How did you get on the internet?" Rafi asked.

Jack took back his phone and admired the picture like it was a newborn baby. "Somebody named Peggy."

Rafi did not like to run, especially not in sand, and definitely not in the world's most poorly made, not-quite-staff, chafey T-shirt, but she did so anyway to get to the other end of the beach as quickly as she could.

She found Peggy sitting under their flimsy clothesline tent, exactly where she'd left them this morning. Only now they were preoccupied with a small object balancing between their thumb and index finger. When Rafi got close enough, she realized it was a fidget spinner. It spun and spun and the randomness of it, along with its spinning, was almost hypnotic. But Rafi snapped out of it, remembering why she'd come here in the first place.

"The internet!" Rafi said. "You got it to work!"

"Yep."

"Were you able to contact anyone?"

"Connection was spotty." Peggy spun the spinner once more. "I'll get it working perfectly, though. It'll just take a bit more time."

All the breath Rafi had been holding came out in one go, but the relief she felt was replaced almost instantly with dread so that now it felt like her breath had been vacuumed out of her. She had to tread carefully with what she said next. "You can't let anyone have it!"

Peggy's spinner stopped spinning, and they cast their lazy eyes on Rafi's frazzled ones. "Why?"

Rafi hadn't thought this far ahead. She had no good reason why they shouldn't try hard to make contact with the outside world. She had only the truth, which included her own selfish desires. But Peggy was practically a friend. If Rafi was going to reveal anything about her ulterior motives for staying on this island, it would be to a friend. A sounding board. Someone with a clearer head who could potentially talk Rafi out of it if her idea was too outrageous.

"Because if everyone leaves the island, then River will leave the island, and if River leaves the island, then I won't get my interview with him, and if I don't get my interview with him, my podcast will be a failure."

The fidget spinner slipped off the axis of Peggy's index finger. "You really are off the rails, aren't you?"

Guess maybe it was more outrageous than Rafi realized. "Please," she said. "I just need a little bit more time. This isn't just about my podcast. This is about exposing a killer and holding him accountable. It's about"—she didn't want to sound too dramatic but—"justice."

"Relax." Peggy tossed the spinner to the side, where it crash-landed on the sand. They stood and dusted off the back of their shorts. "I understand full well what it means to have internet on this island. And even though your plan is deranged—"

"I don't know if 'deranged' is the right word."

"It is without question full-on deranged," Peggy continued. "I will help you."

"You will?"

"Sure," Peggy said. "I'm not exactly in a rush to get back home. And I like when things get a little deranged."

"Oh." Rafi's insides finally stopped feeling like they were being sucked out of her.

"I'm not just going to give the internet to anybody who asks for it," Peggy said. "Not without a price."

Rafi nodded, even though that wasn't exactly what she was hoping to hear. But she didn't worry too much. No, she didn't like the sound of the word "price," but it wasn't like anybody here had anything of value to trade with. For now, Rafi was sure, her plan was safe.

A slow smile spread over Peggy's lips. "Now let's see how deranged things get."

10

Though Peggy had reassured her about the internet being kept under wraps, Rafi was still too nervous about word getting out. Jack, for one, already knew, and he was a wild card. If he told even one other person, then it would be impossible to contain the spread. The more Rafi dwelled on the whole situation, the more worried she got. This wasn't just a wrench in her plans; this had the potential to ruin everything she'd worked so hard for. She was already down a couple grand, already sleeping on sand, going hungry, wearing the worst shirt possible—Rafi was sacrificing a lot for her story. But she was willing to do it all if it meant exposing who River truly was.

No, Rafi couldn't just stand idly by while her entire world unraveled around her. She needed to get ahead of this.

She needed to make a speech.

Rafi had borne witness to the seaport torn asunder by panic, and she'd tiptoed through it in the sleepy morning hours, but she'd never seen it quite like this. There were still plenty of people filling all the chairs, but for some reason there was no shouting or frenzy. Actually, there was a semblance of organization. The chairs had been moved so that they all faced the check-in desk, behind which Paul and Ryan sat, like co-heads of a fraternity going over the rules of the Greek system. Piled on the desk in front of them were stacks of untouched Styrofoam sandwich containers.

Rafi had come here on a mission, but the mood in the seaport demanded attention and quiet, so she found an empty seat in the back and sat.

"Let's focus," Paul or Ryan said, tapping something on the desk that was meant to be a gavel but was actually a conch shell. "If we eat the quote-unquote 'cheese sandwiches,' we will, in effect, be setting a precedent for the type of food we are willing to accept from catering." His voice came out strong and clear, filled every corner of the room. "If we abstain from eating the sandwiches, we send a clear message that we expect better. We paid for better. And we will not be denied."

A boy in the crowd stood to speak. "I vote to request Monte Cristo sandwiches. They're part French toast, part grilled cheese, and meaty. They'd appeal to a wide range of people; plus, they're my favorite."

Another person stood with a counterpoint. "Lobster rolls, though."

A boy with Jesus hair stood next. "I would settle for a Wagyu ribeye and foie gras cheesesteak."

A girl shot up from her seat. "Wait, wait, if we're going to get Wagyu, I want it to be breaded."

"It already *comes* in bread," Jesus Hair said.

"It's not the same thing!" the girl said.

"We are in a desperate situation!" Jesus Hair said, his voice rising. "We are in no position to be picky."

Things were getting heated, and a chorus of murmurs and groans broke over the crowd. Ryan (or Paul) picked up the conch and slammed it down on the desk to get everyone to quiet down. "The dude with the long hair is right!" he said. "When I was nine years old and my sailing instructor fell through our dumbwaiter, I begged my parents for the world's next best sailing instructor, but they told me I couldn't be picky," Ryan (definitely Ryan, Rafi now knew) said. "So too, we cannot be picky now. I say we stick to cheeses."

"In that case, I vote for Gruyère," Paul said.

"Did he say Greer?" the girl next to Rafi whispered. It was the girl who cried hard and often, though she wasn't crying right now. "*My* name is Greer."

"Swiss cheese!" Jesus Hair demanded.

"Plebeian!" Ryan spat.

Paul banged the conch on the desk once more, and it was a wonder it hadn't shattered by now. "Screw it! No cheeses! I say we gather up all the sandwiches into a pile and light them on fire. That'll show the organizers how serious we are about our demands. All in favor?"

Hands shot into the air.

The synapses of Rafi's brain were refusing to spark and connect. It was like she'd taken a megadose of some strong drug because she was totally dazed by the goings-on of this very strange sandwich meeting. It wasn't what she was expecting the festival-goers to be discussing, but it was still an opportunity for Rafi to insert herself. This was her shot to have her voice heard. This was her chance to, possibly, influence the influencers.

"Um, excuse me?" She stood so abruptly that she must've accidentally swiped Greer on the side, because now the girl *was* crying, and Rafi felt bad about that. But she'd have to apologize later. "No one is going to make us Gruyère or Swiss or Wagyu sandwiches." It was probably the wrong way to try to convince them to stay, judging by the crowd's reaction. They regarded Rafi as they so often did: with wary confusion, as though she were an alien, or a DVD player. And then Paul spoke.

"What the ever-loving hell are you talking about?"

Rafi gingerly stepped over the knees of the people in her row until she was at the check-in desk. She fixed Paul and Ryan with an incredulous glare. "When I said you guys should do something useful with your time here, this was not at all what I meant."

"Well, you should've been more clear," Paul said.

"We're just trying to keep the people fed," Ryan said.

"You want to focus on food? Great, but this is not the way to do it," Rafi said. Frustrated, she climbed on top of the desk, despite the sandwiches and Paul and Ryan's monosyllabic protestations. A couple of Styrofoam boxes crumpled under her sneakers while a few others sputtered to the floor, but no one seemed too heartbroken about that. Rafi took her speaker out of her bag, set it gingerly atop a stack of boxes, hooked her mic up to it, and positioned it in front of her lips. "We. Cannot. Burn. The sandwiches."

Her amplified voice gave her words their desired gravitas. Greer stood from her chair, vibrating with fresh tears. "I am not eating those sandwiches."

Jesus Hair raised his hand but did not wait to be called on to speak. "I heard that if you get the sandwiches wet after midnight they multiply."

There was a scream stuck deep inside of Rafi's body that detonated suddenly, but she kept her jaw clenched tight and so no sound came out. After a moment to compose herself, Rafi spoke again. "They're just sandwiches, people."

"They're sandwich people?" someone said, and new murmurs began to froth in the crowd.

"They're regular sandwiches!" Rafi said.

"They can't possibly be regular sandwiches," Paul said behind her.

"I assure you—they are," Rafi said.

"Eat one, then," Ryan said.

Rafi looked at Ryan, and their mutual stare became a confrontation. He did not back down, his chin jutting toward the few remaining sandwiches left on the desk. "If you're so sure the sandwiches are food, eat one of them."

Rafi looked down at the Styrofoam boxes at her feet.

Sure, she would eat one.

Just not right now.

"Look," Rafi said into her mic, "we need to preserve the sandwiches because we might be here a while."

The sounds of grumbling spread out from the crowd, and Rafi could feel that it was just the start of a rising angry tide.

"I know there are a lot of things we were promised that aren't here," she said.

"A gourmet chef," someone in the crowd said.

"The villas."

"The models."

"O-Town," said an ornery Ryan or Paul.

"Yes, all of those things," Rafi said. "But those are just tiny, tiny details. The important thing is the place itself. Look around! We're on a beautiful island."

"It's kind of an ugly island," someone muttered.

"A *beautiful island*!" Rafi repeated, louder this time, trying to drown out the dissenter. "You were all at the beach party earlier—wasn't that fun and beautiful? River Stone was there. You got to party with a rock star!"

Though the beach party had occurred only a few hours earlier, it was as though the coming of the night had erased the concertgoers' memories, because a fog of confusion settled over all of them. A fog so thick, Rafi was beginning to doubt she could cut through it.

It was just at that moment that Jack Dewey appeared beside Rafi. She hadn't even noticed him climb onto the check-in desk. In his hand he held his phone, and she could see the still-frozen post from his Instagram. The picture of him frolicking in the surf with River.

"Oh no," Rafi whispered to herself.

"She may have no sense of style, but what this girl says is

true," Jack said. "Despite every odd being against us, we did actually party with a rock star this afternoon. I have the proof!"

"Oh no," Rafi said again. The irony of the moment hit her like a rogue baseball to the face, and she understood instantly that getting up in front of this crowd had been the wrong approach. She understood that Jack was obviously uncomfortable when someone else was the center of attention, that getting up on the desk had summoned him up here too, and he would now put a pin in her ploy.

She could see Jack start to hold up his phone, but short of slapping it out of his hand, there was nothing Rafi could do. She couldn't think quickly enough, couldn't come up with any good reason to explain away the internet that he'd gotten access to.

Maybe he wouldn't mention it.

"Today I got on the internet!"

A collective gasp rippled through the crowd; all eyes that had been on Rafi, and then on Jack, now swung to his phone, which, to them, loomed as large as an IMAX screen.

"I posted this picture in the afternoon," Jack continued. "It has already reached one point three million likes!"

A million? When Rafi had seen the picture, it'd been only at a thousand-something likes. She had so many questions, but the crowd had more, erupting in a cacophony of voices, sounding surprised, excited, baffled. Rafi could be louder than them, though. Rafi had her microphone.

"Wait, everybody, listen!" Her mic did the trick, and for

once an analog device was enough to distract from something as intangible as the internet. "Okay, so there might be Wi-Fi—fine! But what happens if you get on the internet and show the world what a failure Fly Fest is? The world will see a bunch of privileged morons who got scammed out of a lot of money. They'll laugh at you! They'll think you're all losers!"

More murmurs from the crowd, but this time Paul or Ryan banged their conch-gavel on the desk. "Let her speak! She obviously knows about this topic."

But the conch didn't get anyone to stop and listen, and Rafi could feel herself losing them, like sand sifting through her fingers. And she couldn't lose them. She needed her plan to work. She *needed* to stay on the island, to get her River bombshell—to get her podcast on SteerCat Media.

And to get justice for Tracy, of course.

Rafi looked at Ryan and Paul, trying to settle everyone down; she eyed Jack and his phone; she even searched the crowd, desperate for a spark of inspiration, a final straw to grasp—something that would put her message over the edge. One lone sentence carried over from the masses.

"This is hella random."

"Hella," Rafi said. At first, only Jack heard her, and he let his phone drop to the side, waiting for her to elaborate. Rafi brought the mic to her lips. "Hella is here," she announced.

The crowd quieted down.

"Hella Badid is here?" someone asked.

Of course Hella Badid wasn't here. Hella Badid was too smart to fall for the Fly Fest scam, but Rafi swallowed—her nerves, the truth—and nodded emphatically. "Hella Badid is here!" she said.

"What do you mean, Hella Badid is here?" Jack asked.

"I mean I'm pretty sure I saw her," Rafi said.

"Where?" Jack asked.

"By the mountain."

"*By* the mountain?"

"Like, next to it," Rafi said. The lie seemed to fall apart almost as soon as it left her mouth, but it was picked up by her microphone, amplified and emboldened, and capturing everyone's attention like a magnet. Where once the seaport was filled with loud complainers, they had now transformed into Rafi's captive, quiet audience.

And then something strange happened. Something Rafi could not explain, but it was like someone up there had heard the points she was trying to make and put it upon themselves to add some special effects.

A strange *whoosh*ing sound broke out outside. Like dinosaurs were climbing to the top of the mountain, or like a huge angel with a scythe was thwacking its way through the jungle to kill them all. No one in the seaport could see what was going on, but they all heard it, turning to each other and looking out over the open spaces for the source of the noise.

Rafi took the noise and used it. "That's them, setting the party up!"

And somehow, her lone voice was enough to pull their collective attention away from the sound and back to her. The noise, as it were, went away almost as soon as it came, leaving a stunned silence and all eyes back on Rafi.

"Hella's here," she went on, "and that obviously means that Fly Fest is still happening." The lie did not make Rafi feel bad; instead it filled her with hope, and she could sense the same feeling in her audience. "The festival organizers are obviously in a part of the island we haven't checked yet. Like, the top of the mountain."

"They're still setting up?" came a boy's voice.

"Yes!" Rafi said. "So why don't we wait? Let's wait 'til Hella and the crew are ready to accept us. Because if we show the world the real circumstances here—that we're without proper food and shelter and safety—I promise you, you will never live it down. But if the festival is still happening, then don't you want to be here for that moment? You saw what happened on Jack's Instagram when he posted a pic of him partying with a rock star. A million likes."

"It was one-point-three, actually," Jack said.

"One-point-three! We could all get one-point-three," Rafi said. "Just, please. Don't try to go on the internet just yet. Let's wait."

She liked the way it sounded. Like a political campaign phrase. Something hopeful, a promise of excitement. And as she watched the crowd with bated breath, she felt as though she maybe, just possibly, won an election.

And then, all at once, the crowd ran for the exit in a mass stampede, demanding the internet.

11

T he night bled into day, though Rafi couldn't be sure how much sleep she'd gotten in that time. After her little speech at the seaport (capped by the big stampede through the exit and then the great migration to the internet), Rafi had skulked back to her poor excuse for a tent, dejected. Everyone on the island now knew there was a way to contact the outside world, and though Peggy had promised to keep the internet to themselves, there was no way they didn't cave under the pressure of a horde of angry, starving, influencers.

No, by now the concertgoers would have alerted the world of the festival's failures, probably filed a few lawsuits, and definitely summoned boats and private planes to come and collect them. It was what Rafi expected to see when she pulled back the flap of her tent in the morning. But what she actually saw was two girls, their bikini-bottomed backsides lazily swaying too close to her face.

They were either dancing or having seizures—there was no way to tell which, and all Rafi could do, dumbfounded and tired as she was, was sit back and try to understand what she was witnessing. The girls' movements went from slow to frantic, each motion synchronized. Rafi was able to discern a series of steps, repeated over and over: locked elbows rounding over their heads; two quick hip locks before dissolving into the aforementioned swaying; a little shoulder shimmy; feet stomps; and finally, a full body roll. In the middle of this dance the girls turned and faced Rafi, smiling so widely at her that in that moment Rafi understood why some people were terrified of twins. But these girls weren't twins, and also they weren't exactly smiling at Rafi. Their smiles were directed just above her head.

And then the dance started again.

Rafi stood, wiping the sleep from her eyes, trying to determine if this was a dream. She stumbled into the space between the two girls, and they finally, mercifully, stopped dancing.

"Do you mind getting back inside?" the girl in the leopard-print bikini asked. "We're recording." She pointed at Rafi's tent, or specifically at the phone perched on one of the sticks holding up Rafi's tent.

"Seriously," the girl in the zebra-print bikini said. "You're in our shot."

"Why are you using my tent?" Rafi asked. "Why are you filming here? Why are you filming at all?"

"Because we don't have a tripod and the top of your tent is the perfect height for the angle we want?" Leopard Print said as though it were obvious.

"So can you move?" Zebra Print asked. "TikTok doesn't allow uglies or poors in their videos."

"Ugly?" Rafi had just spoken to Jack about this yesterday, given him a whole speech about feeling confident in one's own skin, but it was a different thing hearing it come out of these girls' mouths. And as it happened, the word elicited a physical reaction in Rafi. It made her stomach drop and her mouth go dry. Who decided what was ugly, anyway? Or was it happening, right here and now? Was it these girls, in stylish animal fabrics, that were the truth tellers, holding up a mirror and forcing Rafi to look into it? She self-consciously patted down her hair.

"We don't make the rules," Zebra said. "It's practically in TikTok's user agreement."

"Ugly" Rafi took objection to, but "poor" was definitely more accurate. And it unnerved Rafi that these two girls could see that word all over her, as if it was written on her forehead. Could they smell it on her? Did her shoe still stink?

"Why do you think I'm poor?" Rafi asked. They were stranded on an island, and people were literally sleeping on sand without any changes of clothes. How could these two girls possibly sniff out Rafi's lack of funds?

The girls looked at each other for a beat, then back at Rafi. Finally, Leopard Print said, "Well . . . your shirt."

Rafi went over to her tent, grabbed the phone placed precariously on the frame, and threw it as far down the beach as she could. It wasn't very far, and all three of them watched it bounce across the sand until it came to a full stop.

"You're crazy!" Leopard Print shrieked. Neither she, nor Zebra, waited for a defense, running off to collect their most prized possession.

Maybe Rafi *was* crazy. Maybe her hair was an ugly mess

sticking up on all sides in perpetual bedheadedness, held aloft by sand and indignation. Maybe her shirt was tacky and her shoe stank. And maybe she was sleep-deprived and looked and felt about a million years old, telling these kids to get off her lawn. But she didn't care. She now knew she wasn't dreaming. No, she'd awakened to a nightmare.

Rafi walked down the beach, heading for Peggy's tent, but when she got there, it was nothing more than a pile of sticks. She looked around for signs of where Peggy may have gone, but all she saw was a girl close by—that forever crying girl, Greer—smiling into her phone's camera.

"Hey," Rafi said, "do you know Peggy?"

"Of course I know Peggy," Greer said. "They're practically saving us."

"By calling for rescue?"

Greer snorted. "By giving us internet. I'm pretty sure I'd be dead if I couldn't go on the internet."

Confirmation that Peggy hadn't been able to keep the horde at bay. "Do you know where I can find them?"

"Tent City. But if you want Wi-Fi, you better bring them a gift."

Rafi took a few steps closer to Greer until she was blocking the girl's sun. Greer looked away from her phone to frown up at Rafi. "You're in my light," she said.

But Rafi didn't budge. "What do you mean, bring a gift?"

"Peggy will only give you the Wi-Fi code if you trade with them. They're very strict about that."

It wasn't hard finding Peggy's new digs. The path to it was littered with people on their phones. Rafi followed their trail like she was observing mice coming and going from a hole in a kitchen wall. Only in this instance the hole was actually the grandest structure in Tent City. It was made up of three individual tents, split at the seams and sewn back together to form one giant hovel. In fact, it was still under construction, and Rafi spied a boy crouched by the eastern wing, crudely sewing one part of canvas to another using yarn and what looked like the underwire from a bra. There was also a boy standing at the front, broad enough to block the entrance.

"Password?" he said to Rafi.

She stared at him. "Uh, Peggy's a friend of mine."

"Peggy has no friends. They have admirers."

It felt like a second ago that Peggy was the most antisocial person on this island. Now they had a boy acting as a human door. The weirdness that started off the day was snowballing, and Rafi needed answers, *now*. "Peggy!" Rafi shouted over the bouncer's shoulder. "It's me, Rafi!"

She waited a moment for a response, she and the bouncer in a staring standoff.

"*Whomst?*" came Peggy's voice from within.

The bouncer smirked and Rafi bit her lip. "We met in the jungle the first hour we were here."

"Can you be more specific?" Peggy asked.

"I'm the one wearing the pink Fly Fest T-shirt?" Rafi pressed on.

"The what?"

"The staff shirt," Rafi admitted reluctantly. "I look like I work here."

"It's a hideous shirt, boss," the bouncer said.

"Rafi Rafi Rafi . . . ," came Peggy's voice again, taking on a singsong lilt as they sounded out the name. "Let her in!"

The bouncer stepped aside without objection and Rafi entered.

The weirdness snowball was officially the size of a boulder now, and threatening to crush Rafi under its weight. Rafi wasn't sure what she'd been expecting to see when she walked in here—maybe simple, curved walls and a single, plastic-covered bed. But she felt like she'd stepped into an *Architectural Digest* house tour. The three combined tents made for a huge living space, and no part of it was left unadorned. Tapestries draped the walls—everything from sarongs to silk wraps to airplane blankets. Peggy didn't have just one bed; they had three, all piled on top of each other like something out of *The Princess and the Pea*. Next to the bed were crates being used as side tables, and on top of them were solar-powered lamps. There were even artworks, or what Rafi was pretty sure was art. Two sculptural pieces were propped on either side of the main door, bundles of branches tied together with twine. Depending on how you felt about wood sculptures, they were either beautiful and introspective, or some kind of shrine to the Blair Witch.

There were people too, lounging on the floor atop throw pillows, heads hunched over phones. And sitting on an inflatable hot pink armchair was Peggy, peering into their own phone. And even though Rafi was standing right in front of them and they knew she was there, it took Peggy a full minute to look up. "Oh, Rafi. Hello."

"*Hey*," Rafi said, her voice heavy with meaning as she gestured all around her. "Where did all this stuff come from?"

"Right, this stuff," Peggy said, as though noticing it for the first time. "Remember when I told you I wouldn't give up the internet without a price? Well, turns out people are willing to pay up."

Peggy looked different, and it wasn't just because they were smiling. They had new duds, too. A fancy, Memphis-style Bonobos dress shirt; pristine, if oversized, Air Jordans; and a cherry Ring Pop on their right index finger, licked halfway to the nub. "I give people the Wi-Fi password, but the genius part is that I'll change the password every day, which means they'll have to keep paying."

"But I thought you were on my side about this," Rafi said. "We were going to try to keep everyone on the island so that I could get my interview with River, remember?"

"Remember?" Peggy laughed. "A harebrained scheme like that is hard to forget. But I don't know if you noticed that even though everyone's got the internet now, no one's actually called for help."

Rafi took a cursory glance around the room, looking at the people lounging on the floor, happily on their phones. She recalled Greer taking selfies on the beach, the animal-print girls dancing in front of her tent. A day ago everyone was desperate to get off this island, and now it was like the Wi-Fi was a pacifier stuck in their pursed lips.

"Why has nobody called for help?"

"They seem to believe Hella Badid and the Fly Fest organizers are still here, getting the party ready."

Rafi let Peggy's words sink in, absorbing them so deep that they pulled her jaw down with them. Because yes, it had been a harebrained scheme—one that, deep down, Rafi didn't think would ever work. But her little lie about Hella Badid still being here had done the trick. People wanted to stay. *River* would stay.

"Nobody's posting about how terrible this island is?" Rafi asked, skepticism seeping through her awe. "No pictures of the cheese sandwiches?"

"Not that I've seen," Peggy said. "They don't want anyone back home to think they're losers."

A zap of glee shot through Rafi's whole body, and she was so giddy she actually jumped in place. People had actually listened to her. They'd heard her, and she was able to convince them of something. Her voice mattered. She'd influenced the influencers.

"Congratulations," Peggy said. "Everyone wants to stay

and I get a bunch of presents. It's a win-win for everybody. But mostly me."

Rafi practically skipped back to her tent. She'd woken up feeling the lowest she had since she'd gotten here, but her mood had done a complete one-eighty. She may have had no bed, and she was starving and itchy in a terrible shirt, but she was happy. Things were finally looking up.

Of course, the moment couldn't last long.

When she got to the beach, Rafi heard a strained cry and saw a crowd gathering around someone. Rafi ran toward the commotion until she saw Greer, the girl who cried a lot. But this was different. She was on her knees and seemed in deep emotional pain. "What is it?" Rafi asked her, not for the first time raking her eyes over the girl to see if she was hurt.

In all her wailing, Greer had only enough breath to say one chilling sentence. *"Sierra Madre is missing!"*

12

"WHAT DO YOU MEAN SIERRA MADRE IS MISSING?"

"I mean she isn't anywhere!" Greer was exasperated, out of breath, and disheveled. Most of her was covered in a thin film of wetness, and it was unclear whether it was snot, sweat, or tears. Probably a combination of all three. Rafi placed gentle but firm hands on the girl's bare shoulders and tried to catch her frenzied gaze.

"Tell me everything," Rafi said.

"I went to her tent this morning to see if she needed anything," Greer said through wheezing hiccups. "I go every morning, because she's amazing and I can't believe I get to be this close to her. I mean, we have a connection, you know? When I met her here, the first day, she gave me one of her rings, which is like, hello? Are you kidding me? I've been following her since forever, and I leave her a comment on everything she ever posts, like I'm pretty sure she looks forward to my emojis? A heart, a teardrop, and the dancing twins. It's kind of my signature comment, so that she knows it's me. She's just so pretty. I'm sorry, but she's just the prettiest person on the planet and that's, like, the *tea*."

Rafi nodded vigorously even though she understood very

little about what Greer was saying. She was still stuck on the fact that Greer went to her tent every morning, considering they'd only been on the island for two days. "Please get to the point now."

Greer took a deep, rattling breath. "I went to her tent and she wasn't there."

Rafi had to admit that when she heard Greer shrieking about Sierra being missing, it was like she'd struck a match and Rafi was the flint. Immediately her investigative reporter instincts got to tingling. But now, hearing Greer explain herself, the morbid thrill slowly seeped out of Rafi's body. And she found herself trying to calm a girl whose defining characteristic seemed to be that she overreacted to things. "Greer, did you ever consider that maybe Sierra just went for a walk?"

Greer shook her head. Though the tears no longer poured out of her eyes, they still clogged her voice. "I looked everywhere. I checked every tent in Tent City. I checked the seaport, I even came here, to the beach, where the dirty people are. Sierra isn't anywhere."

"Dirty people?" Rafi said. "The people on the beach aren't dirty."

"They're sunburnt and sweaty and there's sandflies and they're sleeping on the sand."

"*I'm* sleeping on the sand."

"Oh, well I didn't mean *you* were dirty," Greer said, but she still took a step back until Rafi's hands slipped off her shoulders. "It's been hours and Sierra hasn't shown up *any-where*. You work here, right? You have to find her."

Once again, Rafi was tasked with explaining that she did not, in fact, work here, but instead of doing that she held off. Maybe Sierra Madre had gone for a walk. Or maybe, as Greer said, she really was missing. And as someone who was pretty good at solving mysteries, Rafi owed it to Sierra and Greer to at least look into this case.

"I will," Rafi said. "I will find Sierra Madre."

The first step to solving a mystery was to ask questions. Rafi stopped everyone she could, asking if they'd seen Sierra Madre anywhere, but it took some time to get through to people. Most of them were busy playing around with their new Wi-Fi access, finding a way to be very online even though they were stuck on an island.

There was so much a person could do on their phone, she realized, that was easier and more fun than telling the truth. Because everyone was pretending that the festival was still on, that this was a once-in-a-lifetime experience, that they were having a good time on this island.

Everyone on the beach was taking pictures: a girl doing yoga poses; a group of boys posturing like a boy band; a girl pretending not to be disgusted by a horseshoe crab, squealing and gingerly dragging it back to her side whenever it tried to scamper away. One girl was livestreaming herself sunbathing.

Rafi accidentally photobombed more than a few selfies and interrupted some livestreams, but she still managed to ask everyone the only question she had: Had they seen Sierra Madre today? The answer from every single person was consistent. No.

She went to the seaport next, where non-twin jocks Paul and Ryan held court. If Sierra Madre was on anyone's radar, it would be theirs. When she got there, she found Ryan and Paul outside, lounging on chairs they'd dragged out and gazing at the jungle with their hands linked behind their heads.

"Hey, guys, can I ask you a question?"

"Rafi!" Ryan (or perhaps Paul) said. The boys jumped to their feet, looking way too happy to see Rafi. "We've been giving a lot of thought to what you said," Paul (or maybe Ryan) said. "About how there was nothing we could do to fix the sandwich situation."

"*And* about finding the untapped potential all over this disgusting island. So, as my skeet-shooting instructor always says, we decided to murder a bunch of birds with one gun."

The terminology was off but Rafi got the gist of what Ryan (definitely Ryan) was trying to say. Still, her eyes furtively skittered over the ground, searching for a discarded gun and dead birds. What she spotted, though, was much stranger. "What's happening in the trees?" she asked.

The landscape here was pretty sparse compared to the lush jungle at the center of the island, but there were some pretty big banana plants next to the seaport. The bunches of yellowing fruits must've been twenty to twenty-five feet high, and the plants they grew on didn't look all that sturdy, but

Rafi spied about six different people, barefoot and panting, clawing their way up the trunks like they were climbing a fire-station pole.

"We thought about getting the bananas ourselves," Paul said.

"But then we were like, does that *really* help anybody?" Ryan said. "So instead, we taught those people how to climb."

"And now they're collecting the bananas for everyone."

"And by everyone we mean mostly us."

"Wait." Rafi had come here to investigate a missing person, but suddenly she had a whole other line of unrelated questioning running through her head. "What is happening?"

Paul and Ryan looked like they'd been waiting their whole lives for this question and were about to give the best, most thought-out answer. They smirked and nodded at each other, and Rafi could tell this was the more refined version of their own chest bump. The boys turned to her with their pecs flexed and their fists on their hips and looked at Rafi like she was a shark. Specifically, one of those TV sharks who judged whether or not something was a good business idea and then invested a lot of money in it.

"When you signed up for Fly Fest you expected the world's finest organic gourmet food, didn't you?" Ryan asked.

"Actually, I opted for the 'water' option—"

"And then you got here and all there was to eat were gross cheese sandwiches," Paul said. "Hey, Ryan, did you hear that most of those sandwiches contain gluten?"

Ryan's chin bobbed, concerned. "I heard some of them even contain asbestos."

"They don't contain asbestos," Rafi said, but she didn't know if that was accurate. The boys were uninterested in her comments, anyway.

"What if I told you Paul and I have the answers to all of your food insecurities?"

"That's not the correct use of *'food insecurity'*—"

"We have for you a non-GMO, zero-waste, zero–carbon footprint, zero-carbs, zero-calorie, zero-sum game, nature's candy."

Paul continued the pitch. "This organic, vegan, kosher, locally sourced delicacy is picked by dedicated and specially trained interns, and even comes wrapped in an unbelievable outer layer that is all natural and completely compostable, whatever the heck that means."

"We present for you—"

"Don't say a banana," Rafi said.

"A banana!" the boys said in unison. Paul's left hand and Ryan's right palm came together to gently cradle a banana like it was their precious baby. Rafi stared at it. Though Ryan and Paul had spent far too much time and words explaining it, Rafi had never felt so confused by a piece of fruit before. The questions she had earlier only multiplied.

"Why?" she said.

Paul chuckled first, then Ryan. Their laugher was so befuddled and nervous, it came out like barks. "Why?" Paul repeated.

"Rafi, *you* were the one who told us to find a way to disrupt the food industry."

"I legitimately never said that."

"Well, at the very least you must admit that this idea is very money," Ryan said.

"So money," Paul agreed.

"We're charging the interns eight bananas for every ten bananas they collect."

"For the honor of teaching them how to climb."

"They were just a bunch of lazy dickwads before we came along." As he said this, Ryan plopped down onto his chair and kicked his feet out, draping one over the other. "Anyway, we're good people."

"I feel like I'm doing community service but not because I failed a drug test and crashed my Range Rover into the Salvation Army this time," Paul said. "Like, I'm doing the *community* a *service* out of the *goodness of my heart*."

"And we're gonna make a bunch of money doing it," Ryan said.

"Bunches of money out of bunches of bananas!" Paul said.

They loved this particular turn of phrase and clapped their hands so powerfully that Rafi was almost sure they'd leave bruises.

In the plants, one of the lucky community-service recipients lost his footing and let out a guttural yelp as he *thwacked* through every leaf on his way down. The only sound louder than his screams was the one his back made as it hit the ground.

"My dad would be proud of me," Paul said to Rafi. "You'd understand how huge that is if you had any idea who my father is."

Every time she encountered Ryan and Paul, Rafi understood the world a little less. But she didn't even try to speak their language. She let them have their banana pipe dream. She was here on more important matters.

"Do you guys know who Sierra Madre is?"

Paul and Ryan looked at each other, then back at Rafi. "She's only, like, the most famous influencer in the world."

"Right. Have either of you seen her today?"

Ryan and Paul shook their heads. "We've been busy with our—"

"Bananas, I know," Rafi said. "Find me if she turns up."

She'd covered the beach, the seaport, and the areas in between. The only place left for Rafi to ask questions was the one place she should've started her search.

Compared to the rest of the island, Tent City felt like a luxury retreat. Yes, there were the clay-hard dusty grounds, and the dry bramble backdrop, so prickly compared to the lush green jungle, and the fact that these were clearly tents meant for people displaced by horrible disasters, but something about all the white domes—their uniformity, their pristine cleanliness—made Tent City feel like a wellness resort. Like just around the corner there might be someone in a beige tunic waiting with a tray of heated towels, and tongs with which to give them to you.

Rafi took to the tents like a door-to-door salesman, and the residents of Tent City shut their door flaps in her face accordingly. Of all people, Jack Dewey was the most willing to talk.

He greeted Rafi with a beach towel wrapped around his head so that only his mouth and eyes were visible.

"Still protecting yourself from the sun?"

"I have had public disputes with a lot of people, Rafi. My lying fifth-grade bully, my own mother, the president of the United States. But my biggest enemy to date is the sun. That bitch tries to take me down every chance she gets, and still, like dough, I rise."

If he was trying to quote the famous Maya Angelou poem, he was doing it wrong, but Rafi didn't think correcting Jack Dewey would get her anywhere with him. "Good one."

"It's a Jack Dewey original. I can't stop you if you want to quote me, just make sure to tag me."

"Actually—"

"You know what? Don't tag me. I don't want anyone to think we know each other. If you claim that we do, I'll have to deny it, and if you persist, I'll be forced to have my lawyers send you a cease and desist. You understand, don't you?"

"Sure, Jack. Look, I just have one question and then I'll get out of your hair."

"You're in my hair?" Jack whipped the towel off his head and massaged his fingertips into his red-tinged scalp. "What the hell does that even mean?"

"What? Jack, I'm not, like, a *flea*."

Jack shuddered. "I've heard about you beach people. You're dirty."

Rafi rolled her eyes, regretting ever setting foot in Jack's tent. "Have you seen Sierra Madre today?"

The name seemed to pique Jack's interest. His meticulously plucked right eyebrow cocked. "Sierra Madre? No. Has she asked about me?"

"No. I'm looking for her. She seems to be missing."

Now Jack's left eyebrow joined his right one, and they both hovered close to his hairline. "Sierra Madre is missing? Do you think this has anything to do with Hella being here?"

Rafi had almost forgotten about the lie she'd told about Hella last night. It seemed irrelevant at the moment, but she realized that to Jack—and, in fact, to everyone else on the island—Hella being here was the one thing keeping them all from diving into the ocean and swimming home.

Jack took a step closer to Rafi, seeming to forget momentarily that she was a dirty beach dweller. "You weren't lying about Hella being here, were you? Because Hella being here has made a lot of people very happy."

Now it was Rafi who was taking a step back, suddenly interested in every spot of the tent that Jack wasn't currently occupying. Rafi's lie about Hella wasn't hurting anyone. And if morale really was up, as Jack claimed, then she had nothing to be sorry about. She didn't like to lie, but in this case, its harmlessness made it easy. "I'm not a liar," she said.

The grin that sprang onto Jack's face was spellbinding. For one bright, shining moment, Rafi understood how Jack had managed to get millions of followers online. "I knew it," he said. "You wouldn't lie. You have, like . . . morals."

Rafi swallowed, nodded. "So have you seen Sierra, or not?"

"Nope. But you should check her tent. It's right next door."

Rafi had no trouble getting into Sierra's tent, since no one was there to stop her.

After asking everyone on the island if they'd seen Sierra, and hearing nos across the board, a part of Rafi wondered if Sierra had magically booked it, if she'd somehow found a way, through all of her money and influence, to leave without anyone being the wiser. But being in her tent painted a different story.

All of Sierra's luggage was still there. One carry-on, on the floor. When Rafi opened it she found clothes, all made from delicate, expensive fabrics that felt like butter between her fingers. If Sierra had found a way off this island, she wouldn't have left all of this here. And the fact of that left Rafi with a feeling of dread. An avocado pit sinking in her gut.

Maybe Greer hadn't been overreacting.

Where was Sierra?

Asking about her had left Rafi without answers. Now it was about retracing Sierra's last steps. Rafi tried to think of the last place she'd seen her.

Her breath caught in her throat when she remembered.

13

RAFI DIDN'T HAVE TO LOOK HARD TO FIND RIVER; HE was at his tent, and like the sketchy, probable killer he was, he was in the middle of suspiciously fiddling with something in his guitar case that was definitely not his guitar. Rafi poked her head in his open doorway. "Hiya, River."

River started, and when he saw that Rafi was there, quickly palmed whatever it was he was fiddling with and stuffed it in the front pocket of his soft guitar case, zipping it closed in one swift motion. "Rafi! G'day, mate!"

Suspicious, suspicious Australian. Whatever he was hiding was too small to be the knife. Perhaps a handgun? Like the ones they made that were small enough to fit into women's purses? No, a gun would make the case pooch; this had to be even smaller than that. A corkscrew, perhaps? River could do a lot of damage with a corkscrew.

"Uh, Rafi? You okay?"

Her eyes darted up to his. "Yes. Why?"

"You have the same look on your face that I did when Jimmy Fallon asked me what my favorite body of water was, and I just could *not* come up with an answer."

Rafi remembered the segment. She'd watched the clip

about a million times because it showed the perfect example of River being caught off guard and confused and like he was thinking really hard. She dreamt about interviewing him with her hard-hitting questions and drawing that look out of him. "Jimmy probably thought you'd say a river. Because of your name."

It was like the sun was rising behind River's eyes. "Crikey. You're a genius."

Yes, Rafi thought, but she shrugged, faux-modest-like. She stepped gingerly into his tent, feeling bold enough not to ask for an invitation, but she also wanted to make herself seem like a confidante. If she presented herself as the kind of person who came in for a random chat and made herself comfortable in his space, then maybe River would start to believe that they were something close to friends. It was a risk, though, and as Rafi sat cross-legged under the muted green shade of the muslin roof fabric, she waited to see if River would throw her out.

But he just went on talking.

"People always try to make jokes when your name is an actual verb."

Noun.

"Been happening to me my whole life."

"That a fact?"

River nodded. "What's Rafi short for? Raffle?"

She could feel the features of her face morph back into that confused state from a few moments ago, but she had to remind herself she was talking to a celebrity here. They weren't like regular people. "Um. No. Rafaela."

"Wow, what a beautiful name," River said, his smile wide enough to nearly crack his face in half. He really did have a gorgeous smile, and when he coupled it with a compliment and threw around the word "beautiful," it was easy to see how he'd gotten the world to fall into his charm vortex. Rafi could feel the pull right now. Her guts, always on high alert when it came to River, now swooned inside of her like she'd taken a swig of something bubbly and eighty proof.

"*Rafaela*," River sang. He actually sang it, and the melody, along with the loop de loops the vowels made on his accented tongue, elicited a giggle out of Rafi. It shocked her, and she coughed to try to cover it up.

"The name thing always used to happen to Hella, too," River said. "Like, if there was a jewelry brand who wanted her to hawk their products, she'd be in the commercial saying something like, 'This necklace is hella gold,' or whatever."

"Used to?"

"Hmm?"

"You said 'used to.' Past tense. Does it still not happen to her?"

River had to think about it, even though it should've been an easy question. "Yeah, I guess so. Hey, can I ask you something? Do you know why everyone suddenly thinks Hella's here?"

Of course she knew why. "No idea."

"Weird, isn't it?"

"So weird," Rafi agreed. "So, you weren't at the seaport meeting last night?"

"Rafi, I've been on the cover of *Rolling Stone*, *Vogue*, and *Australian Wines* all in the same week. I don't do meetings."

She had no idea what that meant, but now that they were on the subject of questions, she had one of her own. "Have you seen Sierra Madre today?"

"Who?"

A red flag if ever there was one. Everyone knew who Sierra Madre was. "She's tall, stunning, extremely famous?"

A crease appeared between River's eyes. "What is she famous for?"

The question stumped Rafi. Sierra wasn't exactly famous for anything, she just was. She posted pictures of herself, and that seemed to be the extent of what she did with her life. It wasn't the same level of celebrity that River had, but it was definitely a level above the rest of the influencers here, most of whose posts were ads for tea or antacids or vacuum cleaners.

"She just posts stuff."

River shrugged. "Wouldn't know her. I don't go on the internet much."

"Yeah, but you met her," Rafi said. "On the beach yesterday, I saw you two talking."

The crease between his brows deepened, and he had that Jimmy Fallon look on his face, like a mannequin contemplating the meaning of his existence from inside a store window display. "No, I'm not sure I did."

"You pulled some seaweed out of her hair," Rafi said. *And you walked off into the jungle together.*

"You must be mistaken, mate."

River said all this with a smile on his face, but it was a crooked smile. He was lying.

"Are you sure she isn't in the jungle somewhere, doing boar yoga or something?" he asked.

"You mean goat yoga?"

"No, I don't. Or maybe she's meditating. Being at one with nature—isn't she into that sort of thing?"

"I thought you didn't know anything about her."

The crease deepened, his smile growing only more crooked. River's whole demeanor had changed, and where once he was totally open and willing to say just about anything, now he was suddenly closed off. He shifted his eyes away from Rafi, fiddled once more with the guitar case at his knees. He swung the strap over his shoulder, stood, and crouched through the tent flap, and Rafi followed him until they were both standing outside.

"She's probably definitely meditating somewhere," River said. "This island is a wondrous place. She probably just wants to be alone and at one with nature." He was already backtracking—literally walking backward and away from Rafi. "Good luck finding her."

Red flags rose like goose bumps all over Rafi's skin.

Like the mystery item in his guitar case, River Stone was hiding something.

MUSICAL MYSTERIES
Season 2: Episode 3
"A River Runs Through (Bullsh)It"

Richard Evans was born in Melbourne on an unseasonably cold day in December, the only child of Melanie and Stu Evans. He was a colicky baby, who never gave his parents a moment's rest. As a toddler he talked nonstop, scribbled on every wall of his house, and threw his toys at strangers' heads. Both of Richard's parents have described this period as, quote, "terrible." The boy was an even bigger disaster when he reached school age, unable to trace his letters neatly, making truly hideous macaroni art, and quote-unquote *"accidentally"* killing his pet goldfish.

It wasn't until Richard picked up a guitar, at age thirteen, that he showed any real aptitude for anything. Turned out he could play four chords, could even sing. He even had a talent for writing songs. But although the name "Richard Evans" was perfectly fine, it wouldn't do if he wanted to break into the music biz. No, "River Stone" had a much better ring to it.

He picked "Stone" because that's what "Evan" means in Hebrew. But "River," he claims, is a nickname from childhood. Says people always called him that because he enjoyed "jumping into rivers like a little rascal." Paints a lovely picture, doesn't it? Of a carefree child in an idyllic youth where there were rivers around to jump in and be rascalish. Except, there isn't any record of anyone from River's childhood actually calling him River anywhere. No mention of it in any yearbooks or social media posts. And not a single river anywhere near his house.

The name is just the start of Richard's—sorry, River's—duplicitous nature. There's no telling how many lies he's told in his lifetime. How many times did he tell a girl she had a beautiful name when he didn't really mean it? Has he ever lied about not having any STIs? Who knows, but between you and me: probably. The point is, River Stone is a lying liar who lies. Now, there isn't anything wrong with a few white lies here and there. But when your girlfriend disappears in the middle of a camping trip and everything you tell the detectives about the case is a lie—well, that's a different story.

On the surface, the mystery of River's disappearing first love, Tracy Mooney, is scandalous, to be sure. But let's do something that even the case's detectives failed to do: scratch the surface.

Why was River napping at nine P.M.? I mean, who does that? Especially if he planned to propose to Tracy just one hour later?

And the goodbye note. Tracy uses a pretty unusual word to describe River: "wondrous." In all my time researching River and Tracy's story, I was unable to find a single instance in which Tracy used that word. Not in any of her social media posts, not in any of her videos. River, on the other hand? I've found instances of him saying it at least thirty-seven times.

Not to mention the fact that the handwriting on the note itself looks a lot closer to River's than to Tracy's.

Still skeptical? Okay, then let's take a look at his heroic trek back to civilization. After Tracy took River's car, River had to make it back to the nearest town on foot. But judging from the spot where River and Tracy were camping, and the distance to town, a journey that should've taken eleven hours River was able to complete in two.

So he has superhuman speed, you might say. But then explain the river!

Yes, ironically enough, River would've had to cross a river in order to get back to town in the quickest way possible. By car, you can drive around the river relatively quickly. But walking around the river would've added hours to River's journey. Ugh, say "river" one more time—I know, I know. The point is, in order to get to town, in two hours, River would've had to wade into choppy waters. And yet, when he got to the general store where he famously called the police, pictures show that he was totally dry. His boots weren't even wet.

Maybe he dried off in the sun, you say. But may I remind you that it was the *middle of the night*?

You still don't believe me. Well, what if I told you that there are only tire tracks back to town?

No footprints anywhere on the miraculously shortened trail that River supposedly took to salvation.

I mean, *come on!* The evidence against River's story is overwhelming!

My theory? River went on that trip with Tracy and killed her. He wasn't getting anywhere with his music career. And just being another cute guy on YouTube with a guitar wasn't garnering him enough attention. He needed a *story*, a hook. He needed fodder for his song-writing. He needed . . . a dead girl on his hands.

That's next time on "Musical Mysteries."

This episode of "Musical Mysteries" was brought to you by Nobrand. Ever wish you had some toilet paper because you've been using sandwich bread in a way in which it was not intended? Try Nobrand. They've got you covered. And if you use the code RIVERKILLER, you'll get fourteen percent off your purchase.

Until next time, Mysterinos!

14

Rafi's mind was racing with possibilities, motives, disappearances, and mysteries, and there was only one way she knew how to work through them all. It was a personal project that took her half the day to complete, and when she was done, there was only one person she could think to show it to, and she *did* need to show it. That was part of the process—to talk it out with someone with fresh eyes who could tell her if her hunches seemed sound, if she was on the right track.

It'd been hard to pull Peggy out of their ever-growing tent mansion, but she finally convinced them to come into the jungle. And when Peggy saw Rafi's project, hanging between two trees like a banner, they were glad they came.

"You made a murder board?" Peggy was wide-eyed and slack-jawed, but not disinterested.

It was a cliché, but there was a reason murder boards were so ubiquitous with investigators. It was the best way for Rafi to work out her hypothesis, with the central mystery, the suspects, the motives, and everything else laid out in front of her.

Peggy approached the board slowly, and reached out their

fingers but stopped just short of touching it, like it was a priceless artwork hanging in a museum. Rafi had to admit, she was pretty proud of herself. For someone who had little else than the clothes on her back, she'd managed to make a pretty good board.

"You managed to find cardboard on the island?" Peggy asked.

"It's the bread from the cheese sandwiches, pasted together side by side. Same consistency as cardboard."

"What did you paste it together with?"

"The cheese, what else?" Rafi could've spent hours explaining how she'd achieved such a gorgeous spectacle (the threads linking the different theories were stripped ropes of ivy; the drawings were made in sand art using beach sand and clear lip gloss), but she didn't want to stray too far from the point, which was what the murder board was about.

Peggy still had more questions about the construction, though.

"How did you get so many pictures of River?"

This one was easy enough to answer. "I've been researching this case for a year. I printed out every article I could find about him."

"So let me get this straight," Peggy said. "You're telling me that instead of packing literally any other spare shirt into your carry-on, you decided instead to take to a music festival dozens of pictures of River Stone."

Why was this so hard for them to understand? "I'm an *investigator*."

"Okay, but why are there so many *shirtless* pictures?"

Rafi took one long step until she was standing between Peggy and the board. At this point it was starting to feel like more of a distraction than an infographic. "It's not my fault that River is shirtless in nearly every picture ever taken of him; can we get back to the point? He's a killer. And I think he's killed again."

"Like, on this island?"

Rafi nodded. "Sierra Madre is missing. No one's seen her since the beach party. And I saw her disappear into the jungle with River."

"Lots of girls throw themselves at River."

"But he lied about it," Rafi said. "I asked him point-blank about whether he'd met Sierra, and he claimed he hadn't. I think he did something to her."

Peggy considered this. Or, at least, they didn't seem as preoccupied with the murder board anymore, because they focused on a rock on the ground, kicking it around lazily. "What's the use of looking into this?"

Not what Rafi was expecting them to ask, and it was, in fact, kind of insulting. After all the work she'd done on the murder board? "There could be a killer among us," Rafi said, trying to infuse the proper amount of gravitas in her voice. "And he could kill again."

"But what's the use in that line of thinking?"

Rafi stared blankly, and Peggy sighed and tried to put it in terms that she would understand. "You're better off thinking that River's not a killer. Because if he is, that means he's been let loose on an island, free to kill anyone. It'd be like shooting fish in a barrel. Or dumping a cat into a box full of mice. Or a snake in—"

"I get it."

"He'd be free to keep killing with no one to stop him," Peggy went on. "And, if you think about it, it's all 'cause of that big lie you told."

"Little lie."

"Massive lie," Peggy said. "Face it, Rafi, you managed to keep River on the island. But are you prepared for what that means?"

Rafi let Peggy's words sink in, deeper and deeper until she felt like she was six feet underground.

"I meant him killing a bunch of people," Peggy said.

"I know what you meant," Rafi snapped.

River had his guitar out. The denizens of the beach had left their designated spots in order to sit cross-legged and contented at his feet, their phones held aloft, recording the impromptu twilight concert. They'd come to Fly Fest for the music—well, probably for the bragging rights—but they were finally getting music, anyway. An acoustic set by River Stone. And this song was his most popular one. Rafi listened to the lyrics as he sang.

And that was the last night I saw her / ring in
   my pocket
I was a boat / she really knew how to rock it
Oh Tracy
My heart was big / it was not small
You had a phone / Why didn't you call?

Wordsmith. Lyricist of our times. Rafi wanted to gag. But here was the kicker. The coda. The part of the song everyone always howled in unison:

I call your name in anguish but I'm the victim
   here OH!

Rafi had listened to "Victim" a million times, trying to decode the lyrics, see if there was some subtext that would betray River's lies. As he sang, River managed to make his shirtlessness a vulnerability, the slick strands of hair springing into his face with every key change somehow making him look earnest. He was dazzling them all with his body and his stupid songs.

He was so good at looking like an honest, nice guy. But then, so was Ted Bundy.

Rafi hadn't been able to stop thinking about what Peggy had said. About River being free to kill—and about Rafi's own part in that. If Rafi hadn't told everyone that Hella was here somewhere, still planning to party with them, would Sierra be missing?

Was Peggy right? Was all of this Rafi's fault?

The question gnawed away at her. So much so that Rafi wanted to take it all back—the lie, her part in it. She envisioned herself running up to River, in front of all those people, and ripping the guitar out of his hands so she could get their attention. She'd tell them all the truth, say she hadn't seen Hella, that they needed to get back home, that this place wasn't safe.

Rafi took a few steps forward, ready to make her way to the "stage" when something in the distance caught her eye. A rustling in the trees that blanketed the base of the mountain. Leaves dipped and swayed, like an invisible wind swept through them. Or, more likely, a wild animal. It was coming down fast, barreling through, and Rafi was pretty sure she was the only one who saw it. Her whole body tensed, waiting for whatever monster was coming her way to make itself known. Finally, it reached the bottom and broke through the trees.

It was not a monster. It was a girl. Not just any girl—it was Greer. Crying. Again.

"Not another missing person," Rafi muttered under her breath, hating herself for being more annoyed at Greer's crying than at the prospect of a growing body count.

The crying girl locked eyes with the only person who noticed her and rushed right toward Rafi. Greer had a look in her eyes like she was possessed. Maybe she was, because the few words that came out of her mouth made a chill run down Rafi's hot spine.

"Hell is here."

"What?" Rafi asked. But Greer did not elaborate, choosing instead to run through the concert crowd, kicking up sand, and breaking up the relaxed vibe like an out-of-control pinball. "HELL IS HERE!"

On a trip to New York once when she was a kid, Rafi saw a man in Times Square wearing a big sign over his body with print too small to read, but he kept shouting about the devil. Rafi's mother pulled her by the hand until they were far enough away that Rafi could only hear him in the distance, her attention eventually stolen by the M&M's store. This was kind of like that, except no one was there to pull Rafi by the hand. It was her own intuition, her investigative edge, that pulled her forward, after the girl.

Greer continued zigzagging through the crowd, screaming louder and louder until River was forced to end the song before it could reach its tragic coda. He put his guitar down carefully and stood, placing a comforting hand on Greer's shoulder. "What's wrong, hon?"

"Hell is here!" she said again. "I witnessed it. She revealed herself to me." Greer swallowed and smiled through her tears. "Hella Badid is here!"

15

"EVERYONE, CALM DOWN." RIVER SPOKE WITH THE charismatic confidence expected of a teen idol, but it wasn't enough to tamp down the sudden fervor for more information. People continued to talk over themselves, bouncing on the balls of their feet with excitement—the kind of excitement you'd expect if you'd just heard that the coast guard had spotted you after days stranded on an island. Except it wasn't the coast guard, it was a supermodel.

River wasn't convinced, though. "These rumors are just that—rumors. Hella isn't here," he said. "Believe me, I would know."

"But I heard her," said Greer.

"What did you hear, exactly?" River asked.

"I was walking up the mountain when I heard her. We all know her voice—I wouldn't mistake Hella Badid's voice for anyone else's."

Hella did have a truly distinctive cadence. It was deep but still managed to sound flighty with its Valley Girl accent. She also had the world's foremost vocal fry, all of her sentences ending with a staticky whine akin to the sound a monster might make as it tried to climb out of your TV set. The deep Valley, vocal fry monster voice was occasionally topped off with a small exclamation that sounded almost exactly like a sheep's bleat. Lots of girls tried to emulate it. Few succeeded.

"Wait, you went up the mountain by yourself?" Rafi asked. Her curiosity had led her to the front of the pack, standing right beside River. The mountain was uncharted territory. All paths up its steep incline seemed needlessly treacherous, and not even River, Jack, or Rafi had crossed it when they'd made their exploratory trek. Naturally, Rafi had more questions. "What were you doing on the mountain?"

The features on Greer's face tensed up and turned red. "I don't have to answer that." She looked to River. "I don't have to answer that, right?"

Rafi took a step closer to Greer, and a part of her, subconsciously, was trying to get to the bottom of this—whatever this was—through intimidation. "Why are you being so shifty?" Rafi asked.

"What I do when I am alone with my body is my own business," Greer said, eyes welling up anew, voice cracking.

"Look, we don't care what you were doing up there," River interjected. "Is it possible that you only *think* you heard Hella's voice? Sometimes, when I'm alone, lying in a hammock in my Hamptons estate, musing for inspiration, I think I hear an angel singing, but then I realize it's just me, coming up with new melodies. Could it be that you got excited and thought you heard a voice when really it was the breeze rustling the trees or something?"

"Is that what you think Hella sounds like?" Rafi asked. "A breeze rustling the trees? Have you heard her speak?"

"I've been going out with her for two months, I think I know—"

"It wasn't the breeze," Greer said. "It was her. I've never been more sure of anything in my entire life."

This shut everybody up, including Rafi. It couldn't be. Hella being here was just a lie. A lie that Rafi made up. But Greer seemed convinced. And River seemed tense.

"What did Hella say?" Rafi asked.

Greer sniffed and blinked, clearing away her tears. "She welcomed me to the island. And then she said that things were about to get . . . lit."

It was just what everybody wanted to hear, because the crowd, listening to every word, let out a collective squeal of delight. The bouncing started again, the excitement got louder among them. There was something electric in the air, a buzz, like someone had just turned the music on at a party.

But it was a song that Rafi didn't quite know. And River, whose face was set in a scowl for the first time since they got to the island, didn't seem to hear the music at all.

Rafi had made up the rumor. But was it possible? Could Hella Badid really be somewhere on this island?

"Hella Badid is definitely somewhere on this island!" Jack announced to an explosion of cheers.

He was standing in the same spot where River had been performing just an hour ago, the audience now double in size. And while night had fully fallen, Jack nevertheless wore sunglasses in an attempt to obscure as much of his makeup-free face as possible. Though, they probably also helped to shield him from the glare of the burning torches held up by two of his—fans? Followers? Disciples? Greer was one of them. The flames seemed to make her eyes water.

Rafi wasn't sure what she was watching, but she hovered at the back of the pack, paying close attention. It was fascinating to see who influenced the influencers, and now Rafi had her answer: It was the boy makeup artist. She didn't know why Jack held so much sway over them. Maybe it was the way he spoke—the confidence he had to take up any topic and imbue it with more knowledge than he could possibly possess (stating, for instance, that Hella was on this island, without a single shred of evidence).

It must've had something to do with his skill at courting drama. Online, Rafi had regularly heard more about Jack than she'd ever wanted to know, simply by virtue of all the constant fights he was involved in. There was the time he fought very publicly with a rival MUA over credit for the short-lived slug lips trend; or the time he put out a cover of "Ave Maria" that was so scandalous that the pope denounced him; or the time he started a fight with his grandma because of overdue bar mitzvah money and he made her get TikTok so that people could see both sides of the story, and then she accidentally posted one hundred videos of herself sleeping, and Jack disowned her out of sheer humiliation.

The drama had followed him to Fly Fest, too. He didn't have a grandma to fight with, but Jack picked fights with anyone who was around. He accused a fashion influencer of trying to steal his Burberry fanny pack, a wellness influencer of spying on him while he meditated, and Rafi was pretty sure he was currently in a fight with *her* now, though she didn't know why. It was just that any time she made eye contact with him, his eyebrows arched fiercely, like two expertly plucked question marks that only wanted to know one thing: *How dare you?*

Still, Rafi didn't look away. Despite how ridiculous all of this was, Rafi wanted to hear what Jack had to say. This Hella rumor was the biggest thing to happen to Fly Fest since the implosion of Fly Fest. She herself had started it. And thanks to Jack, it seemed, it was only going to become a bigger deal.

"I know it looks like this festival was a bust. A scam. A lie," Jack told the crowd. "I was ready to believe that, too. But people have heard Hella Badid's voice."

"One person," Rafi muttered to herself. "One emotionally fragile person."

Jack couldn't have possibly heard her, but the way he immediately zeroed in on Rafi with one of his patented narrowed stares—even through the shades!—unnerved her.

"And it wasn't just one person who heard her!" Jack proceeded to look over his followers. "More people have come forward to me privately to say they've heard her, too. We know Hella Badid's publicist has confirmed to all media outlets that Hella has come on this trip. And we also know that Hella hasn't been posting anything on social media, so she's obviously in hiding. My friends, my followers—Hella Badid is *here*. Up on that mountain behind me. I'm not making that up—those are the facts."

Jack paced and his torch-wielders followed his every move, making for a compelling sort of stage show. "I've got another fact for you. Sierra Madre is missing."

No one gasped or seemed at all surprised, but that was probably because Rafi had asked everyone here if they knew of Sierra's whereabouts. But she, like everyone else, waited for Jack to make his connection between Sierra and Hella.

"I've got a theory," Jack said finally. "Sierra was, arguably, the best among us. I mean, I'm up there myself but, as some of you may know, I have sadly lost all of my makeup in this horrific ordeal. I know it is probably physically painful for all of you to have to look at my face, it being as bare and disgusting as the day's first snow. The point is! I think Sierra's been invited."

A subtle wave broke through the influencers as they collectively leaned forward with interest. Rafi couldn't help it. She leaned forward, too.

"We know Hella's here, up on the mountain somewhere. We know she's probably helping to make Fly Fest happen. But what if it's already happening? What if the only ones who are invited are the ones who are *worthy* of being invited?"

"Worthy?" Rafi repeated.

"We know Sierra is worthy. Sierra is perfect." Here Jack paused. Rafi could learn a thing or two from him when it came to public speaking. He had the right cadence, the right starts and stops. He had everyone in the audience wrapped around his finger. And he yanked. "What if this is a test? What if Hella is waiting for us to get it together so we can finally experience the real Fly Fest? Because we all came here expecting a party and we got served a big pile of nothing. It just doesn't make sense."

"Make it make sense!" said a lone voice in the crowd. Jack, emboldened by the audience engagement, nodded.

"Hella is here," Jack said. It was not a question. "Which means the party must be here, too. What if the organizers are watching us, from up on their mountain, and making decisions about who they'll let in? They let Sierra in. Do you want to be on that guest list? I know I do."

Rafi listened, but her mind kept responding with skepticism. *What if there was another level of hoops to jump through just to be granted access to a stupid musical festival?* More like, *What if we all got scammed out of our money, but we're clearly susceptible to scams, and so here's another one to suit your fancy?*

But as Rafi looked around, she didn't see anyone shaking their head or walking away. She saw eyes widening and heads nodding and the kind of devotional tearing up you saw in documentaries about dangerously fanatical cults.

"What if we're one step closer to meeting Hella?" The tone

of Jack's voice rose along with his excitement. "What if Hella and the others—"

The others? This was getting ominous.

"—want us to *prove* we're worthy of going to the festival? We must be perfect to go to the world's most perfect party!"

It was a rallying cry, and it was met with just the cheers Jack wanted. For Rafi, all she was left with were questions. How could these people—with their expensive clothes and faces made smooth by diligent skin-care regimens—get any more perfect? And what did Jack have in mind?

Jack bowed, signaling his speech was over, and the crowd closed in on him, eager to be near. Rafi wasn't sure what to make of Jack's speech, or if it would truly change things on the island. All she knew was that a girl was missing—possibly dead. And now everyone thought she'd been let into a bogus festival on a mountaintop.

Meanwhile, River still roamed free.

Things were starting to unravel, and Rafi didn't have the first clue how to get it all back under control.

And now there was a rustling on the mountain. It was the same type of rustling Rafi witnessed when Greer came rushing down that same pathway to warn everyone about Hella.

But it wasn't Greer who broke through the trees this time.

It was River, calmly dusting off his hands on the back of his shorts and checking to see if anyone was watching.

What had he been doing up there?

16

SHE DIDN'T HAVE MUCH OF A PLAN. AND IT OCCURRED to her that it might be too mentally exhausting to try to be sneaky about this, so it all hinged on River saying yes. She hoped he was just vain and delusional enough to do it.

Rafi stood outside River's tent and knocked. Or, tapped on the fabric, as it were, until it swayed back and forth enough to get his attention. He poked his head out almost instantly and lobbed a smile her way. "G'day, Raf!"

It was fully nighttime, and could this guy be any more Australian? But Rafi served River a tentative smile. She needed to be out with it. "Can I interview you?"

River's eyebrows quirked—not skeptically, just genuinely curious, if a bit confused. "Like, about how I manage to make such good art and stay so fit even though those two concepts are diametrically opposed?"

Um. "Among other things. It would be for my podcast." Rafi held up her phone and mic, her most prized possessions. If he said no, then she'd just blown her one opportunity to get the interview of a lifetime when she probably could've just recorded him without his knowledge. But she needed to do this right, and with the way things were going on this trip, it was time to cut out the games.

River stepped fully out of his tent, standing akimbo. "It would be my pleasure."

Rafi matched his smile. Just because she'd asked nicely didn't mean she would give him easy questions. It was time to get to the truth. It was show time.

They sat in front of their tents, a small campfire that River had built making the night come alive, ablaze and crackling. The atmosphere was akin to two neighbors enjoying a beer on their porches after a long day. Except instead of booze there was the impossible-to-ignore microphone in Rafi's hand. She hadn't even started her interview, but River kept looking at it. It was almost like he hadn't been interviewed thousands of times before.

Rafi stuck the mic in the sand, its soft foam cover sticking straight up like a zombie hand protruding from a fresh grave. She hoped that keeping it out of River's sight line would be enough to make him forget about it. She needed to get him comfortable so that he would talk. She needed him to talk. After all, there was a girl missing who still hadn't turned up.

"So, what's your podcast about?"

"It's called 'Musical Mysteries.' It's about the biggest mysteries. In music." She had to find a better tagline.

"Ah. I think I know what you're going to ask me. . . . You,

like everyone else in the world, want to know when the new album is finally coming out."

No. Definitely not at all. Though, Rafi *was* a bit curious. While most of his fans thought he was just a perfectionist trying to get his album in tip-top shape before releasing it into the world, Rafi had a theory that River was dealing with writer's block. It was only natural, given that his sole inspiration for his first and only album was about the tragedy of his missing girlfriend. Without that tragedy, what did he have to sing about anymore?

"The truth is, for the last year, since I sat down to write the thing, I've been majorly blocked."

She knew it.

"And then, last week," River went on, "poof! It was like a dam broke inside my head and all these songs came gushing out. A whole album's worth."

"Wow. That's lucky," Rafi said.

"Nah, I wouldn't call it luck."

She definitely wouldn't call it luck either. "What happened last week?"

"Hmm?"

"Something must have happened last week to get your creative juices flowing. Something big. Did it have anything to do with Hella?"

River got a funny look on his face, but he avoided looking at Rafi's eyes. He focused his attention on the fire instead, stoking it with a stick. "Don't think so?" he said.

It was the most unsure River had ever sounded. Rafi latched

onto this River—the one who couldn't look her in the eye and ended sentences with question marks. This River was the one who would inadvertently lead Rafi to the truth. And the truth was possibly where Sierra lay. Dead.

"It's weird, isn't it," Rafi said, "that everyone suddenly thinks Hella is on this island." Rafi made no mention of the fact that she was technically the one who'd started the rumor, but that was irrelevant. "Is it possible that she *is* here somewhere?"

"What?" River said, befuddled. "No way. Hella canceled on the gig."

"I thought you told Jack she missed her flight at the last minute." Rafi distinctly remembered him saying that when they all went on their trek together the first day.

"Yeah, she missed it." More stoking of the fire, more avoiding Rafi's gaze. "That's what I meant."

To say River was acting shifty was an understatement. The corner of his mouth pulled itself to the side, like a fisherman's hook tugging the life out of him. His tell. He was lying. Rafi felt suddenly bad for Sierra, that she would trust and walk off with someone so shady. Tracy, too.

"Can I ask you about your relationship with Tracy?" Rafi was walking on eggshells now, trying to get to this portion of her interview as carefully as possible. It was imperative that she didn't spook him. From all her research, Rafi knew that River didn't like to talk about Tracy. The topic was pretty unavoidable when he had to promote his album, but he usually sidestepped it by saying the whole thing was still too recent and hard for him to talk about. It worked in his favor and went a long way in garnering him fans who thought he was *soo* sensitive.

"It's been a long time since anyone's asked me about Tracy."

Rafi breathed, waited for him to say the wound was still too fresh.

"You remind me a lot of her."

It was such a left turn from his usual answer that it took Rafi a moment to process what he'd said, and when she finally did, her cheeks went red. Tracy was a blonde with hair that didn't frizz up at the tiniest exposure to the outside and a constant smile holding up her apple cheeks and a row of straight teeth that were small enough to still look like baby teeth even though they obviously weren't. Point was, Tracy had been beautiful, something Rafi never felt she was. Especially not on this island.

"You mean our personalities?" Rafi reasoned.

"Blimey, no—Tracy was a lot of fun."

"Oh."

"I mean she always used to ask me a million questions, trying to get to the core of what I was feeling and thinking and *hiding*, even. But I wasn't ever hiding anything." River shook his head and laughed to himself, recalling a memory. "One time she grilled me for days—*days*—about how she knew I was lying to her. She said she could tell from my smile or something."

Rafi felt an instant kinship with Tracy then. This small thing that seemed to elude all of his fans was something that she and Tracy both saw. Something that bound them together.

"We could be doing something so mundane, like sharing a bag of chippies, and she'd turn to me out of nowhere and say, '*I know there's something you're not telling me.*' That was the thing about Tracy—she knew me better than anyone. And she was right. There was something I'd been hiding from her."

Rafi didn't move except to lean subtly closer, waiting—ready for something that sounded like a confession. River, for his part, leaned in, too. This close, Rafi could see the patchy stubble starting to sprout on his chin and cheeks. He was usually so neat and clean-shaven all the time, which Rafi always saw as a calculated ploy to stay looking boyish and innocent. Now the dark scruff defined his features more than usual, cut his cheeks, made his jaw sharp as a flat blade. His eyes, both dark pools sparkling with the reflection of the campfire, locked onto Rafi, and she couldn't help but drown in them. This close she could breathe him in, practically. He smelled flowery, fresh. Like jasmine. She inhaled. Why did he always smell so good?

Rafi's lips must've been dry because she licked them. "What were you hiding from her?"

River's own lips, plump and properly hydrated, curved into a naughty smile. "A porcupine."

A porcupine.

River rocked back with a laugh that rivaled the cracking of the fire. "It was a silly birthday present. But she was always talking about wanting pets. The thing is, she was majorly allergic to any kind of fur. Cat fur, dog fur, possum fur."

"Possums?" Did people in Australia keep possums as pets? Were tarantulas next?

"Tarantula fur," River went on. "Bird feathers, too. Once we went to an emu farm, and she was sneezing up a storm all over the place."

"You lost me at emu farm."

"I thought a porcupine would do, you know? Nothing fuzzy that you could pet. Well, you could pet her quills, but who would want to? She was called Porky. I picked the name."

"Original."

River stoked the fire, but when he laughed again there was a sniff tagged on to the end of it. "Tracy loved Porky," River said through a sad smile. "I kept her after . . . afterwards. I tried so hard to keep the bloody thing alive and healthy. I even fed her chocolate bars every day. And then she up and escaped. I think my mum let her out of the house one day. I miss her."

"She sounds like a nice pet."

"She was. But I wasn't talking about her."

He kept his gaze on the fire, but looking at him, Rafi could see how glassy River's eyes had become. It was subtle, but he was emotional. She'd never seen him overcome like this. Not even in the hours of concert footage she'd combed for any hints to this kind of outpouring. She could see it plain as day, how much he loved Tracy.

"I'm sorry."

River sniffed and shook his head back in the way he did when he wanted to get his hair out of his eyes. "Thank you for asking about Tracy. It's been so long since I talked about her."

Rafi nodded but she didn't know what to think. She didn't anticipate River reacting like this at the mention of his long-missing first love. She thought he'd be cagey, suspicious, sly. But he was just a boy like any other, talking about a girl he'd loved and lost. Rafi actually felt a pang of guilt for her ulterior motives in bringing her up.

And she was more confused than ever, because of all the Rivers she'd seen, this one had her the most convinced that he wasn't capable of hurting anyone.

Rafi couldn't sleep. It'd been hours since her interview with River, and she still couldn't reconcile the sweet, vulnerable boy she'd seen tonight with the one in her head—the one with a trail of missing girls behind him.

She needed to know, one way or another, who he really was. Everyone on this island was lying about something. Some were lying about what they really looked like outside of Facetune and filters. Some were lying about what an amazing, beautiful experience this was. River had to be lying about something, too.

And maybe Rafi was crazy for what she was about to do, but it was the only way to calm her mind. If she found nothing, she'd give up the game and admit that she didn't have enough to go on to nail River. But if she found something, then she knew her instincts had been right about him all along.

Rafi knew he wasn't in his tent. Not being able to sleep, she'd seen his shadow outside her own tent, moving away until he was gone. And she waited. She waited long enough that she figured the coast was clear.

She was in his tent now, and she had her sights set on only one thing: his guitar case. Specifically, the front pocket. The same one she saw him hiding something inside.

She knew she was violating something here. His trust, his boundaries, his privacy. But a part of her also felt that she had Tracy on her side. Tracy, who also sensed when River was hiding something, was very possibly cheering Rafi on. At least, Rafi told herself that as she crawled to the back of River's tent, clawing sand through her fingers until her hands were on the pocket's zipper. She pinched it and pulled. And when she saw what was inside, all the breath left her body.

She held it up in front of her eyes to get as close a look as possible. Its shininess glinted in the starlight.

It was a necklace with a rose-gold charm with a name spelled out in cursive. *Sierra*.

17

"WHAT'S YOUR NAME AGAIN?"

"Rafi."

The bouncer at Peggy's door looked skeptical, like he didn't believe that Rafi's name was actually Rafi—like anyone's name could actually be Rafi. He took a bite of a hardboiled egg as he looked her up and down, another already peeled egg waiting in a Ziploc bag in his hand.

"Where'd you get eggs?" Rafi asked. "Are there chickens on the island?"

"I'm the one asking questions here," the bouncer said. "And if you want to see Peggy there's a wait time. And a color-coded sticker system. And a line."

Rafi looked back over her shoulder. The day was barely into its twinkling daylight hours, and there was already an ant's trail of people about thirty deep waiting to get into Peggy's tent. They clutched their phones in white-knuckled sunburnt hands, nearly vibrating with anticipation for their next Wi-Fi fix. Rafi couldn't wait in line. What she had to say to Peggy was too important.

She resorted to the same gimmick she'd employed the last time she'd been desperate to enter Peggy's tent.

"PEGGY!" Rafi yelled at the top of her lungs, so loud past the bouncer's ear the sound made him recoil. Not enough to keep him from blocking the door, though.

"Ambrosius?" came Peggy's voice from their cavernous white dwelling. "Who goes there?"

"Somebody named Razzie," the bouncer responded. "I think she works here."

"It's me, Rafi!"

"*Who?*" Peggy's voice said.

Rafi took a deep breath to try to center herself. "We met on day one. We're friends. I showed you my murder board."

"You showed them your *what?*" the bouncer asked, munching on his second egg.

"Of course, of course," came Peggy's voice. "Come in."

The place looked even bigger than the last time Rafi had seen it, and it seemed to still be expanding. There was someone in the left wing, standing on a stack of crates and cutting a hole into the ceiling. For a sunroom or a second floor, Rafi couldn't be sure, and though it was more than adequate shelter, Rafi couldn't say she was jealous of the accommodations. The place was crammed. All sorts of things were littered everywhere, things Peggy couldn't possibly need, like hand sanitizer or endless amounts of airport headphones, or a Rube Goldberg machine made of Styrofoam sandwich containers that appeared to do nothing more than toss bananas limply on the floor. And there were so many people there, too. It was as though someone from an episode of *Hoarders* was also addicted to hosting parties. Boring parties. All the people were too busy with their noses in their phones, frozen in deep concentration. In fact, except for overworked thumb knuckles and the occasional flying banana, Peggy's tent-mansion was stuffed with inanimate objects.

When Rafi got to Peggy's quarters, she found them eating a chunk of milky white coconut, which was being fed to them by a servant standing to the side of the inflatable hot-pink Fly Fest promotional chair on which Peggy sat. The chair matched the color of Rafi's shirt, and she felt repelled by it, though she wasn't sure if that had to do with the Fly Fest logo or of what had become of the person sitting on it.

"Rafi," Peggy said, licking the last bit of coconut milk off their servant's finger. "What brings you here?"

Rafi held up her hand. Sierra's necklace dangled from between her fingers. "I found this in River's things."

Peggy squinted, and lest their poor eyesight get in the way of this revelation, Rafi stepped closer, until the charm practically grazed Peggy's nose.

"So he wears jewelry." Peggy shrugged. "This is much less alarming than you going through his stuff."

Rafi chose to ignore that last part. "This is Sierra's necklace! Don't you see? It proves River was lying to me when I asked him if he knew her."

"And Sierra's the girl who's missing, right?"

Rafi's jaw came unhinged as she struggled to find words. Honestly, she'd made a whole murder board about this to illustrate her point, but clearly she hadn't done a good enough job at it. "Yes. This proves he knows more than he's letting on."

"And that he probably killed her," Peggy said.

Rafi nodded vehemently. Finally, they were catching on. "And I'm starting to think there may be something to the Hella rumor."

"That you started."

"Yes. I mean, I was lying when I said she was here, but what if she really is here?"

"Lemme guess," Peggy cut in, "you think River killed her."

"I know you think this is a joke, but I'm serious. Look—" Rafi turned to the nearest person, a girl lying on the floor not too far away. "You, could you look up Hella Badid's Instagram for me?"

The girl seemed bothered to be interrupted but also like the type of person who'd check on Hella Badid's socials anyway. And she did. "She hasn't posted anything in days."

"See?" Rafi said, spinning back around to Peggy with renewed vigor. "Hella posts every day, sometimes multiple times a day. Why is she suddenly silent?"

"I guess because her boyfriend chopped her up like he did his last girlfriend."

"Okay, I can't tell if you're being sarcastic, but yes, precisely." Fired up, Rafi turned to the girl with the phone again. "Can you look up Sierra Madre's Instagram, too?"

"Do you, like, not have your own phone?" the girl responded.

"Do it!"

The girl was aghast, but she also followed the command. "Nothing from Sierra either."

Rafi shot Peggy a wide-eyed, self-satisfied look. "These people *live* on social media, Peggy. If they're not posting, do they even really exist?"

This was major stuff. Hella not posting was a huge indicator that something was off. A scandal, celebrities, disappearances—anyone would be intrigued. But Peggy couldn't look more bored. Rafi knew what they were thinking. That she was crazy. That she was once again on a bender of her own conspiracy theories. But this necklace wasn't a conspiracy. It was proof. And Rafi owed it to Sierra—and maybe even to Hella—to get to the bottom of this.

Peggy finally spoke. "So, playing dumb devil's advocate here, let's say River Stone is a kidnapper-slash-murderer. What do you want to do about it?"

"Well, that's why I'm here. I need to get on the internet. We need to tell the police—we need to get River away from all these unsuspecting people." Rafi took a breath. "Plus, stuff's getting weird around here."

"How do you mean?"

"Well, for one thing, Peggy, you're wearing a bear-hide rug as a hat."

The head of the bear was mostly intact, its jaw open and menacing over Peggy's bangs. The rest of the hide draped over their back, like a cloak. And that was only the crowning touch of Peggy's outfit. They also wore at least a dozen necklaces, a pair of orange lace gloves, leather pants, and, for good measure, a satin cummerbund. "Aren't you hot in all that?"

"That's why I have my fan," Peggy said. They gestured toward the boy at their side. Not the one with the coconut, the one fanning them with a paperback spy novel. "Can you believe somebody packed this in their carry-on?"

"People read books."

"I meant this." Peggy pointed to the bear on their head.

"Oh, that," Rafi said. After all the absurd things she'd seen on this island? "Yes."

"Well, I won't apologize for it. It's badass."

"It's not just you—it's everybody. I saw a girl on the beach doing a reaction video with a turtle."

"Like, reacting to the turtle?"

"Like, asking the turtle to react to things."

Peggy chuckled appreciatively and motioned for their servant to bend closer to them. "Get me that turtle," they instructed. The servant was off, and Peggy's attention was back on Rafi. "So you realize your lover boy is a killer, and suddenly you want off the island."

"He is *not* my *lover boy*, and yes, I want off the island. You were right. I said Hella was here, and now everyone's staying on this island because of my lie, and it's making it a lot easier for River to potentially kill people. I don't want to be anywhere near a probable serial killer. Do you?"

"Do you see this?" Peggy held up a jar half-full with a greenish liquid. "Somebody gave me this for five minutes of internet this morning. I'm not sure if I'm meant to drink it or apply it, but it's supposed to make my hair shiny, and I'll be damned if I don't try it. People are just *giving* me this stuff, Rafi."

Again, Rafi was confused at the core concept. Was Peggy complaining here, or bragging? Probably bragging, she realized. It was apparent from the state of Peggy's surroundings that they considered every single thing that people traded with them a kind of treasure, even if it was a liquid of questionable origins.

Well, if Peggy required a trade, then that was what they'd get. Unfortunately, Rafi had nothing of value on her. Except . . .

"Would you take the necklace for five minutes of internet?"

"A dead girl's jewelry and your only piece of evidence?"

"I'm sure Sierra won't miss it," Rafi said.

Peggy examined the necklace more closely, even caressing it with their fingertips, until finally, curtly, shaking their head. "Not interested."

"You're wearing candy jewelry. This is real jewelry."

But Peggy only shrugged. "I'm sorry, Rafi, but I can't let you have the internet."

"What?"

"I'm not ready to get off the island yet. And with all the lying everyone's doing about how great it is here, there's a good chance we could all be staying indefinitely. Everyone in the real world believes that everyone here is living in paradise."

"But it's all a lie. It's a lie utopia!"

Peggy shrugged. "People would rather live in a lie utopia than in a true dystopia. Which is what this island is, let's be real."

"But everyone in the real world must know that Fly Fest is canceled."

"Au contraire. Apparently, the people at Fly Fest have realized all the lawsuits they'd be under if the truth came to light. It's in their best interest to play along with the charade."

"But how are they explaining any of this? No bands. No pics of the accommodations. No video of any concerts!"

"They're playing on the whole secrecy thing. Exclusivity. Don't you get it? The mystery adds to the mystique. It's a win-win."

If everyone was winning, then why did Rafi feel like such a loser? She must've looked like a loser too, because for once Peggy seemed sympathetic. But not sympathetic enough to share the Wi-Fi password.

"I'm sorry, I can't help you," they said. "Now, unless you come back here with something I truly can't pass up, River's just gonna have to keep killing girls with impunity."

MUSICAL MYSTERIES
Season 2: Episode 4
"River Stone and His Girls"

This episode was going to be about Tracy Mooney: who she was, her relationship with River, the legacy she leaves behind. But there have been some developments here at Fly Fest that I have to address.

Sierra Madre is missing.

I'm sorry to have to announce something so alarming and—seemingly—random, but it's true. One of the most followed influencers in the world has disappeared without a trace. A feat, when she was on an island from which no one has come or gone for the last few days.

Sierra's disappearance is a major news event, but you're probably asking yourself why I'm mentioning it here, on a podcast about River Stone. I'll tell you why: because our boy River was the last person to see Sierra alive.

I know. I know. Typical River, amiright?

As for River's current girlfriend, Hella, I'm not sure what to think. Apparently, she's gone radio silent on her socials, which is unusual, to say the least. She was supposed to be a featured guest at Fly Fest, but she is nowhere to be found. And yet, there is a rumor (how it got started is not important) that she is here somewhere on this island. Now, I don't typically put too much stock in rumors—I'm a hard evidence kind of girl. But this rumor has now come from multiple sources. It's picked up so much speed that Hella has almost become more of an idea than an actual person around here. And the idea of Hella has achieved mythic proportions. She is neither here nor there, yet she is everywhere.

No one here can say for sure where Hella is. Well, no one except, probably, River. But any time Hella is brought up, River changes the subject or the story and acts generally shifty. I'm not sure what to make out of all of this. I guess I'm trying to talk it out here, with all of you, my listeners. Right now, it's all a jumbled ball of yarn I can't untangle. But there is one connecting thread that ties all these girls together.

River Stone.

Tracy. Sierra. Hella. Three beautiful girls who knew River. They knew him well enough to have a conversation, were close enough to touch him, intimate enough to be alone with him. Beautiful girls who are now—in one way or another—missing. They followed him into the Australian bushland, a music festival, a jungle. And possibly to the ends of their lives. They were taken in by love, adoration. Manipulated by good looks and mediocre music. But I won't be manipulated. No matter how nice he is to me, or how infuriatingly magnetic the twinkle in his eye is, I won't be swayed by River Stone. I won't follow blindly.

I haven't figured out this case yet, but I believe, now more than ever, that River Stone is a stone-cold killer.

This episode of "Musical Mysteries" was brought to you by Nobrand. Ever have a hankering to wash your clothes because you only have one shirt and didn't anticipate being stranded on an island without a change of clothes? Well, Nobrand has a detergent for that. Go to Nobrand.com and enter code RIVERKILLER for three percent off your next purchase.

Until next time, Mysterinos!

18

Rafi nearly choked on a scream as she stepped out of her tent. River was standing right there.

"Sorry!" he said quickly, hands up in a gesture of apology. "Didn't mean to startle you."

"What are you doing here?" Rafi asked.

"Just chilling."

This was the downside of Rafi's tent being right next to River's. Yes, she had access to him, but he also had access to her, and she wondered how long he'd been standing outside her flimsy fabric door, and just how much he'd heard of her recording.

River answered the question before she could ask it. "I heard you talking to yourself."

She could feel her cheeks reddening but coughed to try to disperse the color. She gauged River's face for any telltale signs that he'd heard what she'd said about him. But he only looked at her with that doofy smile of his. Maybe he'd only heard indistinct mumbling.

"I was recording an episode of my podcast." Rafi held her breath, waiting for him to say something, confront her, but he did none of that. "What did you hear, exactly?"

"Something about detergent?" he said.

Rafi let out a sigh through her nose, relieved he hadn't heard the meatier parts of the episode. "Yeah. Just wishing I could wash my clothes."

River nodded, which was a perfectly normal response to what Rafi had just said, but there was something uncanny about his expression. In the short time she'd gotten to know him, Rafi had become accustomed to River's way of speaking, which was to say he liked doing it. Liked to chitchat, liked to make little jokes to smooth out the harder edges of any conversation. But he remained silent now, the doofy smile slipping subtly from his face. Being this close to him, under his gaze, reminded Rafi of what she really thought of him.

River was dangerous.

"You want to go somewhere?" he asked.

The question was so unexpected, it took a minute for Rafi to respond. "Where?"

"Just this place I know." He shrugged his bare shoulders. "A secret place."

All Rafi wanted was alone time with River so she could get to the bottom of her case. But was she willing to risk her life, going to a "secret" place with a killer? A possible *serial* killer?

"Lead the way."

Okay, technically Rafi said she wouldn't blindly follow him, but all investigators had to make some sacrifices to crack their cases. She practically had an obligation to do this. An obligation to her listeners, to Tracy and Sierra and Hella, and to the truth. Rafi was brave. She was in awe of herself, really. And that was why her heart was beating so fast. Not because she was afraid. And not because she was out of shape and the uphill journey was leaving her kind of winded. It was the adrenaline. With every new step she felt closer to the truth. She would ask him her burning question. She would corner him, confront him, *bear* down until he *broke* down. It wasn't her who should be afraid for not knowing what lay ahead—it was him.

Unlike the other times she'd hung out with River, when there was always the constant hum of human life in the distance, it was as they walked through the lush jungle trees now that Rafi realized they were truly alone for the first time. The rest of the beach, the people, the island, fell away, and all Rafi could hear was the crisp sound of twigs snapping under their feet and fat leaves whacking their arms.

They were thick in the middle of the island, but they'd taken a detour from climbing up the jagged slope of the mountain, going around it instead. And River was evasive. Any time Rafi asked where they were going, River would give her a vague, "You'll see soon enough."

And then he'd do something infuriating, like turn to her and smile, and the beat of her heart would stumble over itself. And no, it wasn't because he was cute. It was *never* because he was cute.

None of him was cute. She would not be distracted by his

deep brown eyes, or the crinkle they got around the corners, or the way all his teeth lined up perfectly and gleaming, or the way his lone dimple popped.

Well, she couldn't deny he was fit. She watched the way his back moved as he walked, his shoulder blades sharp as wings about to break through skin. The elegant indentation of his spine. And his thighs. It was pretty obvious that River did not skip leg day at the gym. His thighs were thicker than she expected, and only sparsely hairy. "Wait." She stopped. "Why are your pants off?"

"Because we're here."

"I feel like that doesn't adequately answer the question . . ." But her comment died on her lips as she took in her surroundings. A pond. Right in the middle of the jungle. Beautiful and clear for at least a yard beneath the surface, burbling at the far end with a waterfall splashing off the side of the mountain. Sunlight bounced off the crystal liquid surface, casting a shimmering rainbow on the waterfall's spray of mist. Even the birds seemed astounded by the unbelievable sight, chirping a soundtrack to welcome Rafi and River.

This was the most amazing place Rafi had ever been.

And to her left was River, whose pants had gone the way of his girlfriends and disappeared. He was left in nothing but boxers, and though Rafi was fully dressed, she felt equally as exposed with the deep flush crawling up her cheeks.

She told herself it was because of the humidity.

"I brought you here because of what I heard you saying in your tent."

Rafi's mouth went dry instantly. She had a talent for assessing situations quickly, and she now saw the scene before her for exactly what it was. River had heard her recording her podcast—probably the whole episode. He'd brought her here, to a place no one on the island knew about, so no one could find them. Just as she'd suspected. And he'd taken off his clothes so as not to dirty them with all of the blood he would surely be spilling.

"You said something about wishing you had detergent," River said.

"Oh."

"And I know you don't have a change of clothing because if you did, you would have definitely changed out of that shirt by now. Not that it's not a nice shirt, but it's also not a great shirt, you know? But what do I know about fashion? I have stylists who tell me what to wear. Sorry, it's a nice shirt, and it definitely doesn't hurt my eyes with how pink it is. Anyway, I figured this was the next best thing." He gestured toward the pond. "Freshwater. It sure beats bathing in the salty ocean."

River didn't want to kill her. He wanted her to take a bath.

And he was apparently part of the long list of people who hated her shirt.

Bringing her to a bath was the equivalent of offering someone a breath mint. There was no way to take that other than as a clear sign that you stink. She tried surreptitiously to sniff her armpit, but not surreptitiously enough, because River chuckled. "I'm not trying to say you smell bad," he said quickly. "I just thought you might appreciate this place."

"I do appreciate it." Usually when speaking to River, every word out of her mouth was disingenuous, but she wasn't lying this time. This place was beautiful. And yet. "I can't go in there." The pond was stunning, but it was deep, and she couldn't.

"Because of your fear of water?"

Rafi turned to River, his words so surprising that they were enough to steal her attention away from the awesome landscape. "How did you know?"

"Rafi, there's a reason why *Australian Lasses* picked me as their favorite artist last year, and it isn't my looks."

"What?"

"It's my empathy. It's what makes me such a good musician. I'm perceptive. I understand people. And your water phobia was immediately obvious to me. Tell me about it."

Rafi stared at him, not sure what to think, but she wasn't going to just start opening up to him about one of the most terrifying moments of her life. She wasn't here to reveal something about herself, she was here to make him reveal something about *himself*. But River watched her with a look so piercing and patient that the rest of her surroundings fell away. Maybe *Australian Lasses* knew what they were talking about.

"I almost drowned," Rafi said. "When I was eight. Family vacation. We were at the beach, and I was in the water alone for some reason. I went out too far. There was a wave so big—at least as tall as my father—and it just went right over my head. It took me under. I couldn't figure out which way was up."

160

"That must've been scary."

Rafi shrugged and shook her head, mostly to try to shirk the memory away. She didn't like dwelling on it too much. "I survived."

"You're very brave," River said.

"For not drowning?"

"For being here. You willingly chose to come to this island, a place surrounded by nothing but miles of ocean. There must've been a real good reason for you to do that."

Rafi took in what River said. There was a good reason she came here. And while Fly Fest may have been a bust for everyone else, this place was tailor-made for just what she needed. And he was standing right here beside her. She liked the idea of them both being in the water. There wasn't anywhere for River to go when she'd eventually ask him what she needed to ask him.

She would jump into this, no fear.

And that was just what she did.

19

Rafi popped her head out of the water, gasping and shivering. Not since she was eight years old had she been so perfectly encased in the thing she feared the most. She was frozen with it, and she had to remember what it entailed to stay afloat. She kicked her feet and tried to pull herself up with her arms, but there was nothing to hold on to, of course. She wanted to scream, but her gasp had turned into hyperventilation, plus there was the pesky problem of all the water pouring into her mouth.

This was how it would all end, she realized. She'd survived her secret detour with a possible serial killer only to die by a little bit of water.

Said possible serial killer bobbed his head right out of that water as rosy-tinged and carefree as a cranberry in a bog. When he saw Rafi, however, the smile on his face slid a bit. "Uh, you know how to swim, right?"

She tried to tell him she'd known how to swim since she was four years old, but through all her splashing and flailing it was hard to get a word out. River seemed to get the message, though, and his patented smile was back, secure as ever.

"May I?" he asked. He placed his hands on Rafi's hips and held her gaze just as strongly as he held her up.

She could see his feet kicking below, but like a duck he was totally composed above the surface. He nodded, prompting her, and she began to mimic him, kicking her own feet, breathing again. She didn't think it'd be possible, submerged in all this water, but her nerves settled down. The fact that she was in this pond was amazing and shocking, but suddenly secondary to the fact that River was touching her.

Knowing what she knew about him, she should have recoiled. But she did not want to.

"Don't let go," Rafi said. Her voice sounded ragged, and she realized just how much water she'd inadvertently swallowed.

"I'm barely holding on."

Rafi looked down. It was just his fingertips on her. How was he possibly holding her up with only his fingertips? "You're so strong," she said without an ounce of irony.

"Yes, I am," River said, without irony either. "But you're also floating on your own."

"I am?"

River let go completely, and Rafi did not sink, even though he looked at her with eyes that could make anyone forget how to breathe. "See? You're a pro."

River did not hold her again, but as they swam in the pond they remained in each other's orbit, as though tethered together below the surface. Rafi didn't know what she expected to happen when she jumped in, but she realized it wasn't so scary here after all. The water felt incredible. Almost as warm as a bath and silky on her skin. It made the turquoise-blue ocean seem harsh to the touch and abrasively salty in comparison. Being here with River was kind of fun, too. He swam like a sea lion released from captivity, but with the muscle memory for performing in front of large crowds. He dove and twirled and splashed, and when he popped back up through the surface of the water, he did that thing that boys with a certain length of hair did, where they whip it so that strands stick sideways and wet to their foreheads.

Like on stage, River loved to perform. He made a big show of climbing up the rocks on the side of the waterfall, then jumping off in a massive cannonball. He invited Rafi to do the same, but there was no way. If she attempted to climb on slippery rocks, she would probably fall and crack open her skull. And she wasn't about to become inspo for River's next album.

It was as she thought of this that Rafi remembered why she was here. Now that she'd conquered her fear, she was ready to conquer the truth.

Rafi watched River swim back toward the spot where they'd left their things. The muscles in his back flexed as he planted his arms on the flat rock and hoisted himself out of the water. He went for the pocket of his pants and rummaged for something inside. The loudness of the waterfall filled Rafi's ears as she watched and helplessly treaded water. What was he getting? A knife? A gun? A candlestick? But why a weapon, when all he had to do was dunk her if he'd wanted to? Taken his big hands, pressed them into her head and shoulders, held her down until—

Her thoughts all vanished when she saw him holding a rectangular white object, small enough to fit in his palm but substantial enough to cause blunt force trauma. Except, it wasn't a stone or a brick or a weapon at all. Rafi gasped.

"Is that soap?"

"Yep!" He dove back in and Rafi winced at the splash. But when she opened her eyes again, River was just a couple of feet away from her, lathering up his shoulders.

"Where did you get that?" Rafi didn't bother to hide the awe coloring her tone.

"Some girl gave it to me. Girls give me a lot of things."

Rafi was aware of the skeevy business of girls fawning over rock stars and gifting them things, and how ethically dubious it was for River to accept gifts, especially since this was a small island and he was likely to see that girl again, and she might expect something from him, or worse, he might expect even more from her. But all those thoughts flitted away to make room for the scent of freshness emanating from the most beautiful rectangular block Rafi had ever laid eyes on. Somehow, her palm was opening up like a lotus flower, and the sudsy, slippery bar was landing on it. "Keep it," River said. "Someone will give me another one."

Rafi finally understood what was behind River's easygoing,

sunny disposition. He never had to worry about anything, because everything in his life always worked itself out. He didn't worry about being stranded on an island, because as a celebrity he knew that eventually he would have to be saved. He didn't worry about staying clean, because someone would always give him soap. And he didn't have to worry about getting away with murder, since he already had.

It was an eloquent thought, if Rafi did say so herself, the kind she might jot down to use later in her podcast. But it was canceled out by how inelegantly she was scrubbing a bar of soap under her arm but over her shirt. She scrubbed everywhere: her hair, her mouth, her jean shorts. She must've looked like an alien who'd been told about soap but who'd never seen it used in practice. And River chuckled as he watched her have at it. But Rafi didn't care if she looked ridiculous. She'd never felt so clean.

When they were done swimming and washing and rinsing off, they dried off by lying out in the sun on the big rock slab at the edge of the pond. River was a lounging marble statue. Water droplets dotted his skin in some parts and casually rolled off in others, like summer rain on a slick leaf.

Rafi, on the other hand, was a soaked, year-old newspaper you find in your gutter and fling unceremoniously onto the street, where it turns into soggy mulch. She glanced over at River and wished she could look so relaxed. Or at the very least presentable. But all she could think to do was bend her knee. Was this relaxed? Did this look sexy? Why was she worried about looking sexy?

River opened his eyes, catching Rafi staring at him, and she immediately darted her gaze up to the sky. She propped herself on her elbow and tilted her head back and tried to whip her hair away from her face, but she almost broke her neck doing so. She dropped the elbow. Closed her eyes. Definitely not sexy.

But who cared? Rafi didn't ever care about looking sexy, not for anybody and definitely not for a serial killer.

Which reminded her. It was time to get on with it. When River serenely faced the sun and closed his eyes again, Rafi slipped her hand into her backpack and felt for her microphone. She always had her mic within reach. It made her brave, gave her a voice. And if she was able to record River's confession without him knowing, then—even if he killed her like he did all the other girls in his life—at least the truth would come out when they eventually found her body. If anyone found her body.

She clasped the mic and she hit record. Time for the interview of her life.

"So, that's pretty nice weather we're having, huh?"

River did nothing for a long moment, then he turned his gaze toward Rafi. He caught her eyes like he had a net, and she found herself unable to break free of it. "You don't really want to talk about the weather."

It wasn't a question, and the way he'd said it unnerved

Rafi. Maybe it was because he'd read her mind. This wasn't what she wanted to talk about at all. She'd been gearing herself up to have The Talk with him. The one about how he was a murderer, etc. It was like he was giving her an invitation to do so without even knowing it. But his net-eyes caught her tongue too, and Rafi didn't know what to say.

So he helped her along. "I'm glad you came out here with me. I wanted to talk to you about something, too."

"Oh?"

"About the thing I heard you say in your tent," River said.

"About the detergent?"

"About me being a killer."

Rafi went so still she wasn't even sure she was breathing. The waterfall roared in the distance, the pond burbled, and birds tweeted. They were the kind of sounds that people selected on noise machines to help them drift off to sleep. But to Rafi it all sounded like alarm bells. Like the musical cues in a horror movie when the villain is about to strike.

"What?" Her mouth was suddenly dry.

"You think I killed Tracy. I heard you say it."

The damning words did not match his even-keeled disposition. Rafi hated that he was so calm while she felt so off-kilter. She was the one who wanted to have this conversation, and somehow he was the one steering the ship.

"If you think I'm a killer, then why follow me into the jungle? Alone? Where no one knows where we are?"

"What are you saying?"

"I'm saying that no one would be able to hear you scream."

168

There was none of that cinnamon-roll, pop-star charm gleaming off him. Not even the hint of a smile. Just an unwavering stare-down. Rafi had to fight not to wither beneath it. Maybe if she said it out loud, she could convince him, and herself, that she could meet this moment.

"I came because I'm not afraid of you." Rafi's elbow dug painfully into the rock as she tried to remain still and composed. "And yes. I do think you're a killer."

River sat up, the movement catching Rafi off guard. But he didn't stop moving. He leaned over her and she froze, unsure what to do but knowing this was the moment. This was the moment River buried this story.

If Rafi was a mouse, then River was the snake, slithering seamlessly toward her, about to swallow her whole. But even as a mouse Rafi was awkward and strange because she didn't try to scamper away. It was almost as if a part of her wanted this.

River was fully on top of her, his dry, smooth body over her still damp one. All Rafi could do was let her elbow fall, and she lay back, looking up at him. Her rough shirt exacerbated the friction between them. When she was in the pond with him, she liked the idea that he had nowhere to hide. Now his face was only inches from hers. She saw the pores around his nose and a scar she'd never noticed on his chin. The tip of one of his incisors was whiter than the rest of the tooth. This close, he had nowhere to hide.

"Tracy didn't just disappear," Rafi said. Her voice was steady as she said the most important thing she would ever say. Maybe the last thing she would ever say. "And she didn't run away. She's dead, isn't she?"

Every second passed achingly slowly as River did nothing but look at her. His glance darted first to her lips, then one eye, and the other. Until, finally, he nodded.

He was reaching his hand out.

It was coming for Rafi's neck.

He was going to kill her.

20

AND THEN HIS HAND PASSED HER NECK. IT PASSED HER face. It went for the backpack she'd left next to her head. He reached inside and took out her mic.

"If you want the truth, it needs to be off the record." River clicked the off button, and Rafi felt like it was her heart that had stopped. But she was alive. River tossed her the mic and she sat up, catching it.

Wait, what just happened? She was sure River had almost killed her. Or wanted to kill her. Why hadn't he killed her?

River sat cross-legged, shoulders slumped and kind of sad. "Tracy didn't abandon me in the middle of the bush like I claimed. She died out there. But I didn't kill her, I *swear*."

Rafi couldn't believe what she was hearing. And she couldn't *believe* that her mic was turned off. But more important, she just wanted the truth. And River was ready to spill it. "So, what happened?"

River let go of such a big breath it almost looked like he got physically smaller. "We went to the bush on a romantic trip. We wanted to sleep under the stars. I mean, we didn't even pack a tent, that's how much we were roughing it. We got there late, and by the time we were done settling in, it was already dark. Tracy spotted these purple wildflowers, and she wanted to collect them. She said they'd be perfect for a photo she wanted to post. I told her to just wait 'til tomorrow, but she wanted them that instant. And then—"

The whole time he talked he'd been looking at his hands, tearing at tiny threads of skin on his cuticles. But now he stopped and looked at Rafi like he'd just remembered that she was there. "This next part is not going to sound real."

Rafi was impatient. She didn't want him to stop and editorialize or even acknowledge her. She just wanted him to let it all out without interruption. She wished she was in a sound booth, a small windowless room, dim and intimate without distractions. But the wilderness would have to do. In her mind, the burbling waterfall and tweeting tropical birds were white noise, providing an ambient cocoon of privacy in which she hoped River could speak freely. "Unless you tell me that aliens showed up to abduct her, I will believe you."

River seemed to think about this, a horrified, faraway look in his eyes as he contemplated extraterrestrials. Rafi was worried she was losing him. "River, focus. What happened?"

River looked at his fingers once more. He tore away his skin until a tiny bead of blood bloomed on the corner of his thumbnail. "A pack of dingoes showed up."

If there had been a desk in front of her, Rafi would have dropped her head onto it. She may have even acted out the motion without realizing it, because River said, "See, I knew you'd think it was ridiculous."

Because it *was* ridiculous. *Dingoes?* Rafi didn't know what to say. All she knew about dingoes was that they were basically dogs with stupid names and a punchline to a joke.

"I'm serious," River said. "The leader of the pack bit Tracy on the forearm and dragged her behind this rocky, hill-formation thing, and she was already pretty far from camp when it happened, but I ran. I ran as fast as I could to help her. But when I went behind the hill she—the dingoes . . . They were all gone."

Rafi sat with this information. She said she'd believe him, but now she had serious doubts. River looked contrite. The boy was practically on the verge of tears. But . . . *dingoes*?

"If this is all true, then why didn't you just tell everyone that from the beginning?"

"Because who would believe it?" River said. "No one believed that real-life story with the lady who said the dingo took her baby, and then it became a Meryl Streep movie, and then they remade the movie with Ashley Woodstone, and it came out *literally* a week before Tracy died, and it was just the worst possible timing, and it's just . . . I went on that trip with my girlfriend. If I left alone and told everyone that a dingo had eaten her, I would've been arrested on the spot. Or laughed at."

"Arrested or laughed at." Rafi snorted. "Which is worse?"

"I'm serious, Rafi. If I told the truth, that would've been it for me. My music career? Over before it even began. I couldn't do that to myself. I had already started writing my album. Imagine what the world would look like today if nobody ever got to hear it."

Sometimes, talking to River felt like an out-of-body experience. Rafi was at once in the moment, having a serious conversation with a boy about his dead girlfriend, and simultaneously coming to terms with the fact that River's autobiography may as well have been a book of Mad Libs.

Shirtless pop star _in the middle of the jungle_
adjective   location

explains how _dingoes ate_ his girlfriend.
noun   verb

"A world without your music?" Rafi responded, continuing the conversation instead of walking out of the jungle and directly into the ocean. "Perish the thought."

"I know!"

"So you made up the story of Tracy running away."

River nodded.

"And you wrote fake diary entries for her where you made her look like an awful person who was always planning on leaving you stranded in the middle of the bush."

He nodded, again.

"So, you were never going to propose?"

"Crikey, _no_. I was seventeen! I just put that in there to make the story more heartbreaking. And it worked! It worked so well, Raf."

He was getting emotional again, and Rafi was almost embarrassed for him. It was the only way she knew how to classify what she was feeling. It certainly wasn't pity. And she didn't have the energy to spare anger for something this idiotic.

"I feel so guilty," River said. "And the only way I know how to deal with it is—"

"Through your music?"

"No. I donate all my money to the Australian Dingo Conservation Society even though that feels totally wrong and not the right charity to give to, but I don't know what is, Rafi. I don't know what is. They buy chew toys for the dingoes, so at least that's training them to chew toys and not humans, right?"

There was a desperate hope in his voice that Rafi, frankly, did not know how to assuage. "*Right?*" River asked again, his eyes turning into pools large enough to rival the one behind them.

"Australia is like a different planet, River. I don't know how things work there."

River sighed, his chin perpendicular to his chest. "My whole life is so stupid."

Rafi nodded until she realized what she was doing and stopped. She hated to admit it, but for the first time ever, she believed River. As he'd spoken, Rafi examined his mouth for any twitch or crookedness, any indication that he might be lying. But there was none. He was giving it to her straight. Literally—his mouth was straight. So she had to believe his words were, too. His story was too ridiculous to be false. And it meant that she'd been right all along. Well, not about River killing Tracy, but she'd been the only one to see that he'd been lying about the whole story and he'd falsified documents to cover it all up. That, at least, gave Rafi some validation.

But validation was not the same as being satisfied, and though she'd gotten to the bottom of this case, Rafi felt a pang. An emptiness. She needed something else—something more.

"What about Sierra?" Rafi asked. "I know you lied to me about her. I found her necklace in your things."

River's lips tightened around a groan he was trying not to let out. There was just so much to explain, and none of it made him look like the good guy he was desperate to present himself as. "People give me things all the time! And then she goes and disappears. I lied because I can't be known as the guy who girls disappear around all the time."

"So you don't know where she is."

"No clue."

"And Hella?"

"I have no idea why people think she's here. But she's not."

River rapped his knuckles on the rock he was sitting on with increasing frustration. "Please swear you'll never tell anyone any of this. I know my music is, like, really good, but deep down I wonder if people only like me because of my sob story."

"Wouldn't you want to know for sure?" Rafi asked.

River's shoulder rose by barely a centimeter. "I just want people to like me."

All this time, in the hierarchy of influencers on this island, Rafi thought River was above it all. He wasn't trying to shill anything like everyone here was. He wasn't obsessed with his phone and his brand and putting out a certain image. But now she knew he cared about that stuff maybe more than anyone else here. At the core, River was just like everybody else. He was selling a story, desperately hoping you looked anywhere but at the real him.

"So you believe me?"

Rafi considered herself a good judge of character, someone who could always tell if a person was lying. And every bone in her body told her that River was telling her the truth about Tracy. It was funny—the truth was all Rafi ever wanted, so why did it feel like socks on Christmas morning? A gift she didn't particularly want and could hardly muster up the appreciation for? The truth of River's case was boring, and worse, off the record. She couldn't talk about it on her podcast, and if she did, he'd never confirm it. Ironically enough, Rafi couldn't tell the real story for the exact same reason River concealed the truth too: No one would believe the absurdity of a pack of dingoes killing a girl.

Rafi saw her podcast, her pending deal with SteerCat Media, her dream of becoming a famous investigative reporter—all disappearing into thin air. *Poof.* She couldn't let all her dreams go that easy, not without a fight. The only way she saw out of this mess was to hold on to some versions of River's truth and not the others. She could choose to believe that River was telling the truth about Tracy's disappearance, but not Sierra's. Her story was still too much of a mystery, and happening in real time, with Rafi right in the thick of it. A new case for Rafi to pursue.

"I believe you," Rafi said. What she didn't say was that she still didn't have enough information to believe him in regards to Sierra's disappearance. Which meant he was still a suspect.

And just like that, Rafi had a new mission: Find Sierra.

21

RAFI STOOD BEFORE HER MURDER BOARD ONCE MORE. Even though there was a new mystery afoot, River was still her primary suspect, since he'd been the last one to see Sierra, so the board remained covered in gorgeous images of him. And since Rafi had no pictures of Sierra, she'd had to use the influencer's wilted flower crown in her place. It turned out to be an apt representation of the girl, once thriving and beautiful, now all but forgotten and probably dead.

The longer Rafi stared at her board, the more amped she was to solve this puzzle, but no matter how many hours she spent focusing, she was coming up with blanks on what to do next.

She needed a snack.

Thankfully, there were plenty of banana plants around. But when she went to shake one, nothing fell out. Rafi looked up. There were no bananas to be found, not even unripe green ones. Rafi moved to the next plant and kicked it, but nothing fell out of that one either. She moved onto the next plant. She kicked hard—really giving it her all, even body-slamming it a few times, panting, sweating, hair in her face. All of her frustrations came out on that plant until the stalk cracked in half at the base and keeled over with a slow, yawning crack. No fruit.

In fact, as she looked up at all the plants in the vicinity, she noticed they were newly bare.

All of the fruit, as far as she could see, had been picked clean.

"Paul and Ryan," Rafi hissed, their names curses on her lips.

Rafi didn't stop moving until she was at the seaport. It was fine—she'd get to the bottom of this fruit situation and interview them as witnesses-slash-possible suspects in the Sierra disappearance at the same time.

Paul and Ryan sat just outside the entrance, a huge pile of bananas, coconuts, and mangoes mounded beside them like a sideshow curiosity. Seemed like they'd expanded their business.

"What fresh hell is this?" Rafi muttered upon seeing the monstrosity.

Ryan and Paul were on their feet immediately, arms spread as wide as their smiles. "Look at this," Paul said. "When you told us to disrupt the food industry, I can't lie—we were a little apprehensive."

"It was a big risk. But as my skiing shaman always says, 'Big risk, painless death.'"

"We weren't sure it was going to work."

"But after a few low points, which included minutes of virtual therapy—"

"And high points, which included three different angel investors—"

"We're happy to report that business. Is. Booming!"

"All we need now is a snappy company name."

"At first we were thinking of going with 'It's Bananas!'"

"Simple, cheeky, great SEO."

"But with the addition of mangoes and coconuts to our line, it just doesn't fully capture what we're about, you know?"

"So then we decided to go with 'ManGoes (Coco)Nuts for Bananas.'"

"But the feedback we were getting from our focus group was that it makes it seem like we only have four bananas."

"And as you can see, we have roughly three hundred times that."

"So we're still trying to come up with the right name, but other than that, *wow*, right?"

"You're big impressed, yes?"

Was there cocaine on this island? It was the only thing that could explain what Rafi had just borne witness to.

But she chose to ignore every nonsensical word that had just come out of Ryan's and Paul's mouths and focus on first things first: getting some food. Rafi approached the pile like it was a stack of Jenga bricks, looking for the loosest fruit to pluck, lest she accidentally cause a fruitslide that crushed every life-form on this island.

The roundness of the coconuts made them too unstable; she wasn't going to touch those. She found a banana that was barely holding on, and grabbed it. The mound stayed intact. "Thanks."

"That'll be fifteen dollars," Paul said.

"What?" Rafi asked. "Fifteen *dollars*?"

"Don't balk at the price, Rafi," Ryan said.

"Balk!" Paul said. "Big impressed with our word usage?"

"Fifteen dollars is a reasonable price—"

"For a single banana!?" Rafi said.

"I don't know if you noticed, but bananas are scarce," Ryan said.

"*Very* scarce."

"We're being generous here."

"Bananas are scarce because you picked them all!" Rafi said.

"You can Venmo us."

Rafi could've chipped her teeth with how hard she was clenching her jaw. "I can't Venmo you, I don't have internet access."

To their credit, both Ryan and Paul looked sorry for Rafi. Paul even frowned as he gently pried the banana out of her fingers, remaining patient when she would not let go. He got it eventually, though. It was mushy now, and the peel had split in a few places, but he got it.

"You can't spare one banana?" Rafi asked. "Just one?"

"I can't just start giving product away," Paul said, as if the concept of charity was untenable. "What would people think of me? What will that do to my reputation? Do you have any idea who my father is?"

The edges of Rafi's vision began to get hazy, and a thin, crackling noise filled her ears, but she could not blame this on the blazing hot sun or even her acute hunger. No, the absurdity of this hellhole, nonexistent music festival was finally starting to get to her. She could feel herself physically deteriorating. Paul and Ryan must've seen it too, because they looked at her funny, though they mistook her weakness for anger.

"I don't get why you're so upset about this," Ryan said. "We're just trying to make some cash. Everyone on this island is basically doing the same thing."

"What are you talking about?"

"We heard there's someone livestreaming from the beach, charging people to have the honor of vicariously vacationing through him."

"And there's this one girl who's just started mindset coaching from her tent. So enterprising."

"*So* inspirational," Paul said.

The noise in Rafi's ears took on the high-pitched squeal of a cat in an alley fight. People had figured out how to make money here? They were getting richer while she couldn't even afford a mushy banana? "They're just influencers."

"Don't knock influencers, Rafi," Ryan said. "They have real jobs. They get products and tell us if they're good or not."

"That is not a real job," Rafi said. "I too buy products and determine for myself whether they are good or not."

"Yeah, but are you making six figures doing that?"

It was funny how quickly Rafi's urge to laugh had turned into the need to sob so hard that her tears could propagate a new growth of fruit all over the island. But Rafi could not let this madness overwhelm her. If she started to think about the big picture too much, she'd be paralyzed by it. She needed to think of the issue at hand, and that was that a banana had just been taken out of hers. "You do realize what you're doing, don't you?" she told the boys. "You've taken something that was free and commodified it. You have a monopoly on the fruit. You've created a *literal* Banana Republic!"

Paul and Ryan looked at each other briefly, then directed their blank stares back at Rafi. "I think you just found our company name!"

"There already is a company called Banana Republic!" Rafi never thought she'd be screaming about a clothing retailer on a deserted island in the middle of nowhere, but here she was.

"I'll get my lawyer on it. By the time Herman's done with them, this so-called Banana Republic will be so tied up in legal fees, they'll have to file for bankruptcy."

"I don't think that's how lawsuits work!"

"Rafi, I've been in and out of litigation ever since I set my pet tiger loose on my nanny," Ryan said. "Please. Leave the rich people shit to the rich shit." He shook his head, having misspoken. "Rich shits."

Rafi left before she was subjected to any more of this conversation. In her rush to get out of there, she forgot to ask the non-twins about Sierra.

22

Rafi stood before Greer, who sat in the shade of a palm tree. The girl was talking, though Rafi was not sure if the conversation was meant for her or the invisible audience in Greer's phone, its front-facing camera never too far from her face.

Whatever Greer was talking about, Rafi wasn't paying attention and cut her off midsentence. "Don't you care anymore that Sierra Madre is still missing?" Rafi asked. "You came to me crying about that."

Greer's gaze momentarily slipped from her phone's magnetic pull to land on Rafi. "Are you kidding? Sierra is obviously at Fly Fest partying with Hella. She's so lucky."

If it hadn't been painfully obvious before that Rafi would not get any help looking for Sierra, it was now. Rafi needed to get back to the reason she was here, talking to Greer.

"I like your necklace," Rafi said. "Is that copper?"

Greer looked down at the space between her collarbones, where a pair of round rings encircled her neck. The necklaces were accented with a few beads, spread equally apart. "Oh, yeah," she said. "They're energy rings. They give you amazing energy and fill your life with good vibes, and in difficult times like these they're great as a gift for yourself or your loved ones, hashtag ad."

Rafi forced herself to smile.

Rafi held the copper-energy-ring necklace up for Peggy. "Each bead represents one of life's essential elements. And as an added bonus, people swear that it's supposed to grant you all your deepest desires. It's handcrafted by at least a hundred different Andean artisans all born after December 1990 but before January 1991. But I'm sure you've already seen it featured in *Vogue* and on Amazon dot com."

Greer hadn't said any of that about the necklace, but it was probably true. And Rafi felt her hopes rise as Peggy touched it, carefully caressing the beads. Until they let their hand drop, leaving Rafi holding the necklace limply. "No."

Rafi wordlessly, desperately, pointed at the hideous branch sculptures in the room, but Peggy didn't see, already back to their phone once again. "Please," Rafi said, trying once more. This was as far as her plan went—making a trade so that Peggy would let her have the internet. Two seconds with Paul and Ryan, and Rafi was beginning to realize she wouldn't get anywhere with the people here. She'd already surveyed most everyone to see what they knew about Sierra's whereabouts, and she wasn't sure she could withstand more conversation. Her street work, as far as Rafi was concerned, was done. Now it was about research. Plus the whole getting-rescued thing, which was also up there on her priorities list, just not before she solved this new tiny little case.

"I need more help if I'm ever going to find out what happened to Sierra. I was going to start doing interviews again, but the people I just talked to tried to charge me an obscene amount of money for a banana."

"Those jock guys?" Peggy asked. "How do you tell them apart?"

"Ryan grew up in a soap opera, and I'm pretty sure Paul has no idea who his father is."

"They sound fascinating," Peggy said, though their attention was almost entirely consumed by the newly minted, internet sensation pet turtle on their lap. They stroked the animal's shell with a gentle hand.

"Is the necklace a new trophy from another girl River killed?"

Rafi had to think about her answer for a second, then laughed nonchalantly. "No. But I actually don't think he killed Tracy anymore."

"You don't say."

"But the jury's still out on Sierra. River may be the—"

"Serial killer of your dreams?" Peggy leaned forward, the turtle sliding forward on their knees like a precariously piled dish full of food. "You have no leads for this Sierra disappearance, so you're pinning it all on River because a part of you can't accept the fact that you're in love with someone who is nothing more than a beautiful, dumb Australian. Face it, Rafi—you're only interested in River if he's a killer."

Rafi was offended by the accusation. Sure, she had her own biases against River, but she also had mounting evidence against him, plus her own finely honed instincts. The Sierra case was important to her, and to the future of her podcast. It wasn't Rafi's fault that River kept bumbling into the role of lead suspect.

"For the last time, I am not in love with River." Rafi took a deep, composing breath. "And I will find out what happened to Sierra. Now, can you please help me by letting me on the internet?"

"No. Can't." Peggy used a leaf to gingerly tickle the turtle's nose. It snapped its mouth back and bit it. "I know what you're going through. I too was once unimportant and desperate. But now that I'm not, I've kind of forgotten what that feels like and can't really help you out."

It wasn't just Peggy and their internet hoarding or Paul and Ryan and their banana scheme. Random moments of bizarreness were cropping up all over the island, distracting Rafi from her case. But none was more bizarre than the presentation she stumbled onto on the beach.

Jack had made his name on YouTube with his wildly popular tutorials that taught people the finer points of shellacking on a coat of makeup. He'd decided to pick up the habit again, but without his pro camera or studio lighting or any makeup to speak of, he had to innovate. Instead of editing and posting a video, he was doing live, in-person tutorials, and instead of a studio, he had a studio audience. Rows of people sat on the beach and watched Jack's every move like he was Bob Ross and his face was his canvas. Though the whole idea of a live makeup tutorial while stranded and scammed on an island seemed like the last thing anybody needed, this was actually well attended, and Rafi could sort of understand why.

The island was starting to wear on people. The relentlessly scorching sun, the precious little supply of sunscreen, and the fact that there were plenty of facial cleansers but not a single sink anywhere on the island was doing a number on people's skin. That was where Jack came in.

And though all Rafi wanted to do right now was sulk in her tent until the sand gathered over her, swallowing her fully into the beach, she instead sat in the back row of Jack's audience. This was where her feelings of frustration and hopelessness had ultimately led. She wondered if this was how cult leaders got their disciples: Find people at their most desperate and then distract them with a show. Rafi was never going to fall for whatever Jack was selling, but she really was curious to see what he would use for makeup when his precious kit had been lost to airport purgatory since day one.

"Let's be honest, we all look like pigs," Jack began from his makeshift stage (a platform of bedside crates collected from Tent City.) "We may not have makeup, but that's no excuse to not be fierce. And if you really think about it, what if the only reason we're not being allowed into the real Fly Fest yet is because we're tragically letting our appearances fall by the wayside? Fly Fest doesn't want uggos clogging their Insta—it wants glamour! And we can be glamorous. We just have to beat our faces."

He'd fashioned a little table out of a trunk suitcase and gestured toward the beauty essentials he'd placed atop it. Rafi craned her neck to see over the rows of heads before her. She wasn't sure what she was looking at, but it seemed like Jack would be fashioning makeup essentials from things found in nature.

"Now, I've showed you some of these already," Jack continued, "but I've been doing research, and you guys are going to go clinically insane when you see my new line of products."

He picked up a jagged thing that fit in the palm of his hand but didn't look like it belonged in anyone's makeup bag. "THIS is tree bark!" Jack took a lighter to it and lit the edge on fire, blowing it out almost as quickly. In one skilled motion he carefully swooped the charred edge of wood over the delicate rim of his eyelid. "Now it's eyeliner!"

The crowd, made up almost exclusively of girls, let out a collective "*Oooh.*"

Jack held up his next beauty product, a cluster of red berries. "You should def remember this from last time, but just in case you missed the show—were you doing something better, you dickheads?!—watch as I turn this into lipstick."

"They could be poisonous," Rafi muttered under her breath. But it was a weak mutter, and she had no intention of rushing to the stage to knock the berries out of Jack's hands.

To her own horror, Rafi was equally invested in the result being a red lip or Jack's imminent death.

Jack crushed one berry after another against his mouth, smearing them around until the glistening juices stained his lips red. She waited with bated breath to see if he would drop dead. But Jack only licked the excess berry juice off his lips like a lion after a kill and smiled at his audience, very much alive.

From a pouch, he pinched a sprinkling of pinkish dirt. "I scraped this off the clay rocks on the cliffy side of the beach. This will work really well for eyeshadow." He used the pad of a ring finger to dab the rock powder gingerly onto both eyelids, and by this point Rafi was pretty astonished. Not because he was painting dirt over his eyes, but because he was doing it expertly, and Rafi couldn't even put on sunscreen without leaving streaks.

"Lastly, my best makeup hack," Jack announced. "This step is essential, and after trying at least ten other different options, I can assure you that I settled on the best one. Behold: the island's best alternative to bronzer."

Jack took something out of the trunk at his feet. It looked like a typical white sandwich container, but Rafi knew there was no sandwich inside it. What Rafi could not know was how arduous the path to this specific product had been for Jack.

He found it in the jungle. He'd lumbered over there one day to find a private spot to sob. He'd been troubled by the fact that there was no Fly Fest, that his makeup was gone, that he didn't have his YouTube channel and his thousands—no, millions!—of fans telling him how great he was all the time. Basically, he felt something he hadn't felt in quite a long time.

Doubt.

And so he went to the jungle to let off some steam, not exactly asking the heavens for help so much as shouting a list of demands and formal complaints. Where was the festival? Where was Hella? Why had his makeup gone missing? How could he possibly overcome this? First his eyes were blurry with tears, but after a particularly dramatic crying jag they dried and cleared. It was like this, with red, stinging eyes, that he saw the sow. A big round thing, oinking away. Slow too, so he could easily catch it without much effort if he truly cared to. And he *could* catch it. Just because Jack loved makeup didn't mean he didn't consider himself an alpha male who could do regressively gender-normative things like catch and kill a big pig and strap it to his back and drag it across the jungle and spit roast it and belch. Jack could do all that, but every day he made a conscious choice not to. And anyway, it wasn't the size of the pig or how much nourishment it could provide that interested him. It was what the sow was doing that caught Jack's attention. Because a pig was more than just food. It provided other useful things. It provided what Jack carefully collected and placed inside the Styrofoam sandwich box.

Jack presented the box to the crowd now, like a prop a magician held in front of his audience for inspection before using it to dazzle them with disbelief. When Jack popped the little tab on the side of the box, he did it slowly, with flair, and paused as the lid bounced open. Rafi was too far away to really identify what was inside. All she could see was that it was brown, which wasn't shocking. This was meant to be bronzer, after all. No, the shocking thing would come soon enough.

"I spent all day yesterday tracking a pig," Jack said, seemingly apropos of nothing. "When that slobbering, hairy sow finally left this for me, it was like the answer to all of my problems. I knew immediately it was just the thing."

Rafi scrunched her face, her mind coming up with conclusions that it desperately wanted to reject. *It couldn't be*, she thought.

"That's right," Jack continued. "Pig dookie."

The announcement was met with silence, and Jack filled it by laughing like what he'd just said was a joke, but it obviously was most definitely not a joke.

"What?" Rafi said to herself. She was trying to understand. Jack followed a pig all day in the jungle, watched it defecate, and his first thought was *bronzer*?

Yes. That was it. That was as simple as the explanation got, and yet, Rafi still could not comprehend what her own eyes were seeing. Or what her ears were hearing.

Jack continued to giggle. "I know it may sound silly, but manure has been used by so many different cultures throughout the ages for so many fascinating things. Like, did you know that some people use manure, as, like, plant food? Wild, right?"

Not wild, Rafi thought with increasing dread. *That* was

definitely not wild. She then watched as Jack bent to retrieve something else from the trunk. A single slice of the cheese sandwich bread. He folded it in half, and of course it did not split like regular bread would. It did not even crack.

"As you know from our other tutorials, this bread is almost the exact same texture as your average makeup sponge, but even better because it's completely disposable and most likely biodegradable. Now, you could just wash it after every application, if you're cheap, but just know that salt water *will* cause the bread to double in size every time. Heck, leave it in salt water long enough and you'd have yourself a cute little floatation device that you could probably float home in! But we're not here to talk about ways to get off the island."

Jack then proceeded to dip a corner of the white bread into a dollop of literal pig poop, and applied it to his cheekbone like it was something out of a Kylie Jenner cosmetic palate. He smoothed it over both cheeks, making them look sharp, popping them out, blending until he looked perfectly tanned and contoured. The crowd was stunned into silence, with a few bouts of nervous laughter sputtering forth from the girls.

"I know, it might seem pretty *out there* if you've never done this before," Jack continued. "But this is also a cool way to turn off your mind. Trick yourself into thinking this is actually bronzer. If you're willing to do anything to get to Fly Fest, then this is nothing. And remember, none of your followers will know what this actually is. As I famously like to say, *you can't smell Instagram*!"

Too many heads bobbed in agreement.

"And there you have it," Jack said. "Don't I look fabulous?"

The absolute travesty of it all was that he did. That weaselly, skid-marked rascal looked like a million bucks. The whole thing made Rafi's gut fill with a heavy dread, and just like that, the Sierra Madre situation took a backseat to a new, unnamable threat. Rafi couldn't pinpoint exactly why Jack's makeup tutorial felt like the harbinger of something terrible, but she couldn't shake the sensation. Like a coming wave when you're already neck deep.

23

She probably should've left well enough alone. Jack wanted to put poop on his face? Fine. Let him.

But try as she might, Rafi was physically averse to letting things slide. Where there was an injustice in the world, she needed to be on the side that would make things right. And while poop makeup wasn't exactly an injustice, it was most certainly wrong.

Rafi had seen a lot of weird tutorials on the internet, but what she'd just witnessed by Jack was beyond the pale. What made it worse, though, was that other people had witnessed the same thing she had, but they *believed* in it. They believed in Jack.

Rafi didn't understand why he had such a big audience. She knew that online, his fans had put him on a pedestal of mythic proportions. Rumors swirled that he had a twenty-three-acre winter estate in Wyoming, that he had a standing ticket on the first spaceship to the moon, that as a baby he'd taken the world's first selfie with Nelson Mandela. Jack could kill a puppy in one of his videos, and Rafi suspected his followers would praise him and be all, "The bitch deserved it!!!"

But the online dedication Jack garnered had fully breached

the confines of the internet and followed him here, to this strange place where logic and reason seemed to have evaporated under the sun's unrelenting blaze. There was a group of influencers getting ready to go hunting for pig feces right now, and Rafi had to believe it was more than just Jack's flair for dramatics or his outsize personality that made people flock to him.

Most of all, Rafi couldn't understand how the power dynamics on this island had so suddenly shifted. She could admit she never really had power to begin with, but it wasn't so long ago that she stood on the check-in desk with her mic in her hand and people listened to *her*. Sure, she'd told a little lie, but it was a million times better than telling people to put crap on their faces!

Rafi found Jack's tent in Tent City, its door flap pulled back. He was inside, busy fiddling with something in his carry-on. This tent was different than Peggy's. Standard size, with a standard cot and a little square nightstand next to it. But it was still the lap of luxury as far as Rafi was concerned. She knocked on one of the rounded plastic poles that held up the structure. When Jack turned and saw her, his face, surprisingly, lit up.

"Well if it isn't Rafi San Antonio!"

The positive response to his tutorial had clearly put Jack in a good mood. "Francisco," Rafi corrected. "I saw your tutorial."

"Oh yeah? Are you here for a makeover?"

"Of course not. You can't tell people to put feces on their faces, Jack."

The corners of Jack's berry lips slipped downward, and he placed his hands on his hips. "And why not?"

"Because feces have, like . . . diseases. Probably. The boars on this island could be sick. And anyway, makeup is the last thing we should be focusing on right now. We need to find a way home."

Jack sighed and took a step closer to Rafi. With only a few feet of space between them, she could see the details of his face. He was no longer that slightly sunburnt boy with the chapped nose, wallowing ankle-deep in the ocean. He was all made up, looking like a secretary right out of the 1980s about to climb the corporate ladder straight to executive assistant. Rafi had missed the part of the tutorial where Jack explained what he used as foundation, but whatever it was didn't match his skin exactly. His neck was a shade deeper than his face, which was pale and vaguely orange. A melting Creamsicle.

"Correct me if I'm wrong, sweetheart, but wasn't it you who stood on a whole damn desk at the seaport and told every single concertgoer present to stay put? 'The party's still on,' you said. 'Hella is here,' you said."

"I lied."

Jack went so still that the only change in him came from the angry heat coloring his cheekbones. It seemed to make the unpleasant odor of his bronzer waft off his face. Jack was a skilled orator, but Rafi hadn't realized just how captivating he could also be without having to say a thing. His silence was beginning to scare her. She needed to intersperse the quiet with more words.

"I never saw Hella. I just wanted everyone to stay on this island for stupid, selfish reasons. But I realize that was a huge mistake. And now that you know that Hella isn't here and Fly Fest is definitely not happening, maybe you can help me convince everyone that we need to send for help and get off this island, like, as soon as we possibly can."

When Jack took his next breath, it was slow and methodical, his chest rising and falling with the action. "Well, you were either lying then or you're lying now. And I choose to believe you're lying now."

"Jack—"

"It's not just you who's seen Hella. Greer saw her, too. How do you explain that?"

Rafi couldn't, and her silence seemed to validate Jack's point. He smiled and tilted Rafi's chin up with the tip of his index finger. "Now, all this flip-flopping—emphasis on 'flopping'—is really causing premature aging to your already-tragic general facial area. You sure I can't offer you that makeover?"

Rafi shook herself free of his touch and took a step back, shivering in disgust at his suggestion. "Emphatically no. Never," she said. "Why *poop*?"

"That's rich, coming from someone who stepped in poop."

His comeback made the kind of no sense that knocked her out for a few seconds. But she snapped out of it. "Once, Jack. I stepped in poop *once*. By accident. I didn't fall face-first into it and decide it was a *whole look*. Why couldn't you use soil? The island is full of soil!"

"Have you looked around?" Jack shot back. "Most of this island is sand or rock! The soil in the jungle is too dry and crumbly, and it doesn't rain enough for mud."

"There's literally water all arou—"

"THIS—" Jack cut her off and pointed to his cheekbones— "is the perfect consistency for bronzer. Do you even know how hard it is to get this kind of viscosity? Did you see how well it took to the bread sponge? Well, *did you?*"

It was hard to tell, but beneath the makeup, Jack had turned red, and he took a moment to compose himself, pressing his fingertips against his temples. "Rafi," he said, calmer now, "why do you hate beauty?"

Rafi's eyebrows pinched together. "I don't hate beauty."

"Really? Because literally everything about all this"—he gestured to her person—"tells me that you do."

"That's . . . offensive."

"You obviously put no effort into how you look—"

"I bought this shirt especially for—"

"Your hair is a mess."

Rafi sheepishly combed her fingers over her forehead only to discover that her bangs had migrated somewhere over her hairline. She tamped them down as best she could.

"Let's face it," Jack continued, "you look like a functioning heroin addict."

"Why are you saying all of this?"

"Be*cause*." Jack gripped Rafi's wrist the way a concerned

friend who just caught you scarfing down caffeine pills might. "You could really use my tutorial."

"I don't need makeup."

"Full offense, but yes, you do." Jack sighed. "It isn't just about the makeup, Rafi. That's what you don't understand. Did you ever think that maybe what people want right now—more than going home with their tails between their legs—is a little bit of comfort? And that maybe that's something that I alone can provide for them?"

"Comfort?"

"Yes, comfort! The people here want something to take their minds off the fact that they're not hanging out with hot musicians, and the villas aren't here, or that their only choice of food is between a ten-dollar banana and a cheese sandwich that might explode if left out in the sun too long."

"Paul and Ryan are only charging you ten dollars?"

"You still don't get it," Jack said. "I'm putting a little bit of beauty back in people's lives. Before I started my tutorials here, people's complexions looked less human and—thanks to that vengeful demon in the sky you call the sun—more lobster. I'm giving them something easy, something that makes them feel good again. Being beautiful is a morale booster. It's what sets us apart from the animals. It's what's saving our lives, damn it!"

As he said all this, Jack's eyes twinkled with the sort of verve that the island had sucked right out of Rafi. She felt jealous that he could be this optimistic when the situation was this dire. But then, his very attitude was proof that what he was saying was true.

The makeup tutorials were making people happy.

Even if it was also covering them in poop.

"But rescue—"

"Screw rescue!" Jack said with an incredulous burst of laughter. "People can't *touch* rescue. They can't *see* it. You might as well be promising them unicorns."

"And you're promising them Fly Fest."

"Oh, that's real," Jack said. "Hella is somewhere on this island, that's a fact."

It felt to Rafi like she was talking to a brick wall. But she finally understood there was no getting through to Jack. He really believed the creators of Fly Fest were just hiding in the shadows somewhere, their little festival so exclusive, so elite, that this island was just a holding area before they could cherry-pick who got in. And for Jack, the only way to gain access was to look as perfect as possible, using whatever means necessary.

Rafi said her next words carefully, deliberately. "Fly Fest. Doesn't. Exist."

Jack took a step closer to her, his eyes suddenly laser-focused and serious. For a second, Rafi saw his delusions slip away. "I have been telling my followers about this festival for months. I did not pay thousands of dollars for something that does not exist." His words were just as deliberate, if a bit icier. "I am not a loser, languishing and desperate on a beach. I will not have the world out there laughing at me. Uh-uh. Couldn't be me."

Jack stepped back and seemed to compose himself, the YouTube-ready smile back on his face with the flip of an internal switch. "How come you never used the lip gloss I gave you?"

Because she'd spent it all to decorate her useless murder board that she was too embarrassed to talk about. "I lost it."

Jack looked disappointed, but eventually shrugged. "I have just the trick." He reached for Rafi's hand, and she felt a pinprick on her finger. She cried out involuntarily, but Jack held onto her hand. She didn't know what he'd pierced her with, but he definitely had pricked her skin, because there was a bead of blood on the tip of her index finger. She was too stunned to move of her own volition, but Jack guided her finger up to her mouth, and she let him. He slid the blood across her bottom lip.

"There." Jack handed her a compact mirror. "Better already."

He was right. Her lips looked rosy and plump, and she didn't look half-dead. And yet. Rafi would not accept that this was now the way of things. She rejected the new normal. And when she locked eyes with Jack, it was with a clearheadedness she had not experienced for days.

"None of this is real," she said. "This isn't real lipstick and that isn't real bronzer and nothing about this is glamorous, no matter how hard you try to convince people it is."

"Oh, young Rafi." Jack leaned forward so that his cheek was nearly touching hers. "Perception *is* reality."

When Jack pulled back, his smile was radiant. "One day you have to let me do a full makeover on you because, I swear, if Hella isn't letting us into Fly Fest because you insist on looking like—"

"I am *not* a heroin addict."

"I was going to say like someone who stuck her finger in an electrical socket, geez! Anyway, if Hella is holding out because of you, I'm going to be really sad." Jack pushed out his bottom lip in a perfect berry-stained pout. "And by sad, I mean violently pissed off, so do think about it, 'kay?"

24

Rafi made her way back to the beach, taking the slowest, most meandering route possible so she could be alone with her thoughts. How did she get herself into this mess? It was easy to look at the totally bonkers shenanigans and schemes these high-key lunatics were cooking up and say she was not a part of it. But that was a lie. Because everything that was happening on this island was, in one way or another, all her fault. Her brilliant Big Lie to get everyone to stay had worked too well, and like a mad scientist working on fumes and ambition, Rafi had turned this island into a petri dish of disaster. Now she felt like she could do nothing but sit back and watch it fester.

Rafi longed for a boat. And when she got to the beach, she thought maybe she had manifested one, because there was a crowd huddled by the shore, and they were waving wildly. There was only one reason to be that excited.

"A boat?" she whispered. Rafi tapped on shoulders and pushed on others, trying to get past the rows of people to see what they all saw. "What is it? What's everybody talking about?"

Finally, someone—a girl with uncommonly long earrings—heard her questions.

"We're on TV!" Earrings said.

"What?"

"Look!" Earrings pointed deeper into the crowd, but all Rafi could see were people's backs. She broke through another layer until she was closer to the center of the inward-facing horde, and that was when she saw it. Greer, holding up her phone and looking into its front-facing camera.

"I can't believe I'm on the news!" she squealed, happy tears streaming down her face. "My grandparents watch the news!"

"Are you live?" Rafi asked, but of course no one heard her. "Is she LIVE?" she asked, louder this time. It was happening. Someone had managed to make contact. The people of the outside world would now know—about the festival being a scam, about the lack of food and accommodations, the total lack of security. The disappeared influencer. The danger. The nonsense! "We're getting rescued!"

But a boy beside Rafi shushed her. "She's being interviewed by Wolf Blitzer."

"Yep!" Greer said, apparently full-on FaceTiming with Wolf Blitzer. "Everything's great here, Wolf! We're having the time of our lives!"

"No," Rafi said. "No no no—" The ridiculousness had gone on long enough. She had to put a stop to this. Jack may have convinced the world that everything was good here with one single Instagram post, but denying the facts would only cause more trouble, or worse. Rafi was about to lunge for Greer, but before taking a single step Earrings, was suddenly holding on to her wrist. "What are you doing?"

"I'm going to talk to Wolf Blitzer!"

"You can't possibly go on TV looking like that."

Rafi blinked. "What?"

"I'm just trying to spare you a national embarrassment. That look of desperation on your face does nothing for your complexion."

Rafi wrenched her wrist out of the girl's hand.

"Nothing for your complexion!" the girl echoed after her, but by now Rafi had gotten away, broken through the layers of people in the circle, and finally reached Greer.

"Greer!" Rafi cried.

"Thanks so much for checking in," Greer said to the phone. "Okayseeyouguyslaterbyeeeee!"

"NOOOO." Rafi yelled it so loud that the force of the sound made her sink to the ground, the coarse white sand biting into her knees. The gathered group dispersed, but Greer hovered over Rafi, wiping the drying tears from her plump cheeks.

"Don't worry," she said to Rafi. "That was only the first interview. Soon we'll get Gayle King, then we'll be on with Hoda Kotb and Jenna Bush Hager, and maybe after that Wayne Brady. But never, *ever* Ellen and her *Game of Games*, because I'm afraid of heights; that lady is a beast with the drop button."

Rafi looked up at Greer, the girl's grinning face blotting out the sun, and all hope. Even so, Rafi had to blink a few times to really see. "I don't understand."

"I paid six thousand dollars to be here," Greer explained. "As Jack says, if anybody asks, we're having the time of our lives."

"But we're not," Rafi said.

"Do you really know that for sure?"

Rafi opened her mouth and closed it again, and for the first time in her life she had the weird sensation of knowing what a fish out of water felt like. Not in the figurative I-don't-fit-in-here way, though that applied, too. But in the literal life-was-slowly-oozing-out-of-her-as-she-lethargically-writhed-on-the-ground-trying-to-breathe way. "Yes," she finally said. "I know that for sure."

Greer leaned down even more. "But do you really?"

Greer did not wait for a rebuttal this time. She wiped her cheeks and skipped away.

Rafi remained on the sand, unable to move. She waited to feel human again.

25

RAFI WANTED OFF. BEFORE FLY FEST THIS PLACE WAS just a crumb on a map, no better or worse than any other uninhabited spit of landmass in the sea. But somehow, without supernatural means; or diabolical, secret mad scientists; or governmental overloads; the people here had managed to turn this place into the stuff of nightmares.

There was no clean water, but all anyone wanted to talk about was a phantom party in the sky. They were all alone, but you'd never know from the pics. Turn over a random rock and Rafi was almost certain you'd find a crab brandishing a selfie stick.

Rafi sat on the sand, using a stick to lazily stoke the small fire she'd made. The strange days on the island started to bleed together to the point that Rafi was beginning to wonder how long she'd actually been here—beginning to doubt phone clocks and calendars. The situation felt, at turns, hopeless, dangerous, and smelly, and the more Rafi dwelled on it, the more the claws of restless anxiety ripped at her insides. Though that may have just been hunger. Rafi couldn't remember the last time she ate. She had an emergency cheese sandwich in her backpack but thought better about reaching for it. She'd heard a rumor that half a sandwich was equal to ten milligrams of LSD, and she needed to keep her mind sharp if she was going to get herself out of this mess. And off this island.

River showed up like a mind reader, though. He found her sitting on a quiet stretch of beach, the tide just threatening to lap up her fire. In his hands were two banana leaf plates with a fish apiece. He held one out. "Hungry?"

Rafi still didn't trust River as far as she could throw him, but she was also starving. "Thank you." She tried not to devour it all in one bite, but it was really delicious. River sat next to her, crossing his ankles in front of him.

"So, what's gotten you down?"

Rafi swallowed the food in her mouth. "I'm not down." Was it that obvious?

"Rafi, there's a reason why I've been nominated for awards and have auditioned for a Spielberg film."

He'd been nominated for four Kids' Choice Awards and had auditioned for an *Elana* Spielberg movie, but Rafi had no idea what that had to do with anything.

"It's because I know about emotions," he explained.

Rafi took another bite of the fish to give herself a moment. He was right, she was down, but she didn't want to sound overly dramatic about it. "I feel like I'm witnessing the fall of human civilization and there's nothing I can do about it."

"Mm-hmm," River said, munching thoughtfully on his own fish. "Yeah, that'll get anybody down."

Being stuck here was bad enough, but Jack's makeup tutorials had only made things worse. People were tracking boars just for their excrement. They were already wearing it on their faces, and some of the boys had even started using it in half-assed attempts to sculpt abs on their torsos. The whole island was starting to stink.

"I just don't get these people," Rafi said. "I'm trying to empathize and think like they do but I just . . . I feel so different from them."

"What makes you feel different?"

"Well, for one thing, I refuse to put poop on my face." It was the obvious, go-to answer. But even before Jack's tutorials, Rafi felt like she didn't belong here. There was a lot that made her different from these people—her values, her interests. But she hated to admit that the thing that ostracized her the most was so surface level. "And I'm not beautiful like they all are."

Rafi had come on this island with a purpose, and she was just trying to get things done and achieve her goals, but at every turn she was reminded that she wasn't beautiful. It was unrelenting, and it was made worse by the fact that it always came out of nowhere, when she was just trying to mind her own business.

Rafi had stopped counting the number of times she'd been called ugly since she got here, but the message had been successfully hammered into her head by now. The only times she usually ever thought about her looks were the few minutes a day she spent glancing in the mirror above the bathroom sink. But here, surrounded by these beautiful people who made their looks their business, the way Rafi looked was starting to weigh on her. The surface of her was all.

"I know I'm so much more than just how I look," Rafi said, "but I never thought I'd have to keep reminding myself of that."

She said all this while focusing on the sand, pinching it, raking her fingers through it like it was her own private Zen island. She was speaking about her feelings, and whenever she spoke about something so vulnerable, she could never do it while looking someone in the eye. But when she dared to cast a glance River's way, she saw a question all over his face, sewing his eyebrows together and tugging his mouth open. "What are you talking about?" he said. "You are beautiful."

Her first instinct was a skeptical one. That this was River lying, saying just the right thing to get her to like him. But that gave way to something akin to understanding. Even if he was lying, it was a kind lie, and it made sense why millions of people hung on every word of his songs. Because when someone like River Stone called you beautiful, you wanted to believe them.

So Rafi chose to believe him, and doing so made her eyes water and her throat tickle. She tucked River's comment away before she let herself get completely overcome by it. "All I care about right now is figuring out what happened to Sierra and getting off this island. But everyone here cares more about their phones or looking good or still getting into Fly Fest, which is ridiculous. So long as Peggy keeps giving them internet and

Jack successfully convinces them to keep smearing poo on their faces, I don't think we're ever getting out of here."

River took another bite of fish and nodded. "I think there's a security-blanket aspect to the whole phone thing."

"Security blanket?"

"Yeah, you know, something that makes you feel good when you're with it. I think it's the same thing with people's phones and posting stuff every day. It's kind of reassuring, isn't it? Safe. Normal. Plus, I think some people—and probably a lot of the people here—are used to posting certain things regularly. A curated list of things to make their lives look better than they actually are. And once you're used to creating a false narrative about yourself, it's hard to break that habit. Not only that—it's really soothing to keep that habit up. Maybe posting about how they wish things would be—and giving off the appearance that everything is perfect and beautiful—feels more reassuring than admitting how crummy things really are."

Rafi watched River as he finished his fish, surprised by how astute he sounded. It actually reminded Rafi of something Jack had said about makeup and comfort. And it made her feel like an idiot for not seeing the same subtext that they were seeing all around them. But still, as nice as words like "comfort" and "soothing" sounded . . . "It's still all lies," Rafi said. "Lies that are hurting us."

"Then it's up to you to tell the truth."

Maybe it was the charm that she swore up and down that

River did not have, but as he looked at her now, with so much earnest belief, Rafi found that she could not look away.

"You have a podcast," River continued. "You reveal the truth to your listeners all the time. Reveal it to them now. And it wouldn't even be off topic—Fly Fest is a musical event. And what's happening here *is* a mystery. Tell the world that it isn't all beautiful and glamorous and that you've been cheated and scammed. Tell the world what it's really like."

His words were like palms on bongos, jolting her, making her nerve endings come alive. River was right. She could talk about the festival on her pod. But as exciting as a shiny new topic to discuss was, her hands were tied.

"I can't get the internet," Rafi said. "I wouldn't be able to upload anything I record until we get back home."

River considered the problem—which Rafi felt was a pretty big one—but like everything else he encountered in life, this insurmountable obstacle didn't seem to be a big deal at all. "Does the timeline really matter?" River asked. "Even if people can't hear it right now, one day they will. And it'll be a true record of what's really happening on this island. You're the only one here who's willing to tell the truth. You have so much power, Rafi, and you don't even know it."

River's words felt as hot and as bright as the fire in front of them. Here was someone who believed in her podcast, believed in *her* and her skills. It touched Rafi, and it ignited something within her. She was starting to feel that spark that she got anytime she had a really good idea. It was a spark that almost instantly blazed into a roaring fire, when all she wanted to do was dive headfirst into a new plan.

"I could talk about Fly Fest being a fiasco—on-the-ground reporting, firsthand accounts. I mean, I've got access that real journalists can't even dream about."

River nodded emphatically, right there with her. He even picked up his guitar and started strumming a tune, an upbeat, yet dramatic ditty that totally matched Rafi's mood.

"And I can talk about Sierra's mysterious disappearance and how nobody here cares because they've all been brainwashed into thinking she found a secret party on an undiscovered part of the island," she said.

River's fingers worked overtime, his song taking on a high-stakes cadence.

"And I can talk about Hella being here."

River's song stopped with an abrupt, discordant note. "What?"

"Everyone thinks she's here," Rafi said. "I mean, again, I have *no* idea how those rumors started, but they are persistent. People keep hearing her around the mountain. And the fact that people believe she's actually here has really changed, like . . . the culture, on this island."

River slowly set his guitar down and leveled Rafi with his most serious look.

"Rafi, please believe me when I tell you that Hella is nowhere on this island."

A crowd was suddenly gathering not too far down the beach, and at the center of it were Paul and Ryan, out of breath. Something was up, and Rafi and River didn't even consult each other when they both decided to see what was going on.

The non-twins had news, and in between gulps of breath they announced it together.

"We saw Hella Badid!"

26

ENCOUNTERING HELLA BADID ON THIS ISLAND HAD become as common as lip fillers on an Insta thot, but this felt different. For one thing, Ryan and Paul didn't usually venture far from their banana business, making this sudden appearance unusual; plus, there was an urgency to what they were saying. But most of all, they'd claimed to see Hella. Until now, people had only heard her voice.

"We were hiking up the mountain," Ryan said, "trying to look for more fruit but mostly also to get some cardio."

"Cardio's gotten a bad rap lately, but it's part of a well-rounded fitness routine," Paul explained to the circle of beachgoers hanging on his every word. "We've been doing push-ups and lifting rocks, which is great for your biceps and triceps and upper-body definition, but it ignores your core."

"As my late personal trainer said as he sank into molten lava, 'You can't ignore the core!'" Ryan said. "Walking up an incline isn't really enough either, though."

"We ran it," Paul said. "We pretended the mountain was a *tour de stade*."

"A *tour de stade* is Chinese for climbing up and down every step of a stadium while being a stud."

"Will you get on with it!" Jack snapped. Rafi didn't realize he was among the gathered crowd, but it made sense: Hella sightings were his bread and butter.

"We saw her, man!" Ryan said. "We saw Hella Badid!"

Rafi sneaked a glance at River. His features had settled into concentrated lines.

"First of all, she called to us with the sweetest, softest angel voice."

Paul nodded vigorously. "Also, boobs: huge."

"Booty: round," Ryan said.

"She looked like a dominatrix supermodel beauty queen," Paul said.

"Body like Jennifer Lopez's."

"She looked like Destiny's Child."

"Yeah, but, with like, Madonna's style."

"With lips like Angelina Jolie's."

"So hot," Paul and Ryan concluded in unison.

At this point Jack had joined them at the center of the circle and turned to the listening crowd, positioning himself between the two jocks like he'd been with them on that mountain the entire time. "You see?" Jack said. "She's here. Hella is among us!"

River tapped Rafi on the shoulder and cocked his chin in the universal silent gesture for *Can I steal you away from these delusional dumbasses?* "They're lying," he hissed to Rafi when they were out of earshot.

"Why do you say that?"

"Because Hella doesn't have the voice of an angel. And

she doesn't look like Destiny's Child or dress like Madonna or have lips like Angelina Jolie. I'm pretty sure Ryan and Paul were just quoting O-Town lyrics."

"For the last time, what the hell is a Ho-Town?" Rafi asked.

"O-Town is an old boy band, and those lyrics are from their song 'Liquid Dreams.'"

Rafi couldn't help making a disgusted face. Why did she always insist on asking questions when the answers were always, inevitably, *so* grody.

"Don't you see?" River whispered. "They're making the whole thing up."

Rafi had seen Hella only in video clips and magazines, but River was right; she definitely didn't look the way Paul and Ryan described her. And even Rafi knew her voice was no angel's. "But what do they have to gain by lying?"

"I don't know," River said. "But something's up. Either they're deliberately doing it or they saw something and only thought it was her."

"Well, what do we do?"

River took a deep breath and gave a curt, decisive nod. He walked back into the circle, breaking up the whispers and questions being lobbed at Ryan and Paul, and now Jack, too. "I don't know what you think you saw," River told them, "but it wasn't Hella. I'll go up the mountain myself right now and prove it."

The whispers in the crowd were replaced by an awed sort of silence. Maybe because here was a superstar, taking on the responsibility of doing something hard, and at such a late hour.

"You'll do no such thing!" Jack said. "I'll go with you."

Rafi stepped up. Like hell she was missing this. "Me too!"

So it was settled. There would be a second expedition with the three of them. This time to find the truth.

Since they left almost immediately, Rafi took with her the only thing she needed: her microphone. If they really did see Hella up there, Rafi would be able to use the mic to record her. Concrete, tangible evidence—the only thing that mattered.

Not that Rafi believed they'd find Hella. Jack was way past delusional, and River was so certain his girlfriend wasn't on this island that there must've been a good reason.

"Who takes a microphone to a luxury music festival on a private island?" Jack asked.

The three of them were already halfway up the mountain, and it'd taken Jack this long to make a comment on Rafi's mic, even though he'd been eyeballing it since the start of their hike.

"Show me a luxury music festival on a private island and we can talk."

"Oh, it's here," Jack said. "Trust me, it's here."

Rafi gripped her mic tight. She didn't want to anthropomorphize it, but she still felt the need to protect and defend it from anyone who scoffed at it. "This mic holds power," Rafi said. "It could save us all."

"I feel like you're about to interview me on a red carpet,"

Jack said. "Or tell me I'm the next contestant on *The Price Is Right*."

The now-perpetual teeth-grinding ache in Rafi's jaw was flaring up again. "It's for my podcast."

"Oh, right, your podcast." Jack quickened his step so he was no longer standing so close to Rafi. "I am so excited to listen to it never."

The thing about mics was that not only could they record sound, but at just the right velocity they made great blunt force objects. Rafi briefly fantasized smacking it against the back of Jack's head. But she was horrified by her own violent reverie; it reminded her of River. Well, the old River. The one from her now-debunked conspiracy theory. Rafi turned around to see him but was instantly blinded by his flashlight beam.

"Where did you get a flashlight?"

"Some girl gave it to me."

Naturally. The sun had gone down fully by now, and darkness creeped through the vines and fronds. The farther they went, the more they needed to use their hands to help guide the way. Jack smacked intrusive leaves out of his face, and Rafi held out her mic, pointing it into the darkness like it could ward off whatever scary thing might be hiding in its shadows. She almost tripped over a tree root, but River's hand was quick and caught her arm before she went down.

When she straightened, Rafi found she was standing too close to him and that his flashlight beam shone only on their feet. River's face was shrouded in dark, his features a muddy, menacing swamp. And though she might not have been able to see him clearly, Rafi could still feel him. The air was warm but he was warmer. The heat exuded out of him with every breath he took, and Rafi felt it landing on her chest.

She probably should've turned away, but she couldn't. Rafi found that she was drawn to the darkness, to the mysterious, humongous hulk of a thing he was. It pulled her in.

"You okay?" River's voice broke the strange spell, and Rafi took a step back, nearly tripping again. "Fine."

"Hey, guys," Jack said, "unless step-and-repeats grow on trees, I think I found something!"

River shined his flashlight up ahead, and the beam of light splashed against a wall. No, not a wall—an eight-foot-tall banner held up by a metal frame that looked like a clothing rack. The banner seemed to be made out of some kind of waterproof canvas, not unlike the tents in Tent City. The words FLY FEST appeared in a pattern all over the banner, and it was the exact shade of neon pink as Rafi's shirt. If she stood in front of it, she'd disappear and look like little more than a hairball on legs. Rafi had seen these kinds of walls before—they were what celebrities posed in front of at award shows or premieres while they got their pictures taken.

Jack saw his moment. He stood before the banner with his phone up, snapping away. But he groaned and muttered, "No flash on my front-facing camera." He tossed his phone to Rafi without warning, but she still managed to catch it one-handed. "Take my pic!" he barked, his angry face switching quickly to a smiling one like he was glitching. Rafi clicked a pic, the flash bursting.

As fascinating as the step-and-repeat banner was, River, who'd seen so many over the last few years, didn't seem to care for it. He was more interested to see what was behind it.

"Uh, Jack, Rafi? We're here."

They'd reached the mountaintop without even knowing it. The place was a razed, flat clearing. Not a small clearing either. The space was half a football field, empty like someone had purposefully mowed down a rain forest worth of trees.

River shone his flashlight on surfaces that glinted and reflected the light back. On the four corners of the mountain peak were huge spotlights, tall as three-story buildings. There was scaffolding all around, a tall platform which was clearly supposed to be a stage. River climbed on top of it, gravitating toward his natural habitat.

"I think that's the stage!" Jack said, way too excited. River and Rafi were taking in the site like it was a cursed ancient archeological find. But Jack was acting like he'd just found buried treasure.

"A performance ground on a mountaintop?" River said. "Doesn't make a whole lot of sense."

"No, it tracks," Rafi said. "This whole festival doesn't make a whole lot of sense."

The metal pipes of the scaffold made it look like a derelict fossil, something that was either just being built or abandoned long ago. It wasn't much, but it was something; a sign that there had been life on this island, at least. That there had been an *attempt* at putting on a festival. It answered the question of whether this fiasco was due to poor planning or if everyone here had just been scammed.

"Don't you people get it?" Jack was practically panting with excitement. "This is proof! This is proof that we're in the right place! That the festival is still on! That we still have a shot to go to it!"

"Uh," Rafi began, "is that what you're getting? 'Cause all I'm getting is *garbage dump*."

"SHHHH!"

Rafi thought Jack was trying to shut her up because he didn't like what she was saying, but then she realized it was because he was trying to hear something else. He whipped his head around, searching for the sound, but Rafi didn't hear anything.

Until, she thought, maybe she did.

A whisper.

Rafi frantically thrust her microphone into the center of the darkness, straining to pick up the sound.

"Do you hear—" she whispered, but this time River was the one to shush her. His dimmed silhouette put an index finger to his lips. He heard it, too.

"Hey, guys."

It was a woman's voice. No inflection. It was impossible to tell if she was excited to see them, or surprised. Whatever she was, she wouldn't come out of hiding. There was no one to connect the voice to, not even the shadow of a person behind the trees. River swung his flashlight fruitlessly. It was a disembodied voice in the dark.

Rafi kept pointing her mic. She tiptoed, following where the voice was coming from.

"I'm so glad you made it," the voice continued. Monotone in its vocal fry. The kind of voice Rafi could easily picture coming out of the lips of a supermodel standing on a white sand beach in a string bikini. "Hella?" Rafi breathed.

"Things are about to get *lit*," the voice said.

Jack, River, and Rafi held their breath. They waited for more, but seconds passed silently on, and the air started to become electric, buzzing with bugs or anticipation.

"HELLA!" Jack squealed, his voice going raspy at the last syllable. The air got louder until it filled with the sound of thunder clapping overhead. Soon the only noise was the fat dollops of rain that began to pound down from the cracked-open sky. "HELLA, WHERE ARE YOU?" Jack yelled.

When no answer came, he spun to face Rafi, whipping around so fiercely that rain flicked off his hair and pelted Rafi in the face. His makeup was decomposing with the rain, all the clay and coal and shit streaming away like a raging sewage drain. "You heard her! She's here!"

Rafi couldn't deny it. She *had* heard. She'd even recorded it. And Jack knew that she had. He swiped the microphone out of her hand and ran.

"HEY!" Rafi yelled after him. "Where are you taking my mic?"

"I have proof!" Jack answered, but his voice was becoming faint as he ran back in the direction from which they had come. "I have proof she's here!"

The rain and dark swallowed Jack up, left no trace of him. Rafi turned to River, who stood immobile, his hair slick and sticking to his cheekbones. Rafi waited for him to say something, because if anyone could explain what they'd just witnessed, it would be him. But for the first time, River Stone had nothing to say.

27

THE RAIN KEPT COMING, BUT IT DID NOT DAMPEN THE party that had spontaneously erupted on the beach. Jack had produced a golden calf: Hella Badid's actual voice, recorded for all to hear. And because she told all who were listening that things were about to get lit, everyone collectively decided that she was right, and made sure her words were made true. Now people from all corners of the island had congregated at the beach, dancing around a fire that grew in defiance of the rain, flames licking the black sky. And Jack, who still had the microphone, played Hella's strange, inimitable voice over and over again. A new favorite song.

It wasn't until Rafi finally caught up to Jack that she was able to wrest the mic out of his hands. But by then the entire beach had already heard the message, and Jack didn't try to take the microphone back. He'd gotten what he wanted, and the party raged on.

Rafi didn't stay, though she couldn't go far, seeing as how she lived mere yards away. So she watched it all from her tent—or, what was once a tent and now mostly resembled an unshapely broken umbrella discarded on a street corner. The fabric she'd used for shelter didn't block out the rain so much as collect it in puddles from where it seeped through like a sieve. Rafi sat strategically in the space that the raindrops sort of missed, knees up and arms wrapped around her legs.

River, on the other hand, was staying pretty dry. His tent was made of much stronger stuff than Rafi's, and as he sat inside it and watched the celebration down the beach, he seemed lost in thought.

Rafi was *all* thought. Thoughts raced through her mind, bouncing off the walls of her skull at such a breakneck pace that she was getting a headache. She stuck her head out just enough to catch River's eye. "You know what this means, don't you?"

River shook his head.

"Jack has evidence now that Hella is here. And look at them, celebrating. He's officially convinced everyone of his delusional idea that the festival is still on. There's no way I'm going to be able to get anyone to send for rescue. Jack won."

"Hella isn't here."

River kept repeating the same thing like a broken record, but it wasn't enough anymore. Not when Jack had proof that said otherwise. Proof that he'd played on a loop.

"You heard her voice. You were there."

"That wasn't her." River shook his head, hearing how silly that sounded. "Okay, it *was* her, but she isn't on the island."

The cryptic way River spoke about Hella had always annoyed Rafi, but now it infuriated her. She'd heard Hella's voice for herself—they both had. Why was he still trying to lie about her? And then Rafi understood. "Because you know exactly where she is."

River said nothing, which was all the confirmation Rafi needed. Her heartbeat ticked up slightly, her old suspicions of a murderous River Stone ramping back up again. "And you're the only one who knows where she is?"

"Yes."

Rafi's heart was hammering in her chest now. With Hella seemingly gone from social media, the entire world thought she was on this island, and yet River Stone was the only one—*the only one*—who knew that she wasn't.

Because you did something to her. The thought cemented its place in Rafi's mind, refusing to budge. "Where is she?"

"I can't tell you."

If she'd had something nearby to throw in aimless frustration, Rafi would have, but for now all she could do was let out an involuntary grunt. The noise caught River off guard, and his eyebrows rose as he looked at her.

"You can stop all of this!" Rafi didn't mean for her voice to come out so harsh, but it did, and she wasn't about to take it back now. "Nothing on this island makes sense. You can make it make sense! You can put an end to this madness, tell everyone the truth and make them see how wrong all of this is."

River shook his head, but Rafi wasn't going to let him go that easy. "You're the only one who can save us," she said.

River looked over at the big bonfire, the people dancing around it. Blissful idiots. "They don't need saving."

"Well, I do!" The loudness of Rafi's voice made River stop

228

and look at her again, his eyes shadowed with pity. But pity was the last thing Rafi needed.

"You talk so much about truth and all the power it has," she said. "But where's your truth now, River? You have the power to change things, and you're keeping it to yourself. You know where Hella is. You probably know where Sierra is."

Sierra's name jogged something in River. He looked affronted. "You still think I had something to do with her disappearance?"

"Of *course* I do! You're shifty and evasive and you refuse to tell the truth about yourself and Hella, much less anything else. I don't trust you about anything."

The rain had fully infiltrated Rafi's broken tent by now, drenching her and her words. River, relatively dry, looked her over with an unreadable expression. But if Rafi wanted something more from him, she wasn't going to get it tonight. River pulled a flap of his tent closed, effectively shutting Rafi out.

MUSICAL MYSTERIES
Season 2: Episode 5
"Where the Hella Is She?"

River Stone is a liar.

He lies about everything. *Everything*. He says his girlfriend isn't on this island, but he can't tell me where she is—probably because he murdered her. *Ugh*. Okay, no, I don't think River is a murderer anymore. I know—plot twist after plot twist after plot twist! I told you this season would be full of surprises! This Hella stuff is probably confusing, so let me start from the beginning.

Hella Badid was supposed to be at Fly Fest, but she never showed up.

Except news has been circulating that she is actually here, hiding somewhere. The rumor that started it all was false. I know that because I was the one who made it up.

Someone here told me that truth has power, so I'm gonna be honest right now. I said that Hella Badid was here, and I did it for selfish reasons. I wanted to keep everyone on this island so I could have more access to River and get the best interview out of him that I could. And why did I need to keep everyone here? Because when we got to the island, we discovered that Fly Fest was a total sham.

That's right. You may believe otherwise, and I

don't blame you. Everyone here has been posting to their social media as if they're chilling in paradise, but they are *lying*. Nobody here is having the fabulously glamorous time that they claim. There isn't a gourmet organic chef—there are cheese sandwiches that everyone is refusing to eat because of increasingly escalating health concerns that I, frankly, can no longer overlook. There aren't villas—there are disaster relief tents, and that's if you're lucky enough not to sleep under a homemade tent you had to make out of borrowed rags.

We've been fooled. Bamboozled. Hoodwinked and throttled. We are all miserable, and the only reason no one is admitting to that is because they don't want you to know it. They want you to keep thinking they're living their best lives.

But no one has a perfect life, no matter how many filters you put on it.

I saw a girl last night who was trying to comb her hair with a sea urchin!

There was a boy who—I promise this is true—was making out with a coconut! And before you ask, no, it wasn't even a young coconut; it was a full-grown, hard, and hairy one. It was obscene.

And everyone's makeup smells really bad!

Telling the lie that Hella was here and the festival was still on was a stupid thing to do, and now I'm paying the price. The lie has taken on a life of its own. People are claiming that they too saw or heard Hella on this island, up on the mountain, inviting them to a party.

And tonight, I finally heard her voice for myself. Pretty conclusive evidence that she's here, right?

No, because River is adamant that she is not. Which is all well and good, but he refuses to say where she is. He is the only one who knows— the only one with the power to come forward and end the ABSOLUTELY ABSURD MADNESS that has overcome everyone on this island—but he refuses to be honest.

I don't know what to think anymore. I thought River was a bad guy. Then I thought he was good again. And now? Now I don't trust him.

Why?

Because River Stone lies.

He keeps secrets.

And I know his biggest one.

Remember his first love, Tracy? The one who abandoned him in the middle of the Australian bushland? Original subject of this podcast? Yeah, her. She never abandoned River. She died on that trip. Killed by a pack of dingoes.

And River lied to you about it. All to ensure that he'd be your favorite Tragic Hunky Dream Boy.

There you have it, folks. Hella is here somewhere. Fly Fest is a scam. And River Stone is a liar. He might be cute and studly and have muscles that scream "Yeah, I do goat yoga, what of it?" But none of that matters, because when you need him the most, he won't be there for you. I can't trust him. And neither can—*Ouch!*

The heel of Rafi's sneaker skidded over wet rock, and her leg went one way while her butt went another. She'd been recording on the run, traversing the island in the dark rain. She'd crossed all the different terrains of the island, from the beach, through the trees, and finally the rocky-muddy grounds of Tent City, but Rafi was finally in front of Peggy's tent.

Unlike every other time she was there, there was no guard at the door. Actually, there was no one inside except Peggy themself. They lounged on their bed, leafing through an in-flight magazine. It looked like for one night only, everyone preferred living life at the beach than spending another night online.

"You've come empty-handed," Peggy said, looking Rafi up and down. "Optimistic of you."

That was when Rafi noticed Peggy's face. One of their eyes was puffy, leaky, and pink. She stepped up to get a better look, but the closer Rafi got, the more she instinctively wanted to keep back. Whatever it was looked contagious.

"What's with your—" Rafi gestured toward her own eye.

"Oh, this?" Peggy tossed the magazine to the side and brandished their face toward the solar-powered bedside lamp. At the full sight of Peggy's eyes, Rafi instinctively recoiled. "Yeah, people pretty much ran out of things to trade for the internet and a few started offering, shall we say, *romantic* favors. Long story short, I made out with someone wearing *a lot* of bronzer, and now I have pinkeye."

Rafi couldn't get off this island fast enough.

"I'm not going to offer you any favors," Rafi said quickly. "I'm just going to beg. One last time. Please, Peggy." She stepped up to the bed until her knees hit the edge, but stopped short of clasping Peggy's hands. "Please let me have the internet."

"Okay."

Wait. Too easy. "What?"

"There's nothing left for anyone to give me," Peggy said. "And I *definitely* don't want to make out with anyone anymore."

Rafi wasn't convinced that it was *Peggy* who didn't want to make out with anybody, and not that people were adamantly refusing to make out with *them*, but she nodded along anyway. Peggy scooted off the bed. "The internet is pretty spotty with the rain, so work quickly. Wi-Fi password is LordOfTheIdiots."

Rafi couldn't believe it. After all this time, she was finally given the keys to her freedom. She took out her phone and found the only hotspot, then typed in the password, quick but careful. It took a few seconds, but the magic word popped up on her screen.

Connected.

She was free.

There was so much she could've done, so many people and authorities she could've contacted. So many people who could come to her rescue. Here was her chance.

But she just needed to get on Twitter real quick.

Rafi clicked the little writing bubble and typed out a new message.

NEW SEASON OF THE PODCAST BEING UPLOADED TONIGHT. Then she took all the files of the new podcast episodes she'd recorded and uploaded them all to her website.

28

IN THE MORNING, THE ISLAND WAS BACK TO BEING QUIET and sunbaked, last night's rain having washed it clean. But Rafi awoke remembering everything that happened. She sprung out of bed, which was to say, she shook off the sand that clung to her skin, and pulled herself from her tent.

She trekked down the beach, through the trees, into Tent City, and didn't stop until she was at Peggy's place. The guard was gone again, but the place was back to full capacity, packed with lazy loungers scrolling in silence. Rafi gingerly stepped over legs and torsos until she reached Peggy's bed. They lay on their back, a teal-silk sleep mask with curled oversize eyelashes covering their eyes. Rafi hoped they were still in the same good mood from last night because she'd come empty-handed again. Plus, she was about to wake them up.

She gently nudged their shoulder until they stirred.

Peggy pulled back their mask, revealing not one but two raging pink eyes. They were so crusted with goo that Rafi had to clamp her lips shut to keep from screaming right in their face. Not that Peggy could see her. They could barely open their eyes.

"Heeeeey buddy," Rafi said carefully. "You look . . . good."

"Don't patronize me," Peggy said. "I'm a monster."

Rafi kept her mouth shut and shook her head from side to side. "You're . . . hot."

If Peggy could've looked skeptical right now, they would have, but all they could really do was twist their eyebrows into something disbelieving. "I am?"

"So hot," Rafi said.

"You're just trying to butter me up so I give you internet again."

Rafi started nodding before she realized what she was doing and quickly shook her head instead. "Not at all. You don't look that bad, honest. And pink is really in right now," she said, pulling at the hem of her shirt.

"Please. If there's anyone who knows what's in right now, it is most definitely not you."

Rafi couldn't really argue with that. No matter, because Peggy pulled their mask back down over their eyes and turned onto their side, away from Rafi. "I didn't change the password today. Go on the internet. Leave me alone."

Rafi grinned and whipped out her phone. Last night, she was only able to post her podcast before the storm kicked her off the internet. But today, she'd finally be able to call for help.

She just needed to check how her podcast was doing first.

She plopped down right where she stood and logged on. The first thing she did was check her Twitter to see how many times her post had been retweeted. But it hadn't been retweeted at all. Actually, it'd gotten only two likes. She checked her website stats next to see how many people had clicked on the audio clips she'd posted.

Five people had listened to the first episode of season two of "Musical Mysteries." Two people had clicked through to the rest of the episodes.

Rafi stared at the number, her whole body going tingly with a numbing cocktail of disbelief and humiliation.

No one had listened to her podcast.

Not the fans she thought she'd garnered over the past year. Not the people on this island who she'd repeatedly told about her work.

Nobody cared.

They were never going to get off this island, and it wasn't because Rafi wasn't trying hard enough; it was because nobody was listening. She wasn't popular in real life, let alone on the internet. She didn't have enough followers, she didn't have a good brand, and after being surrounded by beautiful people here, she knew damn well she wasn't pretty enough to get anyone's attention. She spent so much time talking into the void, hoping someone was paying attention. Well, it didn't work on her podcast, and it didn't work on this island either. It didn't matter if she was doing good work, creating something of substance, diligently researching and compiling. Jack had been right. Without a following, it all meant nothing.

Rafi stared down at her phone. She was frozen except for her chin, which had started to quiver, despite Rafi's best efforts to control it. But just then a beacon of hope popped up on her screen in the form of a new email notification. It was from Nobrand, her lone sponsor. She opened it.

Dear Ms. Francisco. We know we committed to sponsoring your podcast, "The Mystery of Music." Unfortunately, we will not be able to continue on in that capacity as we have gone out of business. Best of luck in your future endeavors.

Rafi threw her phone across the room. A few people looked up from their screens and paused their scrolling to watch the phone bounce off the tent wall and fall to the ground with a depressing thud. Greer was sitting closest to it. She reached out with an arm like a tentacle and suctioned it away, storing it behind one of the folds of her flowy tunic. And just like that, Rafi's phone was gone.

Not that it mattered to her. Nothing mattered anymore.

Rafi's plan for the rest of her life was simple: go to her tent and stay there forever. She would become one with the rags until they inevitably fell with the next rainstorm or slight breeze. Then she and the rags would become one with the sand. And then one day she'd get eaten by a crab.

She didn't want to talk to anybody, and when she got to her tent, River wasn't around to show off one of his fishing weapons or lie to her about his girlfriend, so this was going to be easy. Except Jack popped in, out of nowhere. "Care for a makeover?"

Rafi was not in the mood to talk, which suited Jack just fine because he had plenty to say. "Everyone on this island is either already made up twenty-four-seven or thoroughly beautiful to begin with, so you're the only one who isn't. You don't want to be the only holdout, do you? Because, as I see it, you alone are the reason that Hella hasn't officially invited us up to Fly Fest yet."

Rafi stared at Jack for a long time. His red berry smile did not waver.

If Rafi had learned anything today, it was that it did not matter what she had to say. Maybe the only thing that mattered was how she looked.

"Okay."

Jack blinked. "Okay!" he repeated.

Rafi sat in Jack's tent, on his bed, while he combed her hair with a plastic fork. "I thought you only did makeup."

"In your case, makeup isn't going to be enough."

Rafi almost screamed out—at both the insult and the pain of the plastic prongs pulling apart her knots—but she couldn't even do that because Jack, as always, had more to say.

"This is *a lot* of mediocrity to handle. There really is so much to cover, but while we're on your hair, I'll give you this tip: Normalize using conditioner."

Rafi snorted. "Conditioner? I don't even have a change of clothes."

"There's that no-can-do attitude you're so famous for."

"People think of me like that?" Rafi asked. "But I've been trying to . . . like . . . do so much."

"Where was all that effort when it came to your looks?" Jack asked, making a disapproving sound with his tongue. "And don't snort. It makes you sound ugly. Truly, Rafi, you are fighting this glow up at every turn."

Rafi decided not to fight anymore. Also, this was her first time sitting on a bed in as long as she could remember, and you couldn't pay her to get up. She glanced at the beauty implements that Jack had laid out to fix her. There was an assortment of tools and products, some of which looked like normal things you'd see in normal society. Other things did not belong. Rafi could smell what did not belong. But she didn't have the heart to look at it.

This wasn't the first time Jack had asked if Rafi wanted a makeover. She'd turned him down every time, but now Rafi understood there was no point in saying no. In fact, saying yes was apparently the only way to go through life. No one online, let alone on this island, took her seriously. Today, that was going to change.

"I don't have your exact skin shade for foundation," Jack said. "But I'll just give you the same one I use."

So she would be orange. Great.

Jack worked on her with the deft hand and concentration of a mortuary cosmetologist. "Your brow is very furrowed," he said. "I'm going to need you to stop."

"Sorry," Rafi said. "I was thinking."

"Never a good thing."

She was thinking about what she was doing here. And the more "makeup" that Jack applied, the less she wanted him to. But every touch-up he did was like a hand on her shoulder keeping her in place. "Don't think I'm going to make this a habit," she said.

"Oh, you'll come back," Jack said. "You're hate-following me."

"I'm whatting you?"

"You hate me but you still follow my every move. And you know what? I'm glad. I don't care if you hate me or not. You still care enough about me to be in this tent right now. A hate-follow is still engagement. And it's all about the engagement."

At the start of this hellish trip Rafi wouldn't have taken advice from anybody here, but now she realized that Jack knew of what he spoke. Because he was right. Hate-following was the only explanation for why she was enduring this makeover. If she thought like Jack, maybe more people would've listened to her podcast. Maybe somebody would've alerted the authorities to their dilemma right now and saved them. Alas.

"Time for the final touch!" Jack picked up a small case. Just because he'd managed to pack it neatly in a pale pink

compact did not make it any less awful. It took Rafi everything not to gag.

"Um, maybe we can opt out of the bronzer?"

"Don't be silly. You need it desperately."

"I don't think I do."

But Jack put a hand on her shoulder, preemptively stopping
her from rising. "Right now your face is one tone. You want
to be two tones. Ideally, you want to be at least nine different
tones, but we have limited resources so two will have to do.
Like an overnight oat parfait. Don't you want to be delicious
like a parfait?"

Rafi looked him in the eye. "It's pig poop."

"Tomayto, tomahto!" Jack chuckled. "You get used to it.
Personally, I can't even smell it once it's applied."

Rafi didn't know how to explain to Jack that she could
smell him from a mile away. Nonetheless, she stayed. Everyone was doing this. And yes, everyone looked ridiculous with
a full face of stage makeup on a deserted island. But wasn't
it also true that everyone looked beautiful? Rafi had nothing
else to lose.

She could be a parfait.

She tilted her chin up toward Jack's face. The last thing she
saw before letting her eyes drift shut was Jack's berry-stained
lips curl into a grin.

Rafi pretended not to smell it. Pretended not to feel its warm
gooiness on her cheekbones as the bread sponge smudged the
stuff into her skin. Jack spread it so thin she could even pretend it wasn't there at all.

"*Voilà,*" Jack said.

Rafi opened her eyes to see Jack taking a step back to survey his handiwork. "There. Now you look like a piggy."

Rafi was more confused than ever until she remembered that this was what Jack called his online following. He began and ended all his YouTube tutorials with a salute to his *dear piggies* and even a catchphrase: "oink oink." It was just another aspect of her own generation that Rafi did not understand.

"Why do you call your fans pigs?"

Now it was Jack's turn to look confused, though whether he was confused by the question or Rafi's ignorance, she couldn't be sure. "It's just a joke," Jack said. "It doesn't mean anything."

But words always meant something. Jack may have used the word in an endearing way, but he wouldn't let you forget its scorpion sting.

"Now Hella has to show herself. Now they *have* to let us into the festival."

Rafi had almost forgotten. As sad as she was currently feeling, it made her even sadder that Jack was keeping up this festival charade. "Jack, come on, you know the festival isn't happening—"

"You're a riot, Rafi Santo Domingo," Jack said, cutting her off immediately. You should start a YouTube channel or something."

"I have a podcast."

"Oh. Right . . . Well, this just got incredibly sad and

awkward." Jack did a little sidestep, followed by a restorative throat-clearing. "Anyway! Get out."

Rafi left Jack's tent with no small amount of trepidation. It wasn't just the pig poop on her face—it was the makeover in general. She could feel the makeup like a second skin, weighing down on her, a constant reminder that she looked different—that there was something to look at, period. Her whole thing until now had been about blending in. As a reporter she never wanted to be the story, never needed to be seen. Being made up made her instantly uncomfortable, and all she wanted to do was take cover. But the farther she got from Jack's tent, the more glances she pulled. People stopped what they were doing in order to look at her. Rafi could hear her name whispered on their lips. She touched her hair self-consciously. Jack must've done some magic, because everyone was looking at her. Everyone was talking about her.

And suddenly, that uncomfortable feeling from just a few moments before began to subside, and Rafi began to feel a rush from deep within. A surge. People were looking at her—finally paying attention—and she could show them anything. She could even, maybe, get them to listen. Rafi began to see that the "glow up," as Jack had called it, didn't just have to be a vanity project. It could be a way for Rafi to bring her worth to the surface. Her new second skin began to blend with the first, as seamlessly as the "bronzer" blended with her cheekbones. There was a power in getting all this attention. And Rafi was starting to like it.

And then she heard Jack scream her name.

Rafi turned around. He was standing with someone, who was whispering something in his ear.

"YOU!" Jack yelled, his char-rimmed eyes expanding to double their size. "You told the world the festival is a SCAM?!"

"What?"

"Your little podcast!" Jack rushed toward her until he was close enough that some spittle from his rage-fueled tirade landed on her face.

But Rafi ignored that to focus on the important stuff. "You heard my podcast?"

"Of course not!" Jack spat. "But other people went against their better judgment and did. You told everyone we're a bunch of pathetic losers sleeping on the beach without food or shelter? You told the world we paid thousands of dollars to basically *go camping*?!"

Rafi found herself nodding, despite every bone in her body telling her not to. And she kept hearing her name, kept seeing the looks. People weren't talking about her because she was beautiful now. They were talking about her because they'd heard her podcast. "Have I gone viral?" she whispered.

"Like an STD!" Jack shrieked. "How could you? You're crazy. You're insane."

"I'm not crazy."

"Oh no? Because only a crazy person would—on top of everything—accuse that sweet cinnamon-roll River Stone of being a serial killer!"

River.

She'd forgotten about that part of her podcast. Even though it was the topic of the entire second season.

Jack kept screaming, and at one point he swooned and was about to faint before Greer rushed over to catch him. But Rafi couldn't hear anything that he was saying anymore. Her mind was with River.

She ran back to the beach, straight to River's tent. She pulled back the flap, but he wasn't there.

He must've heard her podcast, too.

She was surprised by the twist she felt in her chest, in the same spot where her heart should've been.

29

Rafi went to Peggy's tent first. She doubted she'd find River there, but she still needed to check everywhere. Also, she kind of wanted to be in the center of the Wi-Fi bubble, to see if it was true—to confirm that, somehow, people really had listened to her podcast.

"Oh yeah, it's the talk of the island," Peggy told her. "Most people here think you're *OMG so nutso* for calling River Stone a murderer. But I've been telling you that forever."

Peggy sniffed, then looked at Rafi. Or, more appropriately, looked in her general direction, since the pinkeye had taken over their ability to see. "Did you step in poop?"

Rafi checked the seaport next. Paul and Ryan were standing in front of their pile of fruit with the desperate eagerness of perfume sprayers at a fragrance counter.

"Rafi!" they said.

"Can we interest you in some bananas?"

"We're having a big sale."

"Only nine dollars."

"Yeah, we gotta move product."

"Remember when we said business was booming?"

"Well, it turns out business is now rotting."

"Who could have possibly known that fruit went bad so quickly?"

"Please, Rafi. Buy a banana. You could really use the potassium."

Once the boys stopped talking, they finally took a good look at Rafi.

"Whoa," Ryan and Paul said simultaneously. They stared at her, and it was only when Rafi touched her hair and felt the stiffness of the hair spray that she remembered her makeover.

"You look . . . different."

"You look like the tennis instructor I had when I was thirteen," Ryan said. "She was good, but I never learned anything because she was really . . . distracting." He swallowed. "Also, she was having an affair with my father."

Rafi wasn't really sure why the boys were acting so strange, and the confusion stunted her in place, making her forget what she was even doing there. Paul grazed her arm flirtatiously with the back of his fingers. "Hey," he said, sotto voce, smirking. "Name-dropping isn't really my style, but do you have any idea who my father is?"

Rafi stepped back, snapping out of her weird trance. This makeover couldn't have been *that* good. In fact, it was too much of a distraction. The attention that she savored earlier was the last thing she wanted. Not only was her makeover irrelevant right now, it was getting in the way of what she was here for.

"Have you guys seen River?"

"River?" Ryan asked. "You mean the guy who murdered his first girlfriend and possibly also his current girlfriend?"

"He didn't murder Tracy."

But the boys only looked at each other and snorted. "Are dingoes even a real thing?" Paul asked.

"They sound like dogs who wear clown costumes," Ryan said. "I mean, that's gotta be fake."

"River seemed so chill."

"Same thing happened with my butler," Ryan said. "He was super low-key all the time and then—*kaboom!*—half the staff turns up dead."

"Is that the guy who's doing time?" Paul asked.

"Yep," Ryan said. Then he turned to Rafi to explain further. "Time is the name of my former nanny. He ran away with her to the Cayman Islands."

Rafi squeezed her eyes shut hard enough that she could feel the burnt powder of her eyeliner crumbling between her eyelids. "River isn't a killer," she said again.

"The internet says he's a killer," Paul said. "And I believe everything that's on the internet."

She would never get through to them. And she was wasting time. "Do either of you know where he is?"

"Um, I obviously can't say this about my man Ryan here, but I don't associate with killers," Paul said. "Do you have any idea who my—"

"I gotta go," Rafi said.

"Wait!" Ryan caught up to her and gently squeezed her hand. Paul was next to Ryan in an instant, neither of them exactly blocking her way, but standing shoulder-to-shoulder, the jocky non-twins cut imposing figures.

"Maybe it's because we never got distracted by the O-Town reunion that never happened," Ryan said.

"Or maybe it's because we're not bogged down by a successful produce business anymore," Paul said.

"*Bogged*, nice," Ryan whispered.

"I don't usually go for the nerdy girl," Paul said.

"Neither do I," Ryan added adamantly. "Absolutely never, ever. Would rather die, probably."

"But I feel, like—"

"Enlightened."

"Like, maybe we could—"

Rafi didn't let Paul finish. "What are you guys—"

"We're saying you can't just go," Ryan said. His eyes were wild, desperate, like he was racking his brains to give her a reason to stay. Like this makeover was really *that* good.

"Why not?"

"Because I need you to teach me to read," he said.

Rafi yanked her hand away and left the seaport.

The pond was just as stunning and serene as the last time she'd seen it. It really was the most beautiful place on the island.

Of course she found him there. He sat on the same flat rock, the one he'd told her the truth on. And though he had his back to Rafi, he must've sensed she was there, because he began to speak before even turning around.

"I listened to your podcast."

She nodded, though he couldn't see her. Some girl must've given him her phone. Rafi assumed he was one of the first people to listen to it, since he'd been gone from the start of the day. And the idea that he didn't go into it already angry—that he sought out her podcast to support her—made her stomach feel like it'd been through a garbage disposal. "I didn't mean for you to hear it like this."

"Did you plan on posting it after we'd left the island?" River stayed focused on the water as he spoke. "Were you going to say goodbye and it was great to meet you and smile and then still post it when we weren't beach neighbors anymore? 'Cause that kind of makes it worse."

It was at that point that River finally turned around and saw her. The new Rafi, all dolled up. She didn't know what she expected his reaction to be. She could do nothing but watch as his jaw slackened slightly. For a long moment he didn't move much else, until he finally pulled himself up, and the closer he came to Rafi, the more his eyebrows drew down, his eyes searching for something within her he could recognize. "What did you do to yourself?"

It wasn't the resounding adulation she didn't dare to hope for. And under River's gaze she could almost feel herself wilt.

Everything she wore on her face, and even the way her teased hair floated above her head, made her suddenly feel like an extra in a community theater production of a postapocalyptic dystopia set in the world of *Working Girl*.

She knew it shouldn't matter what he thought. Intrinsically, she knew to be offended that he would even question what she chose to do or not do with her appearance. But all her empowered, self-assured airs fell away, and instead of feeling like the makeup gave her an extra layer of protection, it felt like it took one away. She stood there, flayed.

"I got a makeover."

River didn't respond, only kept examining her, his gaze like sandpaper over her skin. The longer his silence stretched, the more it put her on the offensive. "Don't say this isn't me. You don't know me."

"No, I don't," River agreed. "How could you record all that stuff? How could you *post* it?"

She didn't know how to answer that. She really hadn't thought she'd ever have to answer for the things she said on her podcast, least of all for the subject of it. She was quickly learning the flaw in this thinking.

"I thought when we talked . . ." He stopped, took a breath. "I thought when we talked, you believed me."

"I did believe you—"

"So you're either lying to me or lying to your listeners and telling the world I'm a killer for, like, ratings, is that the right term for it? I don't know how podcasts work."

"It was just a theory." Her voice came out meek. "It was just the first few episodes."

"And then the last episode," River said. "Where you told the world my biggest secret."

This was the moment for Rafi to try to defend herself. But she couldn't. "I'm sorry. I was frustrated and wanted to get the truth about Fly Fest out. I forgot about everything I said in the first few episodes. And then the last episode . . . I was mad. I was going to edit it, I just . . . I wasn't thinking."

River didn't look like he believed her. She couldn't blame him.

"And you were still being shifty," Rafi added quickly.

"About what?"

"About *Hella*," Rafi said. "Every time I ask you about her, you lie."

"I don't lie—"

"You have a tell," Rafi said. "Your smile goes crooked when you're lying. And you do it every time I bring Hella up."

He was doing it now. Yes, his smile was rueful, but it was also twisted sideways. "I think you might know more about me than any of my most diehard fans," River said. He did not say it kindly.

He took a deep breath, looked up at the sky, and seemed to consider something. After a moment, he looked back at Rafi, most of the anger melting away from his glare, leaving only defeat. "I guess it doesn't matter now." He sighed. "Hella's in rehab."

"Rehab?"

"Yes. For exhaustion," he explained, before muttering, "and other stuff."

Of all the places Hella could've been, Rafi never even considered rehab. Though it seemed perfectly reasonable now. The last time she'd heard anything about Hella, it was a week before Fly Fest, when video spread all over the internet of her shrieking drunkenly at another girl outside of a club while being held three feet off the ground by a bouncer. Along with being a successful supermodel, the girl was also a lush.

"Why didn't you just say so?" Rafi asked.

"Because it's none of your business," River said. "So, yeah, I knew for a fact where she was and I couldn't tell you. But she's not on this island. No one from Fly Fest is."

The trees provided shade but Rafi still felt hot, unspeakably hot under all the makeup. She felt like she was melting, but she didn't think it was just from the climate. It was the way River was looking at her.

"It's funny," he said. "You think you're above everyone here because they're all fake and manipulating the truth about who they really are. But you're doing the same thing. You're painting a whole weird, twisted, false image of *me*. And that's so much worse."

There was nothing that Rafi could say. All the humidity in the jungle couldn't stifle her the way River's words just had. He was right; she was the fake one. She felt it all the more now, standing here like a pig wearing lipstick.

"I'm sorry." It was all there was left to say.

"I wish I believed you." River looked at her face, her eyes, her cheekbones. "But you're full of shit."

Rafi watched him go until he disappeared in the jungle foliage.

She couldn't take the heat anymore. She sank to the ground, and melted.

30

Though they wore their sleep mask over their eyes, Peggy could still sense someone was near. It was the flowery perfume that alerted them. Mixed with the faint smell of pig dung, of course. They knew that smell all too well by now.

"I'm not making out with anyone anymore," Peggy warned, infusing as much authority in their voice as they could. But the nasty aroma lingered. "Okay, fine, one more makeout sesh but that is *it*. I think this pinkeye is getting to my brain."

The smell persisted. This was starting to get annoying, but also mysterious? Which was kind of turning Peggy on. They lifted their sleep mask over their eyes and put all their effort into prying their lids apart. Through the small slit of an opening, Peggy could see Jack Dewey's face an inch away, staring at them. Peggy was back to being turned off. "Can I help you with something?"

"Yes," Jack said. "You gave Rafi Santa Barbara the internet. Prepare to die."

Peggy scooted back on their bed until they were sitting up against the headboard that two sexy and intrepid concertgoers had made for them out of wood and spider webs. "What?"

"I'm kidding about the die part . . . for now. We're here to take your internet." Five of Jack's influencer followers hovered behind him, four girls and a boy, in full makeup, looking just as angry (and also kind of menacingly hungry?) as him. "You can't be trusted with it anymore."

"What?" Peggy asked. "Why?"

"Because that lunatic Rafi told the world we're dirty losers stranded on an island without running water or roofs over our heads!"

"So, the truth?"

"*Ugh*, you're just as bad as she is." Jack turned to his influencers. "Hayes, Stanton, Jayde-with-a-Y, Jayne-with-a-Y, Mahoney: Find me the internet."

Jack's beautiful goons lurched into their rampage. They grabbed anything within reach and overturned it, smashing it on the hard ground. And there was a lot within reach. Peggy's tent was basically a museum of *stuff*—probably the biggest collection of stuff this side of the Caribbean.

There were at least seven other people in Peggy's tent, lounging on the throw pillows on the ground, leeching off the internet that streamed through their phones, but they were either apathetic to the chaos mounting around them or too sucked into their social media worlds to notice it. With no one rising up to help, Peggy was beginning to panic.

"You can't just take my internet!" It was the source of all of Peggy's power. The reason anyone even talked to them in the first place. "You can have the password, no charge—I'm giving it away!"

"And look how good that turned out," Jack said. "The

internet in irresponsible hands breeds disinformation. It needs to be reigned in."

The influencers smashed the ashtray Peggy never used but sorely loved, made by the gorgeous Gio. They ripped down the psychedelic poster Peggy hated but still needed, provided by the stunning Destiny D'Bavio. And they ransacked the drawers of the nightstand Peggy forgot existed but couldn't live without, given to them by the supremely dexterous Nichard Archimedes Bonzalez III.

Peggy shook their head. "You'll never find it."

"Found it!" one of Jack's disciples said, holding up Peggy's satellite phone and grinning with lipstick between every single one of his teeth.

Jack smiled too and held out his hand, where Lipstick Teeth promptly set the brick of a phone. "From now on, *I* control the branding on this island," Jack said. "Nothing gets out without my approval."

Peggy sighed. They were nothing without the internet, and they knew it. Jack knew it, too.

"Let's party!" he told his followers.

There was some sun left in the sky, burning orange and pink as it made its way over the horizon, but River still used the flashlight to wade through the trees as he made his way up the mountain. When he'd left Rafi by the pond, he wandered around for a while, needing to be alone. It wasn't like he could go back to the beach, anyway. By now everyone had probably already heard the sordid claims in her podcast. Everyone probably thought he was a monster. So he stayed hidden in the comfort of the jungle, letting the sounds of nature inform his next moves.

Soon, River found himself going upward. Before he even realized it himself, his feet were guiding him to the spot that he, Rafi, and Jack had explored the night before, where they'd heard Hella's voice.

River knew it was Hella's voice; there was no denying it. He'd been listening to that voice asking him to fetch a bottle of rosé twice a day every day for the last two months. His girlfriend definitely had a drinking problem, which was precisely why he'd convinced her *not* to come to Fly Fest. A boozed-up musical bonanza on a tropical island was the worst place for her to be. To his surprise Hella had agreed and realized it was the perfect time to go to rehab instead. Well, actually, the rehab was ordered by the judge in her assault case, but the official story Hella's publicist was planning to release if word ever got out was that Hella had made the decision on her own. No one was supposed to know, except River. And the week of the festival was supposed to be the perfect cover. People would be too focused on the event of the season to care where Hella was.

Except the opposite had happened, and now everyone here wondered where she was *all the time*, and River couldn't keep up with the lies. Especially not with someone like Rafi asking questions nonstop.

He'd really screwed this up.

But this—this weird disembodied voice in the mountain—this was screwing with River's head.

He needed to find out the truth behind it.

By the time he reached the top of the mountain, the sun was gone and the beam from River's flashlight shone bright enough to illuminate the gnats buzzing in its path. There was the step-and-repeat that Jack had posed in front of. Vines grew over it like it'd been here for a very long time, even though that was impossible. Everything about this festival was last-minute. So last-minute that it wasn't even complete.

The stage platform was bare bones, and though he'd already stepped on it the night before, he did almost fall through a crack in the wooden planks and break his neck. River did not want to take his life in his hands and do that again. So he went around the stage, to the back, where an intricate maze of scaffolding and wires and plant overgrowth ran the length of the space. River didn't know what it was all connected to, but the thing felt alive, like a pumping humanoid heart. He could feel heat emanating from the jumble as he got closer to it. He was hesitant to touch any of it, but he was also looking for answers. He found a compromise. A stick at his feet. He dragged it along the metal and wires, poking some areas that he couldn't see too well and pulling back leaves that obscured others.

Until he found a monitor. The screen was black but it buzzed, like a TV that was still on, even though the cable was off. He tapped the monitor with the stick and it flickered to life. First there was only a grey glow. Then an image came into focus of a beautiful beach backdrop. And then Hella was on the screen. She wore a string bikini, and her face was fixed in its usual expression: bored hottie. "Hey, you," she said to River.

River's mouth fell open. Maybe it was the strange twilight hour, or the heat coming from this part of the stage, or the fact that his girlfriend was suddenly before him, but the moment felt surreal. It was like Hella was looking through the screen, right at River—really seeing him.

And then she continued speaking.

"Welcome to Fly Fest," Hella said. "Things are about to get *lit*."

The screen went black again. And with the darkness went all the magic River felt for that one brief second. And he understood immediately what this was. When Hella had participated in the viral promo video for Fly Fest, she'd also made these little clips, clearly to be shown throughout the concerts. Before the organizers obviously ran out of money and abandoned the whole endeavor.

It all made sense now.

A fly landed on the corner of the monitor, and it was enough to get it going again, the screen coming back to life and Hella there, demanding things get lit once more.

River dropped the flashlight and stick and grabbed either side of the monitor. He shook it and yanked until the thing came loose and a *shzzmm* buzzed out from the screen. And then he ran.

31

"Is it on?" Jack smiled at the camera. Smokey eyes gleaming with wing-tipped liner; drawn-in bold brows in perfect arches; overlined red lips stretched in a supple, practiced smile; cheeks rouged to hell and back; and, of course, to bring the whole look together, contoured cheekbones sharp enough to cut glass brushed and blended with a "bread" sponge and his patented secret ingredient. The orange flames of the raging bonfire nearby danced across his fully made-up face. Jack Dewey had never been more stunning. "We're live?"

He got a confirmation nod from Greer, holding the camera phone. Show time.

"Hi, piggies! *Oink oink* and all my love!" He shaped his fingers into a complicated salute before settling them into a demure wave. "We're coming to you LIVE from Fly Fest where the party is dead-ass nonstop. Now, I don't know what you may have heard, specifically from a total nonentity named Rafi San Bernardino—if that's even her real name—who's been telling people through her podcast—um, who listens to those?—that Fly Fest is a hoax. First of all, I know Rafi, and if there's one thing I can tell you about her it's that *she's* the hoax. She's a bitter, thirsty, nerd who'd never even *heard* of feathered eyebrows before I set her straight. Not an original or smart thought in her body."

Jack beckoned the lens with a hooked index finger until it was zoomed all the way into his face. He tilted it expertly to get his best angle, and spoke his next words as though he were a twenty-two-year-old Academy Award–winning ingenue starring in her first fragrance commercial. "Rafi San Bernardino is a known nobody. A liar. A dirty loser. Just a very nasty girl. Don't believe a word she says."

He breathed in deep.

"Second of all, does this look like a hoax to you?" The camera zoomed out enough to capture Jack with his arms open wide and his head thrown back. All around him were people dancing barefoot in the sand with a raging bonfire in the background. "This is the party of the millennium. And that little pang you're feeling in your gut? That's you wishing you were here."

He started to skip down the beach, but not before winking over his shoulder for the camera to follow him. Jack stopped in front of a girl with a crown of tropical flowers decorating her hair. "Hey, girl, we're live on my Insta right now; tell us your name."

"I'm Emerson, or, I guess, DreamTwoDreamTravelerOne on Instagram." She waved at the camera phone.

"Emerson, you're gorgeous."

"Thank you!"

"What are you drinking?" Jack bent to sniff the coconut husk in Emerson's hand.

"It's the punch."

"Ooo! The Fly Fest signature punch. *So* exotic."

The camera panned to an Hermès luxury titanium-lined suitcase trunk, open on the sand. People were dipping their own halved coconut husks into it and scooping out a murky-colored cocktail.

"Don't stand too close to the fruit punch or you *will* combust," Jack told the camera. "That special juice is full of the richest, most glamorous, secret ingredients."

"I think it's fruit and rainwater," Emerson said, poking her head into the frame. "And hair spray and Listerine."

"Pure, undiluted mouthwash for those of you with a *nasty* mouth; I'm looking at you, Rafi." Jack walked to his next interviewee, a girl dripping freshly from a stint in the ocean. "Oh, look at you!" Jack said. "Skinny dipping in the moonlight?"

"I think I got bit by a man o' war," the girl said.

"HOT!" Jack did not slow his stride. "Hey, look over there!" He pointed up and the camera followed, spanning the cliffside in the near distance until it settled on two boys. They high-fived each other and then jumped, disappearing into the darkness. "We even have cliff diving!" Jack trilled. "It's the *Midsomer* vibes for me."

Jack kept moving, caressing shoulders, shimmying next to dancers, chatting briefly with those who were sober enough to respond. "Tell my followers how much fun you're having right now!" he shouted into one girl's ear.

"So much fun," she responded.

"Do you want for anything?"

"I want for nothing," she said. "Except maybe, like, clean water?"

"She's kidding!" Jack said to the phone. "Hey, look over there! It's the Chainsmokers!"

The camera swung quickly and stopped on two lanky-haired girls, smoking cigarettes. But before the camera could linger on them too long, Jack grabbed it and pointed it in the direction of a boy holding court behind a homemade drum kit of overturned sandwich containers. He was using something peculiar with which to bang on his drums, and Jack's eyes lit up when he saw them.

"You guys are gonna love this," he said to his viewers. "Yesterday we found bones on the beach!" The boy on the drums nodded and banged the bones together in the air.

"One-two-three-four!"

"BONES!" Jack said.

"See, this festival is incredible. Greer, read me some of the comments."

Greer began to read the stream of comments popping up in real time:

> "What happened to those cliff divers? Question
>   mark question mark question mark."
> "I am deeply concerned for the safety of everyone
>   there."
> "Is this a party or a string of ways to kill people?"
> "Man o' wars are no joke."

"The creators of Fly Fest in no way endorse what
   is currently happening at Fly Fest."
"Is that guy passed out on the sand still breathing?"
"Viscerally unsettling."

Greer zoomed in on the guy passed out on the sand, but Jack moved the phone until it was back on his face. "Uh, what?" he asked his followers through the camera. "Guys, no, this is *fun*."

He stared into the phone, as though daring it to respond, but Greer wasn't reading the comments anymore. And though she didn't appear on-screen, anyone tuning in could guess what she was doing.

"Greer, why are you crying?" Jack asked. He rolled his eyes. "Greer, stop crying."

A ruckus broke out behind Jack, and though she still wept, Greer had the wherewithal to zoom out and get a wide shot of the beach. Festivalgoers were cheering for River Stone, who had just broken through the trees of the jungle and run onto the beach. In his hands he held a thirty-two-inch TV screen. His facial features were set in a sweaty urgency.

"Everybody listen!" River said, loud enough to make everybody stop and look at him. "Hella isn't here! She isn't coming! What you all heard was a promo video." River shook the TV screen. It was a useless relic in his hands, but the mere reality of its existence clearly meant something to him, and he was hoping it could mean something to everyone else. "There are screens set up all over the mountaintop. They were playing promos for Fly Fest on a loop—"

"NO!" Jack yelled. The sudden shrillness of his voice cut through the air like a clap of thunder. "You're lying!"

River began to respond but Jack wouldn't let him. "We don't want to hear it! You're canceled! Hella *is* here!"

River shook his head but Jack didn't see it. He was too busy clutching his ears in desperation, trying not to tear the hair out from his temples. "Enough of these lies! We're just trying to live our best lives!" he cried. "Will you please just let me *live*?!"

"Hella—" River began, but his voice was cut off by Jack's, who shouted at Greer to turn off the livestream.

But while Greer may have thought she turned it off, she actually did not. She merely dropped the phone and ran toward the action, her bare feet in stark focus until they got hazier the farther she got from the camera. And although the grains of beach sand directly in front of the lens were the only thing on screen that weren't completely blurry, the camera still captured what was going on in the background. Anybody watching the livestream could see Jack charging for River, and then a stampede of bare feet stomping the sand, spraying the camera with granules of it as they ran toward the two quarrelling boys. It was hard to make out what anybody was saying because all of them were shouting, until their voices blended into an angry chorus. Jack's hand, poking high out of the center of the gang, gripped a nail file like a butcher knife, and it came down in a forceful, terrifying swish.

The phone tipped forward, belly-flopping onto the sand, the feed finally cutting off.

Rafi, standing in a corner of the seaport, watching the livestream over someone's shoulder, stared at the suddenly blank screen in horror.

32

Rafi ran to the beach as quickly as she could, but the chaos seemed to have ceased just as quickly as it had flared up. By the time she got there the party was over.

Almost like something had killed the mood.

River wasn't anywhere, and neither was Jack. A few stragglers were stumbling around on the sand or slumped in close proximity to the drunk-punch trunk that now sat dry and empty beside the dying bonfire.

Rafi bent over a boy who was lying facedown, and pushed his shoulder until he flopped over. "Hello? Have you seen River?"

The boy responded with a belch. It was both minty fresh and toxic enough to style Rafi's hair. She looked around, but no one seemed coherent enough to answer her questions. So she went looking for Jack. But when she got to Tent City she was stopped by the same guy who used to guard Peggy's tent, now promoted to guard much bigger real estate.

"Yes?" He put his arm out, moving it in front of wherever Rafi moved.

Rafi slapped it away. "Is River here?"

"There is no river here, miss. Only a beach."

"River Stone!"

"Beach seashell!"

Rafi wanted to destroy something, and she would've been angrier, but she really wasn't sure if this guy was messing with her or if he genuinely thought they were playing some sort of word game.

"River Stone. The most famous singer in the world right now!"

"Never heard that name in my life."

She'd had enough. "Let me through."

"Are you one of Jack's followers?"

"Not even if my life depended on it," she spat.

"Then I'm afraid I can't let you in."

Rafi didn't have to take this—she was her own independent woman who could go wherever she wanted, and there were no rules on this island. But as soon as she tried to sidestep the guard, he grabbed her around the shoulders and picked her right off the ground like she was a garbage bag.

"Let go of me!" Rafi shrieked.

The guard put her down. "I'll do it again," he said. "But please don't make me."

Rafi tried weighing her options. She could make a run for it, but this guy was bigger, faster, and stronger than she was. All she could think to do was scream.

"RIVER!"

The guard winced. Rafi didn't care. She'd stand there and scream all night if she had to.

Except, after screaming River's name three more times, her

throat was getting dry. And who was she kidding; she didn't have the willpower to do anything all night long. She turned around and headed back to the beach, but instead of going inside her own tent, she went into River's. It was empty, like she'd feared it would be. His carry-on bag was in the corner, his guitar leaning against it.

Rafi was so lost and scared and confused that her mind started running away from her, and she wondered wistfully if maybe there was a secret party somewhere on this island after all. Maybe River had found Sierra and the two of them were there now, having the amazing time that Fly Fest always promised.

But how could River regale the crowd without his guitar?

Rafi sank down and crossed her legs. She'd sit there until River came back.

Because he had to come back.

She stayed in that position for hours, willing her eyes to stay open, until the salty beach air made them feel too dry, and she let them rest.

When she opened her eyes again, the sun was shining flower patterns through the tent's fabric. And River had still not returned.

"Does anyone have any idea what happened to River?" Rafi asked.

She was back at the seaport, asking the same questions she hadn't stopped asking since last night. Most everyone who liked to hang out at the seaport was gone now, defected to Jack's eternal party, apparently. The only people left were Paul and Ryan, who stood on either side of the room, volleying a conch shell the size of a football over Rafi's head. With Rafi having washed all the gunk off her face, Paul and Ryan had gone back to seeing her as little more than a girl who sometimes blocked their peripheral vision.

But there was a new visitor to the seaport. Now that no one was coming to Peggy's tent for the internet anymore, they needed people to talk to, and Paul, Ryan, and Rafi were the only sane people left on this island.

Except for River. Who still had to be here. Somewhere.

"They murdered him, obviously," Peggy said.

Rafi whipped around to face them. "What?" She was usually the one to posit wild theories having to do with River and murder, only for Peggy to call her crazy. Now Rafi and Peggy had switched roles. "Of course he isn't dead, how can you even say that?"

"You saw the same video I saw, right?" Peggy asked. "The one where Jack stabbed River with a nail file and then everyone joined in and then River disappeared into the ocean?"

"No, no, I didn't see any of that," Rafi said. "I mean, I saw the nail file, but that was all. Who knows if Jack even touched him? And River's strong—have you seen his arms? He has strong arms."

"Again with how fit and muscular he is," Peggy said. "Sorry, *was*. You really have it bad for him, don't ya? Sorry, *had*."

"I don't have it bad!" Rafi took a breath and a moment to collect herself. If they were going to find out what happened to River, they'd need clear heads. Paul and Ryan were useless in that department, but Peggy was smart. Peggy was practically a genius. "River is missing. We have to find him."

She was looking for agreement or, really, any sort of reaction. But Paul and Ryan continued their game like they hadn't heard her, tossing the conch over Rafi's head without a break. And Peggy only watched her with mild sadness. "This isn't like one of your podcast mysteries," Peggy said.

"I know. It's more serious."

"No, I mean, there's no mystery about it—pretty sure he got murdered."

Rafi wouldn't let herself believe that River was dead. She didn't come here believing that he was a killer just for him to end up getting killed. That was not how his story ended. And, sure, it was easy for her to believe that anybody could be a killer, but—Jack? The guy could be a little kooky, putting dookie on his face, but he wasn't a murderer. That was ridiculous. The festival—or lack thereof—couldn't have turned him into that big of a megalomaniac.

Could it?

Something shattered, rousing Rafi from her dark thoughts.

Not too far from her feet lay the remains of the conch-shell football. Paul and Ryan looked at the pieces, mouths agape.

"Whoa," Ryan said.

"We've never dropped a football before," Paul sad.

"Not a football," Rafi corrected.

"That's, like, an omen," Ryan said.

"Yeah," Paul agreed. "Like, that bad things are gonna happen."

The two boys turned to Rafi, waiting for confirmation.

"Have you guys heard a word I said?" Rafi asked. "Bad things *have* been happening. River is missing and possibly dead, and Jack may have been the one to kill him. Or capture him. Or *I don't know what.*"

"Don't forget there's an influencer missing," Peggy added.

"Right!" Rafi said, exasperated. "Sierra vanished into thin air. This whole festival is a nightmare—are you just now realizing this?"

Ryan and Paul shrugged and faced each other. "We've been having a pretty chill time, actually."

"We have to go to Jack," Rafi said, because it was true, and because she needed to cut off Paul and Ryan from whatever nonsensical digressions about making millions on bananas they were about to launch into. "We have to know what happened."

"And we have to get my internet back," Peggy said.

At this point, Rafi couldn't care less about the internet. It hadn't helped her when she actually got her hands on it. Actually, it'd only made things on this island exponentially worse.

But if it meant that Peggy was on her side and willing to face down a possibly insane murderer, then she'd go with it.

"And we have to know what happened to O-Town," Paul and Ryan said.

"Okay, then," Rafi said, nodding to herself and ignoring the boys. "Let's confront Jack."

33

Rafi found herself standing in front of the guard of Tent City yet again, but this time she wasn't going to allow him to throw her around like a rag doll. She had Ryan and Paul with her, who each were equally as big as the guard, and there were two of them. Peggy was there too, but apart from a mean—and literal—stink eye, their skill set was minimal in a situation like this.

"I'm usually extremely against violence, but if you don't let us in, these guys will beat you up," Rafi told the guard.

He looked over her head, trading eye contact with both Paul and Ryan. After a short stare-down, he sighed and gave in. "River isn't here."

"We're looking for Jack," Rafi said.

"The MUA holds court at the Cliffside."

The MUA? And also, *holds court?* Rafi vigorously rejected the way any of that sounded, but there was no time to stand around and ask questions. She turned to her small group and gave a quick, curt nod. If Jack was at the Cliffside, then that was where they needed to be, too. She led the way.

The Cliffside was at the far side of the beach, where the sand gave way to something rockier and became the color of bleached coral reef. Until Jack proposed collecting eye shadow from the dusty pink rocks there, nobody ever ventured that far because there didn't seem to be a point to climbing the jagged rocks when there were so many more convenient places to settle. But standing there now, Rafi understood why Jack would choose this place as his new headquarters.

There was a small formation of boulders leading the way to the top of the cliff, and there, with the view of the ocean as a backdrop, was a natural structure that resembled a throne. It had a flat seat, a lopsided but definite back, and uneven armrests, but it was a chair made of stone. And on it sat Jack. There was a person standing on either side of him, one boy waving a palm frond next to Jack's face, and one girl, who seemed to be tasting fruit before dropping the bitten-off chunks directly from her mouth into Jack's. It seemed they'd gone straight from their jobs at Peggy's tent to working for the MUA.

Rafi and her group approached the lip of the shallow rock hill, but Jack pretended he did not see them. He sniffed the air instead, and said, "It stinks. Is Rafi Santa Ana Winds here?"

"For the last time," Rafi stated, her voice steady and authoritative. "My name is Rafi Francisco. And I think what you're smelling is your own face."

Jack finally settled his glare on her. He managed to look

down without tilting his head, or even distorting his perfect posture. It was like he was mid-photoshoot for an ergonomic office-chair ad. But while he usually looked gorgeous, there was something off about his eyes. They were puffy and had a pink tint to them, kind of like Peggy's but to a lesser degree. Now Rafi noticed that the eyes of Jack's grape-feeder and palm-frond flapper were the same shade of nasty. Rafi doubted very much that it was a new makeup trend.

Pinkeye was becoming a pandemic on this island, and it had clearly started to ravage Jack's group. And judging by how it had so thoroughly taken over poor Peggy's face, Rafi figured they had a few hours left before going completely crusty and engorged. She wondered what they'd do about their precious Instagram pics then.

Probably below-the-neck stuff.

"You sure it's my makeup?" Jack asked. "Or is it theirs?" He pointed over Rafi's head, and she turned, unsure what he was referring to. But then Jack's meaning instantly became clear. The Ryan and Paul she thought she knew had been replaced by two big athletic guys with *their faces smeared with poo.*

"What the . . ." Rafi looked up at them, her brain trying to catch up to what was happening. No such luck. *"What is happening??"*

"We thought he'd listen to us if we put on makeup," Paul whispered in response.

"Everyone else is doing it," Ryan said, shrugging.

"Yeah, we didn't want to look like idiots," Paul said.

"Oh, you didn't want to look like idiots, did you?" Rafi said, nodding maniacally, letting her hands fall limply against her thighs. Paul and Ryan hadn't delicately applied and blended. It looked more like they'd just tied for first place in a shit pie-eating contest. "That's not how makeup works," Rafi hissed.

"So we look bad?" Paul asked.

"This isn't, like . . . pretty?" Ryan said.

Rafi did not dignify their questions with answers. She should've realized what they'd been up to by the smell, but she didn't because literally everything on this island smelled bad at this point. Every surface was beginning to attract flies to the point where Jack might get his wish and this could become a Fly Fest after all. *Ugh*.

"Why didn't you stop them?" Rafi asked Peggy.

"And get in the way of this?" Peggy said. "No. That was never going to happen; this is the best thing that I've ever witnessed."

"Your makeup is terrible and borderline offensive," Jack said loudly, in an effort to bring the attention back on himself. "But no worries, I can fix it. Boys, grab them!"

Two boys from Jack's camp materialized from behind the throne and came down to Paul and Ryan, grabbing their arms. Rafi was about to shout out in protest, but Paul and Ryan went willingly. Rafi couldn't even blame them. They really did need their faces fixed. And, to be honest, they were of no use to her right now.

"I guess that just leaves you and Peggy," Jack said to Rafi. "It's only a matter of time before you both see the light and join us here."

"We're not here to join you," Rafi said. "We're here for River. Where is he?"

"Who?" Jack fluttered his eyelids innocently and cupped a hand over his ear.

"Stop playing dumb!" Rafi couldn't help the outburst. She was escalating things far too quickly, but she was done playing. Jack could lead the whole island in a weird cult of makeup and make-believe, but for Rafi this had gone far enough. Plus, she found strength in her loudness. As calm as Jack was pretending to be, her voice was a chaos agent. It was overturning tables. It was a firing squad. It was starting something and ending something right here, right now. Her voice was her most powerful asset. She used it to great effect on her podcast; it was about time she used it in real life, too. "Where are you keeping him?"

Jack giggled and shared a look with his servants, who dutifully also laughed. "I never met River Stone. And that's my official statement."

"Okay, I've heard enough," Peggy said. "I didn't say anything when you stole my satellite phone, and I didn't say anything when you clearly murdered River. And I didn't say anything when you convinced people to start wearing feces on their faces, but I've had it." What Peggy did not say was that, most of all, they couldn't stand the fact that someone other than them had managed to become king on this island. The fun was over now. "We need to go back home, Jack. You know it as well as I do."

"Not until the festival—"

"There is no festival!" Peggy said. "We got suckered into a scam. No amount of poop is going to cover up how bad that stinks. You know, when I first got here, I was upset, too. Then I found a way to make it better. You and I are alike in that way. And it's ironic, because my eyes are nearly swollen shut, but I can finally see something that you so clearly can't. And it's that—hey, what's happening?"

With one flick of his wrist, Jack had commanded two of his people to grab Peggy. They hadn't seen them coming due to the aforementioned eyes-swollen-shut predicament. "Unhand me!" Peggy demanded. But no one was taking orders from them anymore.

"What are you doing to them?" Rafi shouted, watching as the two cronies led Peggy closer and closer to the edge of the cliff.

"We can't go home again," Jack said to both Peggy and Rafi, and no one in particular. "We can never go home again."

As batty as those words sounded, the way Jack spoke them made Rafi finally understand his position. Jack didn't want to go home because home equaled admitting defeat. Admitting the truth. Admitting that there was another reality, an alternate reality to the one he'd made for himself here, where everyone and life itself appeared beautiful.

But Rafi didn't have too much time to dwell on what Jack said, because the words also seemed to be a command for his cronies to push Peggy over the edge.

Like literally over the edge of the cliff. Not being able to see where they were going or what they could grab, Peggy stumbled backward. Their clumsy feet skidded over the gravelly terrain, and their arms pinwheeled, trying to find purchase. The whole thing looked like it was the latest complicated TikTok dance.

"Peggy, watch out!" Rafi yelled. But it was too late. One minute Peggy was trying to hold on to air, the next they were gone.

Rafi ran to the edge of the cliff, stopping just short of the open air. She swung her arms back to try to regain her balance and ended up getting help from the people who'd launched Peggy off the cliff. The influencers caught her wrists, probably to prevent her from unwittingly swinging her fists into their disgusting, beautiful faces. They let her go when she was stable, though, and went back to join Jack's ranks.

Rafi looked down, searching for Peggy's broken and bloody body splayed on the jagged rocks below. But there were no rocks. It turned out this section of land wasn't a cliff so much as a lip that jutted out like a spout. Below, there was deep blue sea. But more specifically, there was—

"A boat." Rafi's breath caught on the word.

The boat bobbed in the sea like a cork, and it was so close—approximately only one story below. And on its bow was Peggy. Not so much broken and bloody, but definitely splayed out and moaning. They sat up, rubbing their back as they looked around. They seemed to have fallen on a pile of debris littering the surface of the boat, a mix of dirty-looking mounds of whites, grays, and yellows. Rafi wasn't sure what she was seeing, but a laugh bubbled up in her unexpectantly. "A BOAT!"

Behind her, Jack was laughing, too. "That's not a boat, sweetie, it's a garbage barge." He tilted his head back to the followers standing around his throne and proceeded to laugh about it with them. "She doesn't know the difference between a boat and a garbage barge."

Rafi was too amazed by the sudden turn of events to worry about the fact that everyone was laughing at her, or to remember just how much she could not stand Jack. "Where did it come from?"

"What do you mean?" Jack asked. "It's been coming every day. The barge stops at different islands collecting garbage. Steve, the captain, stops here for his lunch and dinner breaks."

"*Steve?*"

"He enjoys the shade beneath the promontory you're standing on. If you'd bothered to get to know him, you'd know that."

Just then someone from Jack's group walked over to the ledge with their stem of grapes and threw it over. It landed on Peggy's thigh.

And as Rafi watched all this, she tried to puzzle out the warring thoughts in her head, but there were too many jockeying for her attention. "Wait a minute," she said. "There was a boat coming to this island every day? *Twice* a day?"

"How many times do I have to say it?" Jack said. "It's a *garbage barge*."

"Why didn't anyone get on the boa—the barge?" Rafi asked.

Jack and his tribe looked at Rafi like it was *her* face that was covered in crap. "It's full of garbage," Jack stated, like it was obvious.

The tribe murmured their agreement.

"But we could've been rescued!"

"Me? Get on a boat that transports garbage?" Jack asked, confused. "Honestly, Rafi, you've never lorded over an island full of influencers at the world's most exclusive music festival and it shows."

Rafi rolled her eyes, which was not to Jack's liking.

"If you're so eager to get out of here, go ahead," he said. "Jump on the garbage barge, it's about to leave. And it's clearly where you belong."

Rafi looked down. She looked at Peggy sitting among the muck, at just how much muck there actually was. It really wasn't that long of a fall. With the amount of Styrofoam containers and other bags of cheesy sandwich garbage there, Rafi would probably have a soft cushion on which to land. And she'd finally be off this forsaken island and on her way back to civilization.

The barge was so close, actually, that she could smell it from where she stood. The waves of pungent garbage juice wafted up to her, masking the last of the fresh smells the island had left.

"Jump on the barge!" Jack barked. And he repeated it again, until it was a chant. His followers picked up on it and began chanting, too. "Jump on the barge! JUMP ON THE BARGE!"

The garbage barge. Her salvation. All Rafi wanted to do was follow their direction and jump.

But it really did smell very bad.

And there was so much ocean all around.

The barge began to move slowly, away from the cliff's scree, but Rafi's sneakers stayed glued to the cliff. She didn't move, even as the barge was moving in earnest now, picking up speed and getting farther and farther away.

"You want me to jump onto that?" Rafi said to Jack in a smallish voice. "I could never make it."

Jack shared knowing looks with his followers before turning back to Rafi. "Of course you can't. You don't have that special something that the rest of us do. That *Jenna-say-quack*. You think you're interesting because you have a podcast? *Everybody* has a podcast, Rafi. The sad thing for you is that nobody our age listens to them. Nobody! Also, you're tone-deaf, you have to be the center of attention, and you are far too concerned with your looks."

It was a lot easier for Rafi to take Jack's insults once she realized that everything he said was projection. "And *you* don't look anything like your pics," she said.

The perma-smirk on Jack's face disappeared like a magic trick. Rafi felt like she finally landed a lethal blow. "Excuse me?" he said.

"People only ever saw you with studio lights or behind Facetune or filters or from certain angles. You always controlled the image. But that ubiquitous influencer face? Nobody ever looks like that in real life. The first day here you were sad that you didn't have any of your makeup. But now I realize you were mostly horrified that people would see the real you."

For a moment, everything stopped. None of Jack's follow-ers moved; Steve's barge was frozen on the horizon; even the flies that had been lured by the stink seemed to rest on the rocks. Actually, the only motion came from the nearly imper-ceptible clench of Jack's jaw. Finally, he spoke. "Grab her."

34

RAFI FOUND HERSELF SITTING IN A CAGELIKE STRUCTURE (okay, it wasn't cage*like*; it was a cage, period). It couldn't have been more than four feet tall in any direction, and she was surrounded on six sides by metal bars, much stronger stuff than even the plastic tube frames of the tents in Tent City. She wondered who made this. When? How? Though, as her clammy fingers encircled the bars, she remembered where she'd seen them before. The raw, unfinished scaffolding of the concert stage at the top of the mountain. Where had all these materials and builders been when she needed shelter that wouldn't fall at the flap of a butterfly's wings?

Rafi shook the cage, not so much to demand her freedom but to test the sturdiness of her cell. It was pretty durable, especially considering the fact that it was currently holding her about five feet above the ground. The people who'd set this cage up had put a lot of work into it. They'd found a clearing in the jungle, and a tree with a high enough—strong enough— branch from which to dangle the cage. Like a chandelier from one of their mansions.

But as impressive as the cage was—and, no question, it definitely beat her tent—Rafi was left with only one desire.

I want to go home.

She thought of speaking the words out loud. She had an audience, after all. Every concertgoer on the island was gathered here, in a wide circle below her. Even Paul and Ryan guiltily stood watch, if a bit isolated thanks to the raging stink coming off their faces.

No, Rafi saw no point in saying she wanted to go home. They wouldn't let her anyway. But she realized, as she looked down at the silent, staring crowd, that they were waiting for her to say something. This wasn't exactly the check-in desk at the seaport, and she didn't have her mic with her, and as far as daises went, this one dug into her tailbone. But it was something.

It was time to put an end to the lies and rumors. It was time for the truth. And they needed to hear it directly from her.

"I know some of you have already listened to season two of my podcast, 'Musical Mysteries.'"

"Stop plugging your podcast!" came a voice from down below.

Rafi squeezed her eyes shut, annoyed at the interruption but also at herself. Whoever had said that was right. This wasn't about her or her podcast. She needed to start again.

"When I came to this island, I thought I was better than you."

The faces down below, beneath the clay and crap and crustiness, wrinkled subtly with deep lines of anger, which Rafi knew she deserved. But they still listened, and that was all she asked for.

"I thought I was here to do important work and you were all here to party. And I never cared about what I looked like or how popular I was, but you guys—you all cared about that. It was the *only* thing you cared about."

More angry stares. Rafi was beginning to wonder if their faces were frozen that way now, their makeup casting them like plaster molds.

"But I'm not better than any of you," Rafi continued. "I know now that my need to be a famous investigative podcaster? It's just like you all wanting to be popular influencers. And we *all* care about our looks—it's human nature!"

There were sounds steadily rising from the crowd, a restless grumble, and Rafi could tell she was losing them. It appeared her epiphany was not relevant to their interests. She needed to get to the point.

"I told a lie!" Though she tried to make her voice as clear and loud as possible, the truth still came out shaky and beaten down. But it emerged, nonetheless. "I said Hella Badid was here and that Fly Fest was still on, somewhere in an unseen part of the island. But none of that was true. I made it up so that all of you would want to stay. So that River would stay. So I could get an interview with him. It was wrong, and definitely the worst choice of my life, and you have no idea how much I regret it."

No interruptions, no disgruntled murmurs. It was a good sign, and it spurred Rafi on. "Now that you know that Hella was never here and that there is no festival, don't you want to go home? Don't you want to end the madness and—I don't know—take a hot shower? We've all had our fun. Some more than others, am I right?" Here, Rafi allowed herself to cautiously chuckle and rattle the bars of her cage. "But I think we can all agree that it's time to go."

She knew she wasn't the greatest orator in the world, and she sure as heck wasn't as influential as anybody else here, but she was presenting them with something that was impossible to ignore.

Logic.

The truth was out in the open now from a primary source. There was no more reason to keep up the charade. It was time to wipe off the "beauty" masks.

But Jack—whom Rafi had almost forgotten about—cleared his throat and broke through his circle of followers, strutting into the open circus ring beneath Rafi's cage. He looked up at her. "You really think we're dumb, huh?"

Jack took his time walking the perimeter of the ring, addressing his people. "It's plainly obvious that the organizers of Fly Fest are telling Rafi to say all this. They are trying to test our loyalty. See who the real believers are."

"No," Rafi said.

"Yes," Jack said, batting his eyelashes (or maybe trying to blink away the ooze congealing on his eyelids). He caressed the shawl draped around his neck. It was golden, with thread that looked like it was spun by Rumpelstiltskin himself. Rafi stared at it, sure she'd had this exact thought before, until, finally, it jogged her memory. She gasped out loud.

"YOU!" Rafi pointed with her whole arm through the

metal bars at Jack, who stared up at her innocently. But he wasn't so innocent. Rafi remembered where she'd seen that shawl before. It had once graced the supple décolletage of Sierra Madre!

Instantly all the pieces fell into place, and Rafi couldn't believe she hadn't solved the puzzle earlier. Of course it was Jack. The same person who killed River and threw Peggy over a cliff would've disposed of Sierra, too.

Anytime anyone got in the way of Jack's Fly Fest delusions he had to get rid of them, as proven by the fact that Rafi was currently dangling over the jungle in a manmade cage. Sierra would've been his first victim because she was always too good for this place. She never would've stayed, never would've believed Rafi's lie like everyone else here. If she got her hands on the internet, the first thing she would've done was charter a yacht back home. Jack couldn't have that, so he got rid of her.

Rafi had been so focused on her idea that River was a serial killer that she hadn't even noticed the actual serial killer in her midst.

"YOU KILLED SIERRA MADRE!"

Jack's not-so-innocent eyes flashed in alarm, but it wasn't him who refuted Rafi's accusation. Greer did that for him.

"How dare you!" the girl cried. "Jack wouldn't even hurt a fly!"

"That's right," Jack said. "Now, *kill the pig, cut her throat!*"

"What?" Rafi said. But no one heard her over Jack's rallying cry. There was a frenzy of movement that Rafi couldn't keep track of, with influencers scurrying about and raising their fists into the air and making off-putting ululating sounds with their pointy tongues. But one movement caught Rafi's attention over the others. A rush toward the rope holding her cage aloft. And then there was a *whoosh*—the sound of a roaring flame come to life. There was a torch suddenly, and it was tipping toward the rope at the base of the tree.

"Oh no," Rafi whispered. Below her, the crowd parted in anticipation, like a ripple effect before the pebble ever touched the water. "Oh no no no no n—"

The metal bars broke and crumbled in the crash, but somehow, miraculously, they'd created a skeleton that cocooned Rafi from harm. The top of the cage cracked off like a soda can tab, and Rafi saw her only chance.

She ran.

35

Gravel slipped under her feet and sprayed at her heels, but she was determined not to lose her footing, because if she did, she'd be finished. A scream came out of her that was so primal, it was like a bottle rocket, propelling her forward.

Kill the pig, cut her throat. The words rang through Rafi's ears at the same pace as her racing heartbeat, two thoughts warring in her brain: *Jack has to be kidding*, and *Jack is absolutely going to kill me.*

Just like he did Sierra. And River. And tried to do to Peggy.

Rafi had to stop thinking. Thoughts like these were just weighing her down, and what she needed was speed and distance. And a good hiding spot. There was nowhere to hide on the coastline—her only choice was to get lost in the thickest part of the jungle and hope Jack and his mad pack of followers couldn't find her.

But the roaring sound of them rushing en masse behind her—a crazed stampede of wild and crusty influencers—was impossible to shut out.

Rafi needed to focus. She hoped the mangle of green jungle would provide at least enough cover to give her a bigger head start.

She spotted a thicket of vines and shrubs and ran to it. It was a cavelike structure but only big enough for an animal, like a boar. Perhaps it was a boar's home she was invading. Rafi hoped not. The last thing she needed right now was to upset a wild hog and get herself killed that way when she was trying to avoid getting killed another way. But it was all she had.

The place was hollow and empty. She squished herself through, ignoring the way the bramble scratched at her exposed skin and caught on her clothes. She tried to be as still as she could be, contorting her body to stay uncomfortably hunched over. And then she waited. Maybe Jack's horde wouldn't see her. Maybe they'd run right past, and she could breathe easy and emerge from this prison and come up with a better plan.

"She's in there!"

Greer was the one who'd spotted her. Her pink eyes were runny, but, ironically, this was the one time the girl wasn't crying. A group of people, about a dozen thick, stood behind her. And in Greer's hand—the one that wasn't pointing directly at Rafi—was a torch.

Rafi pretended to be invisible.

"Stop pretending you can't see us seeing you!" Greer said.

Rafi's eyes darted from Greer's face to everyone else's. They all nodded.

"The bush you're hiding in is like a jack-o'-lantern, and your shirt is like the candle you light inside of it," Greer explained. "You really did not pick the right shirt for this trip."

"*Damnit*," Rafi hissed under her breath. This shirt was the single worst mistake she'd ever made in her life, she thought, as she hid in a boar's home from a rabid crowd with torches on a deserted island that she'd spent her life savings to visit. "I'm not getting out of here!" Rafi shouted. "And you can't make me."

Greer approached the bush-cave and bent her waist sideways to look Rafi in the eye. "You sure about that?"

"Yes," Rafi said.

"But are you really sure?" Greer asked.

"I'm serious, Greer!"

"Me also." Greer touched the flames of her torch to the base of the bush Rafi had burrowed into. The dry bramble caught fire immediately.

Rafi did not even attempt to put it out with her shoe before lunging out. "Are you *kidding* me?"

Greer shrugged. Rafi looked around at the others, searching for a compassionate face, someone who might see through the madness and would be willing to help her out. But it was hard to see what any of these people actually looked like behind their makeup masks. All of them—boys and girls alike—were so heavily decorated that Rafi wasn't sure their faces were even faces anymore. They were just mounds of dirt and dung staring back at her. The stuff packed their pores and creases, made mountains out of every bump and blemish, rivers of sweat in the valleys.

Also, the pinkeye epidemic had finally caught up to them, making their faces puffy and grotesque with infection. No amount of berry lip stain and clay shadow and crap bronzer could cover it up.

No, their makeup did not make them beautiful anymore. Rafi knew now that it made them savages.

She ran.

Again.

And they chased her. Again. It seemed like more people than before. It seemed like it was everyone on the island, and everywhere Rafi looked, there they were—torches up, fires *lit*.

Or maybe she was just seeing things. Maybe it wasn't that everyone was holding torches, maybe it was that they'd started setting fire to everything, because she was sweating now, heat fanning her skin from every direction, and her peripheral vision was full-blast hot and orange.

Water. She needed water.

Rafi followed the sound of the ocean waves. It was the only safe place to go.

She touched sand at last, and she stomped so hard that her feet dug in. The faster she ran, the more she seemed to sink into it. But she stopped abruptly when the tips of her sneakers touched the wet part of the shore. This was the end of the road. There was nowhere else to go.

Could Rafi really just walk into the ocean?

She'd gotten over her fear of water, hadn't she? But it was more than that. The water wouldn't stop them. And there came a time when Rafi would have to stop and face the people she was running from.

This was it.

She turned around.

They were all there. Everyone who had come to Fly Fest.

Sweat-soaked kids who were yelling unintelligible things at her. Their makeup nothing more than brown and rosy-hued smears dripping down their faces, leaving angry tracks around their mouths and creases fanning from the corners of their inflamed eyes. They held their sticks and their phones aloft, weapons both.

They were crazed, but they were still cognizant enough to follow orders, and they parted to let Jack through. He walked until he was close enough for Rafi to catch a whiff of his makeup. And though his followers stayed back, a swarm of flies trailed him, surrounding his head like a floating crown. He held up his torch with the grace of Lady Liberty.

Rafi thought about the witches in Salem and wondered if this was what they felt like, watching their executioner approach. She sank to her knees and looked up at Jack.

"Why are you doing this?"

Jack seemed to think about it, his chin tilting upward like the sun was a camera flash. "Okay, yes, maybe this is a little extreme, but can you really blame me? We've been on this island *forever*."

"We've been on this island for *six days*."

"There you go, thinking you're smarter than everyone else!" Jack said. "That's your problem, Rafi. You're a stick-in-the-mud. You're getting in the way of our fun."

"I'm sorry, okay?" The last thing Rafi wanted to do was apologize, but it was a last-ditch tactic to appeal to Jack's humanity.

"Your apology has been declined. Do you have another?"

A tiny whimper left Rafi's lips. "Please. It's just—I was pretty sure you killed—"

"You were never pretty *anything*!" Jack bent low to whisper the next part. "No one will miss you anyway."

"People know I exist. People are waiting for me back home."

"Remind me again how many followers you have?"

Rafi sighed and in a small voice she replied, "About a thousand over three platforms."

A thousand individual people knew about her, believed in what she was doing. Believed in *her*.

"You sad, little Tupperware lid." Jack's flies took turns landing on his sharp cheekbones. They didn't faze him. "Are you really sure you exist?"

Rafi closed her eyes.

Jack lowered his torch, and the heat of the flame was strong enough to force Rafi to lean back. She fell on her butt, her hands clutching the sand behind her. She was practically on her way to doing a crab walk right into the water, guided by Jack. She closed her eyes.

Rafi waited. Minutes passed, and then something strange happened: Jack squawked. Rafi squinted one eye open. Jack wasn't even looking at her anymore. But he did squawk again, a hideous, birdlike sound that emerged from his lips as spontaneously as a burp. But it was not a burp. Jack was looking past Rafi, out to the ocean. His face was openmouthed, frozen with shock, but after a minute it broke into a grin. "Omigawd," he snorted. He bounced on the balls of his feet and squawked again. "OMIGAWD. She came!"

Rafi sat up straight and followed Jack's gaze. At first it looked like a mirage, and Rafi had to squint to make sure she was seeing right.

Butting up against the sand was a small dingy, and coming out of it was none other than—

"Hella Badid!" Jack squealed. He forgot about Rafi and dropped his torch so thoughtlessly it nearly singed her knees before sand eventually snuffed out the flames. "I told you all she'd come!" Jack shouted to his followers. "I told you she'd come for us!"

Hella's feet (bare except for a couple of toe rings and a jangly ankle bracelet) stepped out of the water and onto the sand until they reached all the way to Rafi and Jack. Rafi's eyes roved up Hella's figure, still not quite believing she was real. She wore a short, emerald romper, and her hair was in a topknot. She looked as glamorous and enticing as a bottle of champagne wrapped in crinkly cellophane. Rafi felt bad for the analogy, given Hella's alcoholism, but the girl looked fancy and Rafi was parched. The supermodel towered over Jack, which was fine since he seemed mostly interested in slobbering at her feet.

"Hella." His face was a mess of wet, happy tears. "I've been holding down the fort until you showed up. I've made sure we were all worthy. I would never want you to be disappointed in us."

Hella didn't seem to know what to say. Her normally stoic, dead-behind-the-eyes look, which had graced so many magazine covers, had a little bit more life in it as she stared at Jack. Then she scrunched up her nose and sniffed. "You smell," she said.

The confusion seemed to transfer from Hella's face to Jack's. Hella turned to Rafi and held out her hand, helping her up. "You're Rafi, right?"

Rafi nodded.

"I've heard all about you." Hella looked back to the dinghy bobbing in the water, where River was trying to keep it anchored.

36

IT WAS THE REAL HELLA. NOT JUST THE MYTHIC IDEA OF her that had filled the minds of the concertgoers. And the sight of her had been so bizarre that Rafi hadn't even noticed River. Or the huge yacht in the distance that had brought them to the island in the first place. But now River was all Rafi could see.

While the rest of the beach fawned over the supermodel, Rafi stood numbly, watching as River pulled the floating raft to shore until it was stationary on the sand. And when River straightened and looked around, it was Rafi who he settled on. She was so happy to see him alive. But she couldn't say if he was happy to see her. His face, with his mouth usually on the cusp of a smile and his eyes sparkling, remained neutral as he regarded her.

It was a stare-off. Their gazes unwavering, focusing only on each other, even as everyone on the beach started running straight toward the ocean.

Eventually, the rush of people hurtling past them was too big a distraction, and Rafi and River turned to see what was going on. Hella was pinching her nose and breathing through her mouth, which must've triggered everyone to realize they were wearing poop on their faces. They were suddenly desperate to wash it all off, Jack chief among them. He splashed his face compulsively and scrubbed the abrasive salt water into his pores.

In the end, he had been right: All it took was Hella finally showing up on the island to save them all.

Rafi turned back to River and the two approached each other, stopping with a few feet of space between them. They both knew that there was a lot to say, and that this wasn't the spot for it.

"I know a place," River said.

They only went farther down the beach, to their tents. The same spot where they'd had so many of their conversations. Only, Rafi's tent barely held together anymore, and River had definitely outgrown his. He looked strange before it, like he'd come back to visit a childhood home that didn't belong to him anymore. Or maybe it was just that he was actually wearing a shirt for once. He looked like a brand-new person.

They sat in the sand, side by side, close enough to the commotion on the shore but far enough away to have a private moment alone.

"I am so glad you're alive," Rafi said.

"Did you really think they killed me?"

"I wouldn't put it past them."

River seemed lost in thought at the terrifying memory. "They jumped me. And I think Jack tried to file my nails.

Anyway, I was able to get away, but they chased me to the cliffs and ended up pushing me off. Good thing I had somewhere to land. Did you know there's a garbage barge that comes to the island every day?"

"Just found out about it."

"Steve's a great guy."

"Oh yeah?"

River nodded, and there was a lull in the conversation. Rafi could've continued talking about Steve the garbage barge captain all day if it meant avoiding the hard stuff that she and River had to talk about. Luckily, River brought something else up.

"Sierra Madre is fine, by the way."

Sierra. In all the madness, Rafi had nearly forgotten how certain she'd been that Jack killed the world's most prominent influencer. "Where was she?"

"She called for a helicopter to come get her. Remember that weird whooshing noise?"

This bit of info was shocking, until Rafi began to think back on that time on the island. Now that she thought about it, the whooshing did sound like it could've been a helicopter's propellers. And there *had* been a lot of talk with the word "hell" in it for a good couple of hours there. Of course, Rafi had just heard that word and assumed that people had been talking about Hella. But she realized that was all conjecture on her part. They easily could've been talking about seeing a *hel*icopter.

As outlandish as it was, this made the most sense. And it also tracked with how Rafi collected and processed rumors and news. Where there were hoofbeats, she thought zebras instead of horses. She chased the conspiracy theory instead of stepping back and assessing all the evidence in a rational way.

She was a bad investigator.

Rafi was wrong. Often. About a lot of things. She looked at River, knowing there was no way to avoid this part of the convo any longer. "I'm sorry about the things I said on my podcast. It was wrong to accuse you of all that stuff. And then to share something you told me in confidence."

She meant it. She really did. Thinking about what she'd done to River made her stomach twist. "I don't expect you to forgive me. What I did was unforgivable."

She deserved all his wrath, and she braced herself for a storm, but River didn't say anything. And he didn't look angry either. Not like he did the last time they'd spoken.

"I've appeared on *Entertainment Tonight* thirty-four times, Rafi. I've heard way stranger conspiracy theories about myself."

Rafi nodded, but River's reaction was almost too kind for her to accept at face value. "I'll take the podcast down. I'll post a retraction."

River shook his head. "I've been thinking about what you revealed about me. And, weirdly, I'm okay with it."

Rafi wondered if she heard him right. She knew a lot had happened since their fight to put her podcast into perspective, but this was the last thing she expected him to say.

"I mean, the first few episodes—your theories about me being a serial killer—that stuff is . . . pretty out there. But the rest of it? It's the truth. You told it without my permission, but now that it's out there . . ." River took a deep breath, and his toned shoulders rounded and fell. It was not his usual always-on, stage-ready posture. But he actually looked kind of comfortable. "I was getting really tired of lying. It's kind of a relief not to have to do it anymore."

Rafi took a deep breath, too. Hearing him say all that made a huge weight lift from her chest. She felt relieved, invigorated, free. Though some of that definitely had to do with the huge boat in the background ready to rescue them finally. The point was, Rafi was happy. River wasn't mad, Jack wasn't currently trying to kill her, and they were all saved.

And then River said something that Rafi really didn't expect. "What if I give you an interview?"

"Really?"

"Yeah," River said. "A real one. I'll be up-front about whatever you want to know. The truth."

This was the only thing that Rafi had ever wanted. The reason she'd come to this wretched music festival, her ticket to a legitimate podcasting network, presented to her on a silver platter. Everything inside of Rafi screamed *Yes!*

"No," she said.

River looked surprised enough for the both of them. "No?"

"I think I need to step back from the investigations for a little while," Rafi said. "I wasn't delivering news, I was creating theories. And it—clearly—got completely out of hand."

"But your podcast. I thought you were really passionate about it."

Rafi nodded. She couldn't deny that. "I'll come back to it. But for now, I think it'll be good for me to step away, enjoy the real world for a bit."

River nodded and smiled. Together, he and Rafi looked out wordlessly at the shimmering ocean, unbothered by the influencers in it frantically washing the muck off their faces.

MUSICAL MYSTERIES
Season 2: Episode 6
"Where Are They Now?"

Hi, Mysterinos. It's been a while, huh? Six months, to be exact. Six months since Fly Fest became the butt of every joke. Six months since I touched this podcast. But it felt like the right time to come back.

By now, there have been countless news stories about what happened on that island in the Caribbean. You don't need me to rehash why the organizers of the festival abandoned it on day one of construction, and we probably don't need to go over the zillions of lawsuits the concertgoers launched as soon as their feet touched American soil. In fact, maybe you're getting a little tired of hearing about Fly Fest completely. You're probably thinking I should move on, time to get over it. But I still think about the week I spent at that music festival with neither music nor festivities. And I think about the people that I met there, and what they're up to now.

Paul and Ryan successfully sued the organizers of Fly Fest, the social media platforms that helped promote it, and the retailer Banana Republic. Though they jointly describe their time on the island as "not very money," they acknowledge that it made them experts in the world of produce and have since started their own line of gourmet bananas. I'm not sure what that means, but as they would say, business is booming. They had a launch party in Malibu and got O-Town to perform.

As it turned out, Peggy wasn't just trading bad tchotchkes for access to the internet—they were also accepting personal information, like phone numbers, email addresses, and Social Security numbers, which they then sold to third-party buyers. It was all kind of illegal, but they collected enough money to buy the island we all stayed on, where there is no extradition. They just finished construction on a mansion that rivals the size of their massive tent, and employs a staff of twenty.

Jack's reputation took a hit once the truth came out about why everyone's bronzer looked so . . . shitty. People were appropriately disgusted by his island makeup methods, companies dropped him as their spokesperson, and he lost a hundred thousand subscribers after the *New York Post* called him "gross." Jack subsequently tried to salvage his brand by releasing a special twenty-four-hour apology video marathon, where he posted a new apology video every fifteen minutes. Jack started his first video with the words, "This is a conversation that needs having. It's time." His last video was just seven minutes straight of him sobbing while perched on the edge of a Sealy Posturepedic. But by then he had lost the rest of his followers.

Hella had no career setbacks despite having actively promoted a sham festival. Anytime she's asked to comment about the mythic role she unwittingly took on in the concertgoers' eyes, it takes her a moment to recall the scandal at all. For Hella, Fly Fest was an hour of work that took up no space in her mind. She's since cut a lot of things out of her life, including alcohol, deals with shady festival people, and River Stone.

River. He came clean about what actually happened to Tracy in a sit-down interview with Oprah. It garnered even more sympathy than his original lie about being abandoned in the bush on the eve of his planned proposal. He's writing a new album about it all, and even his time at Fly Fest. It's called *Deep as a River, Hard as a Stone*. People continue to love him. And I understand why.

As for what I've been up to for the last six months? For a long time I blamed myself for the role I had in making Fly Fest an even worse experience than it would've been all on its own. I never fully realized how much influence my words had on those who listened to them. For six months, I was too afraid to say anything at all. So I stayed away.

But that's no way to go through life. I still have a voice and things to say. I just know now that the truth is everything. You just have to be careful how you wield it.

And River, if you're listening . . . I think I'm ready for that interview now.

THE END

Acknowledgments

Depending on whether you like/hate this book, here is a list of people you and I can thank/blame, for helping me bring this story into the world.

I had a long talk with my agent, asking her whether I should go forth with this story or dump it in favor of something more traditional, more palatable, something that "young adult readers will actually want to read." My agent said absolutely not! That I should write this story like only I could. So, Jenny Bent, thank you/this is all your fault. And to Gemma Cooper, for your valiant wheeling and dealing. Thank you so much for your endless and unwavering support of my stories.

Through no fault of their own, many editors were burdened with whipping this manuscript into shape. The first was Tiff Liao. Truthfully, I was terrified that Tiff would take one look at this book, print it out, and then set it on fire. But to her credit, Tiff did no such thing! She texted me as soon as she'd read it to tell me how much she liked it. She then left for better job opportunities. I can't say my book lead to her departure, but I also can't say it didn't. Tiff, I am eternally grateful for that text, for your thoughtful notes that truly made this book better, and for the time and patience you had for me and my work.

Sarah Levison also had to edit the heck out of this book.

Sarah, I can't imagine what you were thinking when I saddled you with this, but I'm so glad for your guidance through the many iterations of it.

Dana Chidiac, I think you had the most difficult task of all, looking at this almost-finished beast, maybe (probably) wanting a whole rewrite, but with little hope of me changing much. Thank you for coming through on this journey with me, and I can't wait for the next one!

Did you think this book had enough editors? Well, joke's on you because it had even more! Ann Marie Wong, what an absolute surprise and delight it was to have you on board the team! I worried those other editors didn't know what was in store with one of my manuscripts, but you had to have known. And still, you were my cheerleader the whole way! It was such a gift to know I had your support. Here's to Mr. Henry Holt for bringing us together and footing our bills!

Jennifer Abbots, publicist extraordinaire! This wild ride is sweeter with you in it.

Writing a book is a lonely endeavor, but making one is a team effort, and I want to thank everyone at Henry Holt, especially Jean Feiwel; Jess Harold; Rich Deas; Alexei Esikoff; Lelia Mander; Mariel Dawson, Melissa Zar, and their team, especially Leigh Ann Higgins; Brittany Pearlman; Sara Elroubi; Molly Ellis; Mary Van Akin and her team; and Jen Edwards and her team.

Thank you to: Sonia and Irina, for giving me the time and space to write when I needed it. Yasmin, Maayan, Hadas, and Akiva. For Tove, my Silly Billy, and Imri, my Silly Goose. Being silly is the best. It can get you paid!!!

And for Alex. The absolute worst ideas in this book are also the best ideas in this book, and they're usually always yours. You giggle across the table, making jokes about my characters and suggesting they smear [redacted] on their faces and you so innocently think, "She'll never do that. I'm just saying stupid stuff because there's no way she's going to put that in a traditionally published book." And I throw my napkin on the table and I think, "Well, damn." Because the ideas are so stupid, so good, that how can I not put them in a traditionally published book? How can I not. So, thanks/I blame you the most.